VISION
OF THE
HUNTER

HARPER & ROW, PUBLISHERS, New York

Cambridge, Philadelphia, San Francisco

London, Mexico City, São Paulo, Singapore, Sydney

VISION
OF THE
HUNTER

JOHN TEMPEST

FIRST EDITION

Designed by Alma Orenstein

Library of Congress Cataloging-in-Publication Data
Tempest, John.
    Vision of the hunter.

    I. Title.
PR6070.E44V57   1989   823'.914   88-43004
ISBN 0-06-015684-8

88 89 90 91 92   WB/HC 10 9 8 7 6 5 4 3 2 1

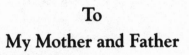

To
My Mother and Father

CHAPTER
ONE

▲ ▲ ▲
▲ ▲

BEFORE ANYONE ELSE in the tent had stirred, Finn had awoken and thrust his head out through the tent flap into the light. To do so without disturbing the other sleepers was a simple matter for not only was Finn of necessity adept at moving silently but his place, as befitted an outsider, was by the door. Even so, and despite the bitter wind that had rattled the deerskin tent on its frame, he had spent a good night. There was lots of room in Hann's tent with only three other occupants—Hann himself, owner of the tent, and leader of this and the nine other tents crammed with kinsmen that clustered around his great hearth; his wife Mata; and their son. As hearth leader Hann must soon be up and about his duties while Mata saw to the lighting of the fires, but the boy would not rise, perhaps would never rise again. On his hands and knees in the tent doorway, Finn looked back over his shoulder to the small bundle of skins where the child lay asleep. He always thought of him as a child, for although the boy was as old as he, his mind had not kept pace even with his body's slight growth. The sight of these three, the nearest he had to a family, at peace for a while, was

1

almost unbearable, and he dragged himself out gratefully into the early morning light.

Hauling his deerskin smock over his head he made his way through the circle of tents, past the ashes of the great hearth and the dozen or so smaller ones that ringed it and out onto the bare rock beyond. There was no one awake, neither at Hann's hearth nor at any of the other great hearths that stretched away to his right along the rocky ledge; here the camp perched high above the valley below, at the mouth of the great cave. This cave, so lofty that Finn could scarcely hit its roof with a stone, was the only home the ten hearths of the Burnt Shin tribe had ever known. It was the focal point of their public life, their meeting place for Councils and feasting, and in severe Winters their final place of refuge. Yet to Finn it always appeared vaguely menacing, as though the mountain might at any moment close its great jaws on them all. He had never dared to give voice to this thought that—as well as causing great offense—would have been put down at once to his being a stranger, a foundling, and not properly of the people. Yet even now in the dawn's cheery glow he could not escape a feeling of unease, and he turned his back on the cave to look out over the treetops to the far side of the valley. Before him the ledge sloped down to a steep shale escarpment and then down to the tree-line and the valley bottom; it was here at the shale's edge that he took his seat to enjoy the first of the sun and survey his world.

Across the valley were more mountains; the skyline there was turning blood-red now, and in a matter of moments the sun would appear, flooding this side of the valley with warmth. Its rays would turn the whole camp behind him crimson, and in time its light would dance on the waters of the stream far below. Even in the half light he could see the stream at various places through the trees. His eyes followed it back to its source deep into the ever-thickening forests away to his right, to places he had never been and probably never would. He could imagine its

2

coldness at this time of day and he shuddered involuntarily, turning to his left to follow it down to the valley mouth, where it rushed to join the river. Away to the left the trees thinned out. With narrowed eyes it was possible on a clear day to see where the tree-line gave way to the open ground on the river's banks, and beyond that to the first ridge-line of the rolling grasslands beyond. How far the grasslands went no one knew. Hann had once said that a man could walk his entire life away and never see the great salt river that lay at their end, the river where all rivers ended.

Yet although few of the people had ever wandered that land it was there that all their hopes were centered and to them, especially now as Autumn approached, that all eyes were turned. For it was across those grasslands that the deluge came that was the lifeblood of the people. It was coming on the wind, *this* wind, first portent of the Winter that would bring the Reindeer back to the forests to feed. Fat and sleek from the Summer grazing, antlers at their highest and hides in prime condition, they would flood the river's banks and the valley mouth with a seemingly endless river of flesh. For three or four days they would cover the earth so densely that hardly a patch of bare ground could be seen—bucks, eager for the rut, clustered at the edges of the herds, does in the center, and last year's fawns, first antlers sprouting, still unwilling to leave their mothers' sides. Even now at the Summer pastures they would be growing restive, feeling on their backs the cooler air that heralded the Winter. Closing his eyes Finn could see them filling the valley; watch their breath rising through the trees like the smoke of a thousand fires; hear the coughing and grunting and the clicking of their ankle bones as they passed deeper into the forests, and smell their rank smell. Then would come the massive slaughter that meant life or death to the ten hearths: hunters massed at the river pitching spears into the passing throng, the smell of blood and fear, the butchered carcasses steaming, strewing the ground for as far as the eye could see.

Finally, at last, the feasting: the taste of fresh meat after a long Summer, the songs and laughter, the joy of knowing that they would live till the Spring when the deer passed again on their way to the salt river.

Noise from behind him startled him out of his thoughts. Almost at once, it seemed, the camp had come to life. At all of the hearths women and infants were crouched about the cold gray stones piling bunches of sticks or blowing life into the smoldering kindling. The hunters were up too, arming themselves with switches as the boys of the tribe tumbled naked from their tents. Shouting, laughing, and leaping over newly lit fires —pursued by the women's angry cries—they raced for the shale. Here and there a fugitive was caught, lurking among the tents for devilment, and was driven out from shelter by stick-wielding fathers and brothers. This was the morning ritual of the Burnt Shins' youth—a headlong race down to the stream, with stripes across the back for laggards, and at the end an icy plunge for all. For a moment Finn watched enviously as the last stragglers bolted from cover. The morning swim was for those who would soon undergo initiation, to prepare them for the hardships to come. Although he always joined in, Finn would never be initiated, never be a hunter, so no one compelled him. To be driven as the others were was for him the stuff of dreams. Before the last of the boys could pass by him, Finn had climbed to his feet and begun to haul his smock over his head. As he drew it over his shoulders, temporarily blinded, something hit him in the small of his back, sending him tumbling down the bank. As he rolled, then came to a stop, he heard laughter, and struggling free of his clothes he saw Venn of Hann's hearth standing over him. Bruised but glad to be included in the fun, he grabbed for Venn's ankle, but the other boy danced out of his reach, turned and raced down toward the trees with Finn in pursuit.

From the edge of the scree he could see the others entering the trees, jostling and fighting for a place on the track. Not far

4

behind them their fathers and brothers drove them downward in a straggling line, like wolves driving deer. Over to the right the girls, on their way down to the watering point farther upstream, shouted encouragement to their brothers and favorites. Ahead was Venn picking his way carefully among the loose stones of the escarpment. Over level ground or uphill Finn knew Venn could escape him. Anyone could run *up* a hill, it was descending that was difficult. Even as the broken stones bruised his feet Finn knew he was gaining on his quarry. He tore down the loose shale with the ease of a boy who has been running over rough ground all his life—the life of an outcast had prepared him well for this. Halfway down he slipped, tucked in his chin, rolled and came to his feet in one movement. He was gaining on Venn; he laughed out loud.

By the time he felt the soft grass beneath his feet and the lower branches of the first scattered pines lashed his face and arms, he could see the objective of this stampede, though he had lost sight of Venn. The gap in the trees that lined the stream was wide enough for ten men to stand side by side; the pool below it, although neither wide nor deep, was the best place for swimming that the stream afforded. It was here that the whole tribe would gather to lie around and bathe on warm afternoons after the Spring kill, when the meat was laid out on the scree to dry and the day's gathering was done. It was here, too, that the boys were driven on cold gray dawns such as this, hardening their bodies for the life that lay ahead.

As he descended deeper into the forest the branches overhead blotted out the sky. Finn could see the crowd less than a stone's throw ahead. Yet he had lost Venn. Before he could begin to comb the crowd in search of him, he was caught up in a press of bodies driven forward by the switches of the hunters. Many of the younger men took it as a personal affront if a single youth of any hearth returned to the ledge unmarked. At the water's edge some boys, memories of warm fawnskin beds still fresh, shivered on the edge, peering furtively at the gray, uninviting water below. Others barged past and leaped in, keen to get it over with, though one or two turned on their pursuers to wrestle with them. In the trees around the pool echoed, as had echoed for generations beyond number, the sounds of laughter from dozens of small fights that ended, as always, with the younger participants being hurled headlong over the edge. Finn was not so sure of his standing yet, as to throw himself into any of these contests, yet he would wrestle with Venn if he could find him. Making his way through the throng he paused at the water's edge. Below him the kicking and thrashing of those who had already braved the water's chill made the whole pool seethe like a pot full of boiling meat.

There was no sign of Venn, and no point in delaying the inevitable. Pausing only to pick his spot Finn drew up his knees, clutched at his ankles and launched himself into the air. For an instant after hitting the water he felt nothing, then the cold knifed through him, and suddenly all was dark and silent. The cries of the swimmers, the shouts of encouragement and laughter from the bank, all were lost as he sank. Only the kicks and buffets from countless arms and legs thrashing around him in the pool reminded him that he was not alone. By the time his head broke the surface and he gasped for air, the shock of the cold had passed, and the clamor filled his ears again. Even the hangers-on at the bank were in the water now. In ones and twos the hunters were starting to make their way back up the valley side to the ledge. With heavy limbs numbed by the water's chill, Finn, too, made his way to the bank, and hauled himself out of the water.

The pool was emptying fast as he shook himself dry and looked about him. At last he saw Venn, still in the water and swimming toward the bank. He was racing Gronu of Llin's hearth; reaching the bank Venn turned back to shout to him over his shoulder. As he did so he reached to pull himself out, unaware of Finn standing over him. Half out of the water he saw him, only when it was too late. Finn's foot on his shoulder propelled him back in, and before he had resurfaced Finn had taken to his heels. He had reached the bottom of the scree before Venn caught him. They fought, laughing and rolling in the grass. At last tired and starting to shiver, they climbed up to the ledge to where the thick columns of smoke indicated that the cooking fires were now well established.

"You'll eat with us?" said Venn as they dressed. If it smacked more of a command than an invitation, it only reflected the truth. Finn lived happily and unashamedly in Venn's shadow. Venn was all Finn wished to be. Venn was both taller and broader, with the muscular build covered by a protective layer of fat typical of the Burnt Shins. Typical too was his long brown hair (how Finn hated the reddish tinge of his own), slightly snubbed nose, strong jawline, and perfectly regular white teeth, marred in Venn's case by a front tooth broken while mending a spear. It seemed that all the world from the old men to the young women loved Venn. Strong, generous, straight-talking, more given to action than to words, he was the one among all the hunters-to-be of whom the most was expected. That he was also the only one among them who treated Finn with any respect, who would seek him out and talk with him, was entirely in character. If in their dealings he spoke from a position of conscious superiority, it was a superiority they both recognized.

"I lost you on the way down," said Finn. Nodding a greeting to Venn's sister Laela who tended the fire, they seated themselves on two of the large stones that ringed the hearth.

Venn laughed. "You were standing right by me for a while. I hid in the bushes, crouched at your feet."

Finn shrugged and smiled ruefully; it was no disgrace to be thus outwitted. Venn's skill at movement and concealment was well known to him from their childhood games.

"It's movement that gives you away," Venn went on. "If you keep low and still most things will pass you by."

Finn smiled again. He did not, as others might, resent being

7

lectured. Venn was justly proud of his prowess, and Finn, lacking a father, was keen to learn from anyone even if, as now, it was a lesson he knew by heart.

"Listen to him!" This was Laela. "Talking like an Elder. You'd think he had a beard down to his chest instead of a chin as smooth as mine!"

"You worry about feeding the men," said Venn as his sister lowered a flat cooking-stone onto the flames. "Never you mind their talk! How long will it be now?" He gestured to the wooden pot into which she was mixing meat from small game, and herbs and water from the stream.

"As long as it takes," she stirred the cold broth. "Longer if I have to step over there and beat a *boy* who's forgotten his manners."

Venn laughed. Despite her threatening tone, this banter between them was incessant and always good-natured. To Finn he said loudly and for Laela's benefit, "Better a boy who forgets his manners than a woman who forgets her place. It's this day, it always affects them this way."

Unwilling to be dragged into their running battle, Finn looked away shyly. Today was the day of the Fire dances. By midday, every woman and girl would depart the ledge and not return until morning. What took place at the ritual no man knew; none had ever seen and lived to speak of it. Fire was woman's business, woman's gift to the world, purchased at a terrible price. Fire *was* life. It animated every living thing— why else did butchered carcasses steam in the Winter air, or the dying grow cold as their life drained away? When a man died the Burnt Shins said "The fire has gone out of him." So those who produced life, those who brought fire into the world, tended that fire *in* the world. However much a man might learn of hunting from his father and brothers, he learned of fire from his mother.

Getting no response to his last sally, Venn turned to his sister once more. "What do you women get up to down there, anyway? Perhaps I'll come down tonight and see!" Alarmed now, Finn reached out to still his friend's tongue. Laela saw the gesture, and nodded at him. "He has more sense than you," she said, addressing her brother. "Do not delve into matters that don't concern you. That is dangerous."

From her tone Venn knew he had gone too far. In a year he would be a man and could say what he pleased; in the meantime he was still a child and must defer. There were limits even to Laela's love for him. Anxious to change the subject he turned to where the stone lay in the fire. "The stone's ready!" he declared, rubbing his stomach and treating her to his most winning smile. Laela said nothing, but Finn noticed, as she carried the pot over to the fire and lifted the stone with wooden tongs, that she struggled not to smile. As she balanced the stone on the edge of the pot for a moment, Finn saw the stump where the little finger of her left hand had been severed—a sign of mourning. Laela had not been lucky. Venn's senior by five years, she had married a hunter of Llin's hearth. Two Winters ago he had been drowned in the river at the Autumn slaughter; she, being childless, had been returned to her father's hearth as a "useless mouth." Yet she was kind and humorous, and though no beauty, had a pleasant face. Finn felt sure that she would marry again.

The cold water of the broth hissed as she lowered the stone into the pot, and Venn, eager to placate her, wiped three bowls with moss and laid them in a row on one of the flat hearth stones. As the steam from the broth filled the air with the scent of herbs even Laela's set face softened at last. With the almost religious respect accorded to all food, especially now at the tail end of the Summer, before the deer returned, the broth was poured, and the bowls passed out. The boys ate in silence, if the slurps, belches and grunts of satisfaction that accompanied any Burnt Shin meal could be so called. When they had all eaten, Laela rose and looked about her. Among the tents of Hann's hearth, and at the other hearths all down the line of the camp, groups of women and girls were gathering. Soon it would be time to be off—the men must fend for themselves until morning.

Donning her hooded deerskin cloak Laela turned to her brother. "Tell father that is the last of the smoked meat in the bag by the door. If you want anything more, go and check your traps, or there are salmon in the river."

Venn pulled a face. He shook his head, grinning at her. "The only food I like is meat!" Almost as if by a signal all three looked away over the treetops toward the river. Nothing was said to express their longing—no words were needed. The Fire dances were the last of the Summer rituals. Soon would follow the Reindeer dance, heralding the coming of Autumn, the coming of the herds.

When Laela had gone, joining the lines of women and girls descending the scree to the tree-line, Venn slapped his knees as the men did when they had come to a decision, and stood up. He stretched, sniffed the air and gazed up at the sky. Noticing for the first time the clusters of high white clouds drifting over from the grasslands, he narrowed his eyes as though trying to pick out something among them. Failing to do so, he turned to Finn.

"Will there be pictures in the sky?" he asked, suddenly a child begging his father for a story.

This was Finn's moment. It was his gift—a gift that only Venn had bothered to discover—to see things as others could not. With his eyes closed he could conjure up people, objects, animals as vividly as if they were there before him. He did not fool himself that these visions were real, nor was this gift of benefit to anyone but himself. Yet it was for this as much as anything that Venn prized his company.

For Venn a thing was either there or it was not; when he closed his eyes he saw darkness. It was a constant delight to him to lie by Finn listening to him describe the things he had dreamed up—things they had both seen, things that had happened in the past, people who were far away, or were dead and in the dreamworld. Finn brought them to life so vividly that he wished he could enter Finn's head and see them for himself. It was that same gift, he supposed, that those men had who had painted the walls of the ritual cave. He would see that for himself on that eagerly awaited day when he would enter into manhood. Whatever the gift was, Venn envied it. The sight of the clouds caused him to invoke it now, for Finn's gift took one other form. As well as presenting pictures for his closed eyes, it enabled him to see in everyday things shapes and images that were apparent to no one else. He could look at a rock, a tree, or a branch and see a man's arm throwing a spear, an old woman gathering sticks, a bird in flight, or an animal crouched in the bushes. Best of all, though, was the way he could impose order and meaning on the random patterns of the clouds.

Finn scanned the clouds, taking his time, enjoying the moment—*his* rare moment of power.

"The sky looks good!" he declared suddenly, and without another word both boys took to their heels, dodging through the tents, sprinting across the open ground between the tents and the scree where the hunters sat talking as they fashioned flint spearheads or mended traps. Scrambling over the loose stones on the scree they tumbled down in the direction of the river and the valley mouth. At the tree-line they turned to the left, following it along to where the valley's sides opened out, to where, though still among the trees, they could see to the river far below and out across the grasslands.

Immediately below them was a flat bare rock warmed by the sun on which they would often lie and gaze out over the land below or, if they chose, roll over and stare at the sky. By the time they had settled themselves in their familiar places the clouds had moved. The farthest edge of the rock formed a lip that sheltered them from the wind. For a while they were content simply to bask. Then Venn grew impatient and watching Finn searching among the clouds began asking him, "What's there? What can you see?"

Without taking his eyes from the sky Finn whispered reverently, "I can see Annu!"

At the utterance of their God's name, Venn's jaw fell open. Yet try as he might he could see nothing above that suggested Him.

"Where?" he demanded.

"There!" Finn's arm pointed to where the sun rose in the mornings.

Just above the horizon Venn could see the form that had suggested to Finn the Father of the Burnt Shins and the Creator of the worlds. A long blunt-muzzled head, topped by a vast rack of antlers, had slowly emerged from the mass of cloud that crawled across the sky toward them. As yet no body was discernible, but the cloud mass was breaking up and the great deer's head was drawing clear of the rest.

As happened so often Venn found that he could see what Finn saw, once it was pointed out to him. Yet this time something troubled him.

"Why Annu?" he said softly. "Why Him? Why not just a deer? I cannot see his body." As he spoke the cloud mass changed form, and below the huge Reindeer head the torso of a man appeared.

"Yes!" Venn cried out. "I see. It *is* Him!"

Finn smiled as the image of Annu—who was part deer, part man, and much more that was neither, He in whom man and nature became one—drifted toward them. Without him, Venn would never have noticed it. It would pass over the camp, and over the grove where the women were gathering for the Fire dances, and none would see it, or if they did would not spare it a second glance. This vision was his, born of his gift, and now made a gift to his friend.

"You knew before it moved," Venn whispered, awe-struck. "How?"

Finn pointed once more. "Because I saw His daughters first! See? There are the three dancers, and there, above the trees, is Aela running with the stolen brand."

It took a few moments for Venn to see the completed story that Finn had picked out of the sky. But at last under his friend's guidance he saw it unfold.

The Burnt Shins loved stories, loved them as much as singing or dancing. At work or at rest, roaming the forests in search of food, or huddled round their fires at night, their appetite for stories new or old was insatiable. Venn was no exception. He himself was no storyteller, lacking the wit to invent new ones or the facility to remember the old. But Finn had even the longest of the old tales word-perfect. Nothing less would do for the people of the ten hearths. A storyteller who strayed even slightly from the track of a well-known tale would soon be interrupted and politely corrected. If he persisted, he would find himself embroiled in lengthy arguments about the smallest of details. Often loud and always fiercely contested, such arguments were one of the tribespeople's chief amusements.

"Tell the story!" cried Venn eagerly. "I want to hear it. Quick, before it goes!"

Finn needed little urging. Proud of his learning, it was all too seldom he had the opportunity of displaying it. As the clouds floated across the sky, Finn told the tale of the daughters of Annu.

"When Annu first created the earth he made from clay the images of all the things he would people it with. Then he went back to the dreamworld where his dwelling was, beside the great fire that was the source of all life. From the fire he took a brand and returned to the earth with it. Everything He touched with the brand took life from the fire. With this fire He gave life to everything on earth. But first of all he touched the men

13

and the women and the Reindeer, whom He loved the best, saying that they should be called His children, and that they should live together in peace.

"For a time all was well. The people and the Reindeer lived together in the forests, and the people were never cold for the sun warmed them by day, and by night they lay down among the deer. The deer had fawns and the people had sons and daughters. They all sported together and knew neither fear nor want. Then one day the Reindeer grew curious, as is their nature. They wanted to see what else Annu had made. They set off across the grasslands, for they had heard of the great salt river and they wanted to see this above all else. The men and women ran after them, reminding them that Annu had said they should live together. But the people could not keep up. They called out to the deer to stop, but the deer were so consumed by their curiosity that they left the people on the plain.

"Such was the speed of the deer that first the women and children and finally the men failed and fell back. When the sun, like the deer, had vanished over the horizon, the people grew cold. Now, having no fur of their own, they could only huddle together for warmth. The next day the men set off in pursuit of the deer. The women waited in the forest to watch over the children. After three nights the men had not returned. The women, fearing for their children's lives, sent Aela, first of the daughters of Annu, and her three sisters to the dreamworld. They found Annu sitting by the great fire. The three sisters approached and told him they had come to dance for him. Annu was delighted to see his daughters dance for He loved them dearly. While he was distracted, Aela crept up to the fire and snatching up a brand raced back to earth. The dance over, the sisters followed Aela back to earth, where the women and children and the returning men rejoiced by the many fires they had lit from the brand.

"In the dreamland Annu returned to the fire and soon discovered the theft, for the fire burned lower. He came to the

14

earth. In turn he asked all the beasts if they had taken the fire. He found the Reindeer by the sea and, because they had wandered, and because they were too busy grazing to answer Him, He took away their power of speech. At last he came to the men and women where they sat in the forest. They had hidden the brand in a cave and they denied the theft. But their shins were burned from sitting close to the fire, and He knew what they had done. He asked them, 'Why have you done this thing?' 'The Reindeer left us and our children grew cold,' they said. And Annu grieved in His heart, for He loved them the best of all His Creation. And He said, 'Because of what you have done, the world will grow colder still, and the sun will not warm you, nor the grass feed you. You and the Reindeer shall live apart all Summer, but in the Autumn they will come to you, and you will eat their flesh and warm yourselves with their skins, and there shall be bloodshed between your children and theirs until the end of time. The blood of the deer shall be on the hands of my sons, and the secret of the fire shall be my daughters'. And as you toil apart so shall you worship, neither knowing the rites of the other until you are with me once more in the life that is to come.' And so it has remained."

By the time he had finished the image of the girl Aela had passed out of sight behind the trees, leaving only the trail of cloud that was the smoke from her flaming brand to mark her passing. Venn sat up, gazing at Finn in wonder. Finn whose voice, when using the words of another, was stronger and more confident than normal, now resumed his customary diffidence, and smiled back shyly.

"A good omen," announced Venn, "on this day of all days."

"And only we, from the whole tribe to see it," added Finn.

"Only *you*," corrected his friend, "for it would have passed me by." He shook his head. "We have seen a wonder today. You must be favored by Annu."

When at length Venn left to go and check his traps Finn watched him until he had disappeared from sight. He was glad to have been able to share his gift with his friend; gratified too, to be the object of his envy. Yet he wondered, as he turned away, if Venn realized how enviable was his own position.

He knew that Venn envied him that world behind his eyelids that was his refuge, to which he could retreat at will, and in which things were ordered to his choosing. How much more enviable then, to have no need of such escape. At thirteen Summers, in his last year before manhood, Venn was like him in all outward things, but different in that he truly belonged, was not tainted, *marked* as an outsider. Venn had been born in the camp; had been the cause of songs and rejoicing round his father's hearth. At night he slept on fawnskin in his father's tent, by day he learned from him the skills of a hunter. In another year he would be a hunter, in another three he would marry. He would choose a girl from another hearth and, she and her family being willing, and the match being ruled lawful by the Elders, Venn with his hearth companions would appear before her father's tents on the appointed day. Her father and brothers would form up armed and challenging, there would be mock fights and protests, and he would carry her to his father's hearth, to the tent his mother and sisters had prepared. Her family would follow, protesting; they would be appeased with gifts; and there would be feasting. All night the people would sing around their fires of his prowess and of her beauty and wisdom.

For Finn the future held no such promises. He would never be initiated into the ranks of the hunters, would have no hearth companions, would never marry. What girl would favor him, son of a strange tribe, ragged and primitive, who had tried to enter the valley one Winter years ago? Attacked by the Burnt Shin hunters they had put up little fight, then fled, leaving no trace of their passing but a child abandoned by the riverbank. Those had been fat times for the Burnt Shins. Able to afford the luxury of pity for a foundling, they had carried him home with them. Yet pity had its limits. Though the tribe had spared him death, it had condemned him to a life of scavenging on the fringes of the camp, belonging nowhere, accepted at all hearths but welcome at none, and marked forever by the only thing his own people had left him, the tribal mark, a leaping salmon, tattooed on his left forearm.

▲   ▲   ▲

Finn sat up and examined his arm; he was reconciled now to the fact that it would not fade with time. One year he had tried to remove it with one of the bone scrapers the women used to clean the deerskins. His arm had swollen and he had nearly died, but the salmon remained to mock him. Long ago he had acquired the habit of wearing his cloak slung over his left shoulder to hide the offending mark. But it was of no avail. It was always there to remind one and all of his rightful place in the world. It had even given him the nickname "Smolt," after the young salmon that came up the stream each Summer—with which they taunted him when on occasion he was tempted to assert himself and was chased off or beaten for his impudence. After a few moments he shrugged and threw back his cloak; his mark and all it meant were too familiar to darken his mood for long. The sun was shining, Venn was pleased with him, and he had work to do. Not the tasks that fell to the other youth of the tribe, he was at least spared those, but a task of his own choosing.

When he was sure Venn was gone and there was no possibility of his being observed, Finn began to climb, skirting the mountainside, to a place where the grassy slopes gave way to steep cliffs. Here, with the ease of long practice he shuffled along a ledge until he reached a great crack in the rock, and checking once more to be sure he was not watched, slipped in. The space within was just large enough for him to sit or lie in, and still see the sky. It was cool on Summer days, and in the

Winter sheltered from the worst of the wind and weather. Neither concerned him now, though, as he groped down into a fissure in the rock that surrounded him until his fingers found a small skin bundle, then drew it out and emptied its contents onto the earth floor. There were two pieces of flint and a small oddly shaped piece of wood. The two flints had originally been one, one of the sharp hand tools the women used for jointing slaughtered deer. Having broken up the middle, it had been flung out onto the scree to be retrieved by Finn and carried away here to his bolt-hole. The wood, too, had been discarded, though brought home as firewood by a small girl of Hann's hearth. It was resinous wood; anyone who had burned it would have been smoked out of his tent. In the hard way of the tribe she had been sent out at once, dark as it was and despite her fear of the woods at night, to gather more and better wood. Finn remembered how Hann the hearth leader had watched stern-faced as the child had set off, then had followed her secretly and brought her home laughing, on his back, with armfuls of firewood. This first piece had lain disregarded until Finn had seen it, and had seen what it could be.

Now as he worked on it, remembering Hann's kindness to the child, it seemed appropriate that this should be a gift for Hann's own child, the sickly boy who lay day and night at the back of Hann's own tent. Hann's benevolence, which extended to all Creation, had not been rewarded in his son. Simpleminded, with his spindly limbs and odd misshapen head, he was an abiding sorrow to his parents, and the object of much cruel comment by those who envied Hann's strength and wisdom.

Finn looked at the wood in his lap. It was roughly worked but the shape he had first seen in the wood had begun to emerge. The workmanship was crude; evidence that, whatever tribal laws might say, Finn was still a child, yet it pleased his child's eye. From a discarded lump of wood he had worked an image of a buck Reindeer, nose thrust into the air so that its antlers lay across its back, trotting forward to meet a threat. Finn's tools were ill-suited for the work he had to do, and he had cut his hand many times. There was much more that needed to be done. The legs were not right, and the toy had not yet become all that he had envisaged. But something inside him told him that he was running out of time. He would present the gift tonight, before it was too late.

The boy had grown weaker despite Hann's best efforts; rarely now did Mata bring him out onto the ledge to sit in the sun or look out over the valley with those eyes that seemed to see nothing. Finn had missed him; alone among the Burnt Shin youth, he had had time for the boy, and the boy in turn had always greeted his arrival with a cry of delight that gladdened his heart. Apart from Hann and Mata, Finn was the only person the child could recognize, knowing him as the one who would come in from the woods bearing gifts—flowers and leaves and brightly polished stones. This gift would be the greatest gift of all and, Finn feared, the last.

The sun was dying as Finn climbed up the scree to the camp, and made his way over to the right-hand cluster of tents which was Hann's. The camp was strangely silent as it always was on this day, mainly, ran the joke, due to the absence of the women. What took place down there in that sacred grove, what weird rites, invocations, re-creations of age-old myth, was unknown to any of them; yet the men's voices as they talked around the fires were muted in acknowledgment of the awesome power that was abroad that night.

Hann was seated at the door of his tent, repairing the stitching on his great Reindeer mask. Even at such a time as this and even though Finn was not of his hearth there was something reassuring to the boy about Hann's massive presence. His stout squat frame, with broad thighs and shoulders heavily muscled, black beard wide as a hand span and unkempt locks overhanging his brow, all were real enough to dispel the air of unreality that hung over the camp. Seeing Finn he smiled a welcome, then, guessing the reason for his visit, shook his head.

"He's asleep," he said. "He tires easily these days." His soft voice and benign manner belied his wild looks.

"I wanted to give him this." Finn's voice faltered as he held out the toy. Tucking the small bone needle, absurdly small in his powerful hands, into the fur of the mask, Hann lifted it to one side and took the proffered gift. He looked it over for some time, conscious of the boy eyeing him anxiously, and nodded his approval, one craftsman to another. Finn's face lit up at the unspoken praise. Hann returned the gift, saying, "Tomorrow."

But the man saw the disappointment in the boy's face, and, as their eyes met, something more—the boy feared, as he did, that tomorrow might be too late, that the child who lay within had few tomorrows left.

"Wait here," he said as Finn's eyes brimmed with tears. "I'll get a light. We'll wake him."

Cradling the gift, Finn followed Hann into the tent. It was lit by a shallow stone bowl filled with deer fat. It was rare at this time of year when fat was scarce to see such a lamp, but with Mata at the Fire dance Hann feared lest the child should wake in the dark and be afraid. There was no fear now, though, as he shook the bundle of fawnskin where his son lay. Finn saw the thin arms reach out to embrace the man, and saw Hann turn the frail body to face the tent door where he waited. Seeing him, the boy cried out in joy. It was a weak cry, almost indistinguishable from the few other sounds that were the child's only language, but Finn recognized in it his own name. He crawled forward into the light, holding the toy self-consciously, reveling in the sleepy child's ecstatic welcome. Without a word Hann left the tent, and Finn saw his shadow settle once more outside the door.

Now that they were alone Finn held the carving up into the lamplight, and to his delight saw the boy's face light up. As he reached out to touch it, Finn saw for the first time the toll the past few months had taken. The wispy hair on the child's head had thinned still further and Finn could almost see through his skin; his arms were thinner than ever, and as his eager fingers closed round the toy and Finn relinquished his hold, it fell to the floor between them. Weakened by even this effort, the boy lay back. Finn turned him—how painfully light he was!—onto his side. Taking up the toy, he began to walk it along the floor toward him, imitating with his tongue the clicking of the deer's hooves. The child laughed, remembering perhaps the time during the Autumn migration three Winters ago when he had been strong enough to be carried down to the valley bottom to see the deer pass by. Until the flame was guttering in the stone bowl, Finn played with the deer, re-creating the sounds it made: the startled cough when threatened, the satisfied grunts as it fed on lichen beneath the snow or moss in the Summer grazing grounds, in search of which Finn took it on endless migrations across the floor of the tent. At last the child grew tired and reached out a hand for the deer. As Finn placed it gently by him, he drew it under the fawnskin and was asleep in moments, clutching it to him.

Finn too was tired, and lay down for a few moments beside his friend. The camp outside was hushed now, and from below in the valley deep in the forests came the sounds of the women shrieking and ululating at the Fire dance. It was an awful, eerie sound, conjuring a thousand fearful images before his eyes. Venn had joked about going down to see the Dance, but Finn had little doubt that he too was chilled by the sound, which was enough by itself to deter anyone from venturing into the woods that night. He thought of Laela, and how her face had clouded at Venn's joke. Could it be possible that she, for all her love for him, would have denounced her own brother if he had carried out his threat? It had happened in the past, he knew; boys speared by the hunters to save the tribe from the misfortune attendant on breaking age-old taboos.

The steady breathing of the child beside him distracted Finn from such grim thoughts. The boy's face in repose, freed from the strain and frustration of trying to communicate with those around him, seemed calm, as though he might wake at any moment and talk to him. Finn wondered if he was in the dreamlands, and if he was whole and happy there. Outside, the fire of Hann's hearth flared, silhouetting his body against the wall of the tent. Struggling to keep his eyes open Finn watched the shadow change shape as Hann lifted his great mask up into the light of the fire to examine it more closely. The shadow of the mask merged with the body, replacing Hann's head with the long neck, blunt muzzle and mighty antlers of the Reindeer. For the second time that day Finn beheld the image of his God, and under His benign shadow he slept at last beside his friend.

CHAPTER
TWO

▲ ▲ ▲
▲ ▲

THE WIND HAD DIED, and in the absence of rain the pools were low; it was a perfect day for fishing. It was the day after the Fire dance; the women had returned to the camp, and the strange atmosphere that always prevailed for a while in the wake of their rituals had vanished with the morning dew. By midday the camp was in the grip of a new excitement. For days now the stream had been filling with salmon in unheard-of numbers. As soon as the morning's instruction was over, the boys of the tribe had raced to their tents for their fishing spears and tumbled down the scree to the stream. Finn had been among the first of them, proudly brandishing a fishing spear of Hann's making, a gift in return for a gift. Like everything made by Hann it was the best of its kind, with a light slender ash shaft and three barbed bone prongs delightfully sharp to the touch. As the boys crowded the banks, jostling for space, Finn knew he would have to be content with a spot no one else wanted. Venn would not come fishing; he avoided things at which he did not excel. Finn alone was neither strong nor well placed enough to secure one of the best stretches. That would be where there were rocks and

23

shade, or a gravelly bed. But the spear and what it represented were more than compensation.

When the crowd had shaken out along both banks of the stream, Finn found himself at an unpromising spot. At least the shade of a great old alder took the glare off the water, but the bed here was bare, and offered little shelter to the fish. Silence fell now as the boys crouched, spear arms raised, and stalked the banks, feeling for footholds among the rocks and the mossy alder roots, peering into the pools and eddies below.

Eyes strained through the patterns thrown by sun and trees upon the face of the water. As they grew accustomed, they began to pick out silver among the shadows; the pink under-sides of the males in their breeding colors, and the darker, mot-tled females. Never in the memory of men had the stream held such abundance of salmon. They seemed as numerous as the leaves overhead, woven in and out among the tree roots below the bank, lurking under rocky ledges or in the calmer waters behind boulders, still, save for the swaying of tail fins that held them in the stream.

It was a sight to stay even the most eager hand. The silence that settled on the riverbank, the silence of the hunter, became for a moment the silence of the devout. They stood, unmoving as the surrounding trees, as though arms raised to strike had become branches and naked feet had taken root in the mossy soil. It seemed as if they would always remain there, forever poised to strike, forever holding back; as if this scene, earth and trees, sky and stream, hunters and prey were all of Creation, and this moment all of time, and to break either would be a blasphemy.

It was Gronu who struck first, from his pride of place on the gravel bank; Gronu, half a head taller than any of his fellows, with hair as sleek and black as a raven's back and brows like a raven's wings. His pale green eyes, eyes that saw everything and wanted what they saw, had never for a moment stopped search-ing the depths while the others had merely stood and gaped. In his impatience he had forgotten that below the surface things were never what they seemed; his spear points struck gravel as a silver shape darted for cover. Before he could even curse, another boy upstream had hit, and was raising his spear with its wriggling burden skyward to the delighted shouts of his hearth companions. From that moment the contest began in earnest as each strove for food for the tribe, his own glory, and that of his hearth.

Gronu was not slow to redeem his mistake. His was the best stretch of bank, and his spear flashed into the water like the beak of a heron. That spear was the envy of all, except Finn now, and seldom left the water unladen. Such was Gronu's status that when the younger boys arrived at the bank, drawn from their tasks with the women by the cries of their brothers, most, in spite of all considerations of hearth or kinship, splashed across the stream. Ignoring the angry shouts of their Elders they gathered behind Gronu. There they cheered him on and fought among themselves for the honor of gathering and clubbing his catch.

Alone under the giant alder Finn made short work of what few fish came under his spear. He was fast with the fish spear, fast as life among the Burnt Shins had made him, and he had mastered the trick that water played with men's eyes. From where he was, at the end of the line, he could see all the youth of the tribe thronging both banks. Their numbers had been swelled now by the arrival of the girls who had dropped their bundles of firewood and handfuls of berries and sprinted down through the woods. The older women, left behind, smiled to each other, remembering days when they had done the same. Now the rivalry intensified as the girls joined in the clamor that greeted each catch and, when silence fell once more, pointed out targets to their favorites. When Gronu turned to shake his latest catch from his spear there were plenty of fair young faces smiling up at him, but among them was not the face he had wanted, or expected to see.

25

Shani had been standing beside Finn for some time before he became aware of her presence. He had been staring into the unpromising stretch of bare rock on the stream bed below him, thinking what wonders he could work with his new spear if he were downstream where the gravel was. In any case, if he had been looking for Shani, as he would have sooner or later, he would have expected to find her in the crowd behind Gronu. Even now, though she was by his side, she showed no sign that she was even aware of his presence. She was standing with her weight on one leg, the other bent slightly, staring intently at a stretch of the earth bank below and to her right. Finn had never been this close to her before. He could hear her breathing, almost hear her heartbeat, still fast from the race down to the stream side. Her short, tightly belted fawnskin smock barely covered a body slender and straight as a spear, not yet a woman's but already more than a child's. The fine down on her arms and legs, almost invisible normally, shone golden now in the light that filtered down through the leaves. It was her face, though, that haunted him, both in his dreams and in his waking moments; the long straight nose, mouth a little wide perhaps for perfect beauty, the even white teeth with sharp canines that flashed whenever she laughed, and above her high cheekbones brown eyes as lovely as any doe's. She had tucked her light brown hair behind her ears, and as Finn gazed at her, rapt, a bead of perspiration trickled down over her soft cheek to the line of her jaw. He longed to take it gently on his fingertip, to capture some small part of her, the essence of her, which would be his and his alone forever, but he dared not.

Often, daydreaming in his bolt-hole, Finn had tried to think how it would be to be like the other youths of the tribe. He would picture in his mind all the great events of life that would never happen to him: initiation to manhood, hunting with hearth companions, marriage to a girl of his choosing. However these dreams might vary, one image alone was constant—the image of Shani. All the others were mere notions, the *ideas* of friends and family, shadowy figures who came and went, changed according to his moods, bearing little relation to the people among whom he lived. She alone was real, for how could she fade or alter when he had her living image daily before him? The pain of passing from dreams to bitter truth had caused him countless times to forswear this world behind his eyes. Failing that, he had tried to keep the two apart, but in Shani both worlds met. She gave his dreams enough of truth to make them sweet, and his life enough of magic to make it bearable.

A splash and a shout downstream distracted Finn. A boy of Hann's hearth had landed a large female and his comrades crowded round him while the others called angrily for silence. Finn was watching the youth, envying him the congratulations of his friends, when he felt Shani's hand upon his arm. Only once, years before, when he had been about to leap into the river from a high ledge, longing to jump but afraid too, had Finn felt such a sensation as that which now rose in the pit of his stomach and spread up and across his shoulders and down his back. The people of the Burnt Shins lived closely together and touched often, but Finn, existing on the fringes of the camp and used to rough handling from his fellows, had learned to avoid contact. This small hand resting gently on his arm, his marked arm at that, was a new sensation to him. It thrilled through him. He turned his gaze upon her but she was not looking at him. Still holding on to his arm, she was peering down into the water, into the twisted roots of the great alder below the bank.

Feeling his way carefully with his feet, Finn crept closer to the water's edge. He wanted to see what it was that had caught her eye. At the same time he was loath to move lest she remove her hand. Her hand moved with him, though, as woven among the roots Finn discerned a cock salmon, the largest he had seen, at least as long as his arm. Silence had fallen downstream; the fish had grown cautious and the kills were fewer and less frequent. A slight breeze disturbed the trees, turning the pattern on the water into a turmoil of green and gold. Still, through it all, Finn could see the silver and pink of the fish as it wound its way sinuously through the moss roots. Alerted by the splashing downstream it was biding its time before moving across to the shelter of the rocky ledge on the far bank. Finn knew that he would get only one shot at it. To strike too soon would be to risk hitting wood and then to try to wrench his spear points free as his quarry darted away. He would have to wait until it emerged, then strike fast and true. As once more it began to move slowly toward the open water Finn raised his spear arm. Sweat stung his eyes. Then came a splash and a curse downstream; Gronu had missed for once, and Finn's fish slid back into the shadows where it lurked, its lithe body still visible among the roots.

Finn felt himself weakening; the closeness of Shani, and the strange sensations it had aroused, the excitement of the hunt, and the fear of failing her, all were wearing him down. He longed for the fish to appear, for the ordeal to end one way or another; and yet part of him wished that this moment could go on forever. He felt the soft mud oozing through his toes, and to relieve his tired eyes he looked down at them. Suddenly he felt her fingers tighten on his arm. A memory flashed through his mind—the moment he had actually leaped from the edge and the feeling as he began to fall—the same feeling as now. The fish was emerging again. Finn could see its head now, its hooked lower jaw; an instant more and he must strike. He glanced at Shani. She was biting her lip, the sharp white canines crushing the lower lip, turning it pink, salmon pink. He struck. She cried out, and he felt the spear sink into flesh. Taking the weight of it in both hands he wrenched the spear points clear of the stream, showering both their faces with water. The fish flew over their heads to land heavily in the grass behind them.

Shani was on it almost before it had landed, snatching up a stick and clubbing it while Finn leaned on the shaft of his spear and caught his breath. At Shani's cry all eyes had turned to them. Even as the fish finished its thrashing a crowd had begun to gather around her. Finn moved to go forward and join her, but Shani was already surrounded by most of the youth of the tribe and the remainder were splashing across from their places on the far bank to see this prodigious catch. They parted before him as Finn made his way to where Shani knelt, struggling to lift the fish. All around him he could hear their acclaim; someone even clapped him on the shoulder as he passed. He felt the sun warm his back as he approached her. His catch in her arms, she at her brightest, reveling in the attention, answering as best she could the questions that came at her from all sides.

"There's always one there, I've seen it many times!" she was saying to a boy of her own hearth. Then she dug him in the ribs with her elbow. "You go round with your eyes shut!"

As Finn approached she smiled at him, and held out the fish.

"Yours!"

Finn was shy now, abashed and suddenly wary at finding himself the center of attention in the midst of so many people. Words failed him. It was all he could do to stammer out, "No. It's yours."

She seemed to sense his confusion, for she stepped closer and spoke more softly, her eyes not leaving his, "Ours then." In that instant Finn could not remember when he had been so happy. This act of public recognition from a girl so widely admired was worth all the fish ever caught. All around him were smiling faces, the sun turned the grass golden, he thrilled to her touch again as she loaded the fish into his arms. Then the crowd parted once more; Gronu had crossed the stream to find

29

out what had caused the commotion. Finn looked toward him; a good word from Gronu, the undisputed leader of the young men, would complete his happiness. It was not too much to hope for; Gronu was not often among his tormentors. Generally he was above such things, and it was his generosity as much as his strength and prowess that had earned him the regard of his peers. Joining them in the center of the circle, Gronu gazed down at the fish in Finn's arms and, thrusting out his lower lip he nodded, recognizing, though grudgingly, the size of the catch. Then turning to Shani—as though Finn were not there —he said, "Why tell him, and not me?"

Not defiant so much as amused at his anger, she gazed back at him. "He was nearer." Neither of them had so much as glanced at Finn during this exchange. He felt himself slipping back once more to the fringe of things. What was happening was between the two of them; he was unimportant, something she could use to tease Gronu, as she was so fond of doing. Now, seeing the look on Gronu's face, he was grateful not to be no-ticed. If he could not gain Gronu's approval he would be con-tent to escape without offending him. Then Shani spoke again, breaking the silence that had settled over the glade. "Besides, Finn is faster than you with the spear. *You* might have missed."

In the crowd someone gasped, and Gronu turned his gaze for the first time on Finn. Finn could see—Gronu too was trapped. Stung by Shani's words he had to do something. But he would not risk losing face by bickering with a girl half his size. He looked Finn up and down scornfully. His eyes rested, as Finn knew they would, upon his tattooed arm, and Gronu nod-ded at the fish. "It must have taken you for its brother," he sneered. Laughter from behind him showed the mood of the gathering had shifted: Gronu, undisputed leader, had spoken with his hearth companions at his back. Others were quick to echo the gibe.

"Go and bury your brother, Smolt!" cried one.

"If you cannot bear to eat him," added another, and was

followed by a mocking chorus of "Murderer!" and "Cannibal!" from the crowd.

Finn knew better than to answer; in the absence of Venn there was no one to speak up for him. Shani seemed to have stepped back into the crowd, as if answering his silent hope that she would spare him the shame of her defending him. Taking up his spear, and clutching the fish awkwardly to his chest, he began to shoulder his way through the press.

"Be thankful that our fathers did not eat *you* when *you* came up the river," Gronu jeered.

Finn knew as well as any the truth that lay beneath this joke. He had been found in fat times; but he had heard of lean times in the distant past, when children vanished mysteriously. Gronu seemed satisfied now, and the incident would have ended there but for Finn. His one moment of glory had turned quite suddenly into another humiliation; the accumulated anger and frustration of many years welled up inside him. Before he had time to think he had lashed out with the butt of his spear and, caught by surprise, Gronu fell on the grass, as the salmon fell from Finn's arms.

When Gronu sat up, blood was trickling from the corner of his mouth and Finn's rage gave way to fear. He turned to run; but his way was blocked. He was thrown, sprawling, onto the trampled grass. Before he could rise, Gronu, on his feet now, had brought his spear shaft down across his back. Finn winced with pain, and buried his face in the grass, aware of Gronu's companions crowding round to join in the beating. No other boy would have taken such a thrashing; his hearth companions would have leaped to his defense, right or wrong. A general brawl would have ensued. There was no one to help Finn, though, as he crawled through a forest of legs to his escape. Even so, he could hear amidst the angry shouts of his enemies and the shrill cries of laughter and encouragement that some voices were raised in protest. At last he reached the main body of the crowd and, though some boys kicked him and pulled at

31

his hair, others—he knew not who—hauled him through the throng until he could see open ground in front of him. Battered and dizzy as he was, Finn knew that he could lose them in the woods, that none were as fast and surefooted as he. Before his persecutors could force their way through this thickest part of the crowd—where the young men of Shani's hearth, gathered in a body, seemed somehow to impede their progress—Finn was away.

▲　　▲　　▲

They hunted him through the woods for some time; Finn could hear them calling to each other as he crashed through the undergrowth, ignoring the brambles that tore at his arms and legs. His cheeks burned as he heard their taunts, and he wondered as he gained his haven, whether Shani had been among his tormentors. It was not impossible; the Burnt Shins were fickle, their moods changed faster than the winds. That she had seen what had happened was bad; that she had used him as a weapon in her running battle with Gronu was worse. Worst of all, though, was the thought that she might have been among those who had laughed and encouraged Gronu and his friends.

Settled between the rock walls of his niche he looked himself over. He was not badly hurt. He watched the clouds drift through the sky, confident that by now his pursuers had tired of their sport. Only if Shani was among them was he in danger of being discovered. He could remember a time two Summers ago when he had lain in this same place looking up at the sky, and had suddenly seen her face looking down at him. Shani was known for her curiosity; it had earned her many beatings as a child, and some said it would be the death of her. But Finn's fear had been for himself now that his hiding place had been found. She had said nothing, only smiled and moved on, and he had remained undisturbed. He remained undisturbed this day too. As dusk began to fall, he eased himself from between the rocks and made his way, aching now, back toward the camp. No doubt by now all would be forgotten and he would be able, as usual, to get a meal at one of the hearths. The Burnt Shins were not cruel—they had, after all, given him the gift of life. What more had he any right to expect? Nor did they hate him. He had received many kindnesses. It was just that he was no one's kin, no one's responsibility.

Before he had reached the camp, Finn saw ahead of him in the half-dark a lone figure seated at the base of a tree. As he drew closer he saw that it was Hann; he was seated with his back against the trunk of the tree. His spears lay abandoned in the grass beside him. Finn approached hesitantly. What could have drawn Hann out into the woods at this time? He could not have been visiting Sanu; the holy man's cave was up the mountainside beyond the camp. The cooking fires would be burning high now. What reason had Hann to be away from his hearth? Silently as he moved, Finn expected at any moment that Hann would turn and greet him. But he was almost standing over him before Hann became aware of his presence. As their eyes met, Finn read in Hann's drawn face the reason for his wandering alone out here. Sometime that day, while he had been fishing or hiding at the valley mouth, Hann's son had relinquished his frail hold on life.

Finn howled in pain; what the blows and curses of his tormentors had not achieved the loss of his first friend had, and his tears flowed freely. Without a word Hann reached up and drew the boy to him; with his arm about his neck Hann wept, at last, himself. In the way of the tribe their grief was unrestrained. They howled like wolves, tearing at the earth with their hands, showering their heads with dust. Together they sang their loss to the surrounding darkness, Hann mourning the only son he would ever have, Finn the one person in the world who had greeted his coming with a cry of joy. When at last they had exhausted their bodies, if not their grief, Hann rose from the cold earth, took up his spears once more, and taking Finn by the hand led him away toward the camp, where the women were keening around his hearth.

▲　▲　▲

From where Finn was, near the front of the procession, the murmur from the tribe assembled above sounded like the humming of bees. Hann led the way up from the valley floor to the burial place high among the rocks, where the women had been busy since before dawn preparing the boy's resting place. Behind Hann four men bore the child's body, wrapped in fawnskin and garlanded with flowers, and behind them trudged the remainder of the men and boys of the hearth. The wind was colder than ever today. In recognition of the chill the whole tribe had that morning donned their winter furs. Even Finn, walking close behind the body—the place accorded to those who had been closest to the dead one—was for once resplendent in a cloak of doe's fur lent him by the boy's mother. He walked alone. There were few enough who could or would wish to claim the privilege in this case. Even Venn's position close behind was a tribute rather to his friendship with Finn than to any rapport with Hann's son. Finn had attended many such burials before, but always as an onlooker. Both his station at the head of mourners and his fine fur cloak were unlooked-for honors. At first he had declined his place in the procession, fearing his presence there would cause resentment. Yet to his surprise his arrival, and Hann's ushering him to the head of the column, had been accepted as perfectly natural and had passed off without comment. All that remained was for him to fulfill his role, and lend to the boy's passing that dignity that had been so lacking in his life.

As they cleared the last of the scattered pines and came in sight of the burial cave, the murmuring subsided, leaving only

34

the throbbing of a single drum. The whole tribe were there drawn up on three sides of the open ground before the small cave, one of many that pocked the cliffside. To the left sat the women and girls, to the right the men and boys of the other nine hearths. In the center stood Sanu the holy man, beating with an antler on his deerskin drum, to drive away evil spirits and summon those of Hann's ancestors to guide the boy on his journey to the dreamworld. Within the cave Mata crouched over a small fire, blowing life into the kindling. The flames cast an inappropriately cheery light over the roof of the cave where the women of Hann's hearth had laid a bed for his son. As he took his place among the boys gathered at the cave mouth he could see Mata rocking to and fro crooning to herself as she placed the meat on skewers—the last meal she would ever prepare for her child. Her hands were as yet unmutilated, and her cheeks unmarked; that would come later in the woods when the men had departed.

Taking a place among the boys and seating himself in a space cleared for him by Venn, Finn watched the procession move on into the cave as, led by Sanu, the whole tribe raised its voice in prayer to Annu and the spirits of their ancestors. Even as they sang, though, Finn noticed the eyes of many of the men straying back down the valley in the direction of the grasslands. The winds were blowing stronger each day, and the deer were coming—there were more pressing concerns than this business of the boy. There were even those, chiefly among those who had mocked Hann in secret for his idiot son, who whispered that his judgment had been affected, that it could not be trusted in the all-important matter of the deer. Finn glanced at the indifferent faces of the boys around him. Hann's child had been a stranger to them; few bothered even to feign a sense of loss, and what sympathy was shown, by Venn and his companions, was for the sake of Finn rather than the boy.

They had laid him down in the shallow grave the women had prepared, arraying him with the food, tools, and weapons

35

he would need for his journey. Finn could dimly discern Hann's face, stony in the gloom, looking down at his hope for the future—shortly to disappear beneath the great flat stones that leaned against the cave wall. Hann stood for what seemed an age, then, just as Finn was wondering whether he had forgotten his promise, appeared at the cave mouth and beckoned to him. Finn scrambled awkwardly to his feet, to his surprise receiving a helping hand from Gronu seated beside him. He felt the eyes of the whole tribe following his back as he entered the cave, fumbling in the unfamiliar folds of his borrowed cloak for what he had cradled inside his smock since dawn. Making his way to the front of the small crowd clustered round the foot of the grave, Finn forced himself to look down. The inside of the trench was stained red, the color of blood, of life and of death, but the boy lay on a bed of moss and fawnskin, curled to one side as though asleep. Finn thought of the last time he had seen him alive, the day he had set off for the fishing, cradled in Mata's arms, sucking deer fat from a skin bag she held to his lips. His eyes had never left Finn's for a moment; his face had seemed suddenly old and wise as if, Finn thought now, he had known what was coming and was saying farewell.

Choking back a sob, Finn knelt and placed the crude wooden Reindeer among the objects that surrounded the boy. The toy looked strangely out of place among the hunter's things—bowls and cups, spears and tools—that his hearth companions had provided him, but it was all Finn had to give. He knew that his friend would soon be re-born, whole, among his ancestors, to hunt with them the spirits of the dead deer across the endless grasslands that lay beyond the sky. There, it was said, all earthly sorrows were forgotten. But Finn hoped that the toy would remind him of his friend, and that when his own time came he would not go into the next world as unwelcome as he had been in this. With one last look at his friend's peaceful face Finn left the cave. The men laid over the body a framework of saplings decked with flowers. As he took his place

36

once more among the youth, Finn heard the great stones being dragged into place. Then Mata and the women emerged blinking, into the light, and the keening began.

Taking her rightful place at their head, Mata led the women in this weird chant whose words had been old long before the Burnt Shins had ever crossed the river. They sang of the sorrows of motherhood, of the pain of birth, life and death. At times the song seemed about to break down into a meaningless babble as some moaned and some muttered their private griefs or shrieked them to the sky, tearing at their hair. Yet always, somehow the old tune and the old words would reassert themselves, and the song would rise once more to a crescendo, crashing against the mountainside and echoing over the treetops. To Finn as to many another, that song at that moment seemed more terrible than death itself. In company with all the boys and men, Finn left the burial ground before the women had finished the keening. Glad now to be free of that place and its dreadful associations, Finn glanced back to where the women sat row after row behind Mata. She lay prostrate, her clothes rent. He caught a glimpse of Shani's pale face among the crowd that gathered round her. Soon they would carry Mata off to the woods. Their ceremonies would go on well into the night, terrifying rites of self-mutilation—gashed cheeks, bloody tears, a finger severed at the knuckle—of which the boys whispered as they crowded down the slopes toward the camp.

In the camp silence reigned that night, while the women were away. Hann sat apart from his hearth companions staring into the fire. No one spoke at his hearth; what talk there was elsewhere was confined to necessities and conducted in whispers. All down the ledge, it seemed, the only sounds were of flames licking at logs and flaring in the freshening wind. Still huddled in his cloak, Finn too sat apart. He had refused with a shake of his head the food Venn had brought him, and now he stared into the night pondering a world that was emptier and a future that was bleaker than he had thought possible. A knot

37

crackled in a log on the hearth fire, startling Finn. He glanced across at Hann who, roused too from his thoughts, stood up as though he had reached a decision. Ignoring the questions of the hunters who sat at a respectful distance, he strode to Finn, and saying only, "Come!" walked to the outer edge of the ring of tents. There, where Finn had left his few belongings, he stopped and, looking down at the small bundle of rags that constituted all his wealth, stooped to pick them up.

"Is this all?" he said without turning to face the boy.

"My cloak . . ." muttered Finn fumbling under the flap of the tent where he had left it, wondering at the same time what the man meant to do.

"Your spear, the one I gave you?" Finn could hear in Hann's voice the effort this attempt at talk was costing him.

"Venn has it," Finn lied, unwilling to explain that it had been lost in the fight by the river.

Hann nodded and turned, leading the boy back to where his own tent lay. He spoke no word to the group of hunters. As Finn passed them they nodded to one another as if in confirmation of something they had all expected. Lighting a small oil lamp, Hann drew back the flap of the tent and led Finn deep inside to where the child's bed had lain just days before. Placing to one side Finn's ragged bedding he laid a mat of soft doeskin across a bed of moss. With his hand he gestured for the boy to lie down. Shrugging off his cloak and smock, Finn obeyed, lying in the place his friend had lain. Tears ran down his cheeks, splashing the pillow Hann had slid gently beneath his head, and as the man drew a fawnskin cover over him Finn tried to speak and failed. Such tenderness was new to him. However well he had borne himself that day, he was still just a child. With a shake of the head and a finger laid upon his lip Hann silenced him, blew out the light, and placing himself at the door of the tent settled down to await his wife's return.

Despite all he had been through Finn slept heavily, and dreamed a golden dream. In it he sported with a young fawn in

38

a sun-splashed glade. He called to it, and it came trotting across the soft grass, snorting its sweet breath onto his hand as he stroked the soft fur behind its ears. Finn had never seen or heard of such a thing; he had only known deer to flee at the approach of men. So enraptured was he that nothing could rouse him from his sleep; not the return, still keening, of the women bearing Mata in their arms; not Hann and Laela carrying her into the tent, nor the whispered talk between her and her husband. Not even when Mata, in all her pain and anguish, dragged herself over to his bedside, ran the fingers of her unmutilated hand through his tangled hair and, humming softly, stroked his cheek, did Finn cease to wander, arm about the young fawn's neck, through the forest of his dreams.

CHAPTER
THREE

▲ ▲ ▲
▲ ▲

IF FINN HAD DOUBTS about the meaning of Hann's gesture on
the night of his son's burial, they were soon to be dispelled. In
the manner of the Burnt Shins Finn had been taken into
Hann's tent and without a word being spoken on the subject
had achieved the privileges of kinship. Thinking back in later
times he realized that all the signs had been present from the
start of that day, and that what he had missed had not escaped
those around him. On waking in the morning he found, where
he had left his deerskin smock and ragged cloak, a bundle of
winter furs. Creeping from the tent, past the still sleeping figure
of Mata, he drew them out behind him and examined them in
the light. Finn had never seen such clothes as these. Unlike his
own, the smock fell to below his knees, and the leggings had
neat sinew ties at knee and ankle. The boots had soles of head-
fur to give firm footing on snow, and the hooded cloak, of
winter belly-fur, fastened at the neck with an ornamented bone
toggle. It was not possible that they could be meant for him,
and he was about to crawl back in to search for his own when
Hann called to him from the great fire.

41

"The broth is ready," he shouted. "What are you waiting for?" He nodded at the pile of clothes at his feet.

Hurriedly Finn dressed and, a little awkward in his new finery, joined Hann beside the fire. A space was cleared for him, as though it were the most natural thing in the world that he should sit by the hearth leader. After Hann's greeting there was silence at the hearth fire, a silence which Finn for one was not inclined to break. After they had eaten, some of the hunters tried to steer their talk toward the subject of the herds, but Hann seemed withdrawn and preoccupied. Re-filling his bowl, he smiled briefly, reassuringly, at Finn and then strode away toward his tent.

Unsure of what to do, Finn stayed there, watching the faces of the men around the fire. He did not like what he read there —some were worried, some openly scornful, most merely con-fused, but all said in one degree or another the same thing—that Hann had lost his power. For the Burnt Shins death, most especially the death of infants, was a fact of life and everyone knew better than to invest too much love in a child who might not live beyond its fourth Winter. There was a feel-ing in the air, even here at his own hearth, that what little grief Hann had displayed was already too much, and that his sorrow had unmanned him. Finn was uncomfortably aware too that his presence at Hann's side would come to be cited as further evi-dence of his derangement. Finn did not blame them; he could understand their fear. If Hann's judgment was affected now of all times, it could mean starvation for them all, death and bur-ial for their children.

Hann had gone to the tent to tend Mata, whose condition served to remind Finn what had brought about his changed circumstances. If it was true, as it seemed to be, that he was henceforward to be regarded as Hann's son, this privilege had been purchased at a terrible price. Her wound had festered, and she had grown feverish, not even recognizing Hann when he came to bathe her forehead, dress her wound, and feed her a stew of herbs. Still sleeping when Finn returned to the tent, she presented a ghastly figure with her gashed cheeks, matted black hair, and mutilated hand wrapped in a bloody rag. At that moment it seemed to Finn almost as if he had brought this distress upon her, who had shown him nothing but kindness. Gazing down at her troubled sleep it pained him that his good fortune should be so bound up with her suffering.

There was no escaping the truth, however. No sooner had he left the tent, glad, for all his pity, to be free of the hot fetid air and the smell of sickness, than Gronu approached. His jaw still bore the mark of the blow Finn had struck him; not so severe as Finn's injuries, but more than he was used to. It took an effort on Finn's part not to turn and run, but what he saw in Gronu's hands stayed him. It was the fish spear Hann had given him, which he had abandoned in his flight from the river bank. "I kept this for you," was all he said, and smiled ruefully. It was a smile that said much—proclaiming that the past was forgotten, and that from then on things would be on a different footing between them. Nothing that had yet happened so brought home to Finn his changed circumstances. Even Venn showed in his manner that something had subtly changed between them. As open and good-natured as ever, he had—probably without ever realizing it—dropped that patronizing tone that Finn had accepted as right and natural, and was treating him as an equal. Overnight, it seemed, his world had changed beyond recognition; the future that had seemed so bleak the day before now held undreamt-of promise.

Within a few days Mata had recovered sufficiently to be brought out into the light. Weak as she was, she insisted on at once beginning Finn's education. Both she and Hann knew what had scarcely dawned on Finn, that if he was to take his proper place in the hearth he must be initiated in the Spring with the other boys, and had therefore much to learn. Finn's delight at her recovery was matched only by his eagerness to please her.

"Go to the tent, little wolf," she whispered on the morning of that first day, still using the pet name bestowed on him long ago from his habit of warily approaching the firelight, "and fetch the long bag by the door."

Finn rushed to obey, knowing that the bag contained her fire-lighting block and spindles. Seeing his expression she smiled. "You are smiling now," she cautioned him gently, "but before the sun is overhead you will curse those sticks, I promise you!"

So it proved; what Finn had never in his life been called upon to do, and what looked so simple as practiced by the women and girls, proved backbreaking and fruitless. For what seemed like an eternity he rolled the pine spindle in the hole in the block, running his hands up and down, forcing the spindle downward to no effect. The end of the spindle grew warm, and Finn grew tired and angry.

Watching him wipe the stinging sweat from his eyes, Mata smiled. "You see how well it works?" Finn frowned, seeing no such thing.

"It may not light a fire . . ." she laughed, "but it keeps you warm!" Finn smiled grimly and returned to his task.

Mata let him struggle for a while longer, then smiled weakly and said, "Try a little sand in the hole. It's there in the small pouch." The sand, from the riverbank, increased the heat of the spindle end but nothing more. At last, frustrated, Finn dashed down the spindle and slumped beside her, chafing his aching palms. Having thrown himself into the task with such enthusiasm, so keen to win Mata's approval, it pained him to have failed her. Mata was unperturbed. "You were almost there when you gave in," she whispered, stroking his shoulder. "You must have patience!"

Finn's head dropped as she went on, "You will need patience to stalk the deer!"

He sat up. "I will have. For that! But this is different."

Mata smiled and shook her head. "How different? How will

44

your deer keep you warm in the forest? Will you slit its belly, and crawl inside? And will you eat it raw?"

A group of girl children wandered past on their way down to the river, and she nodded at them smiling.

"They light fires every day. . ." she taunted him gently, and in an instant he was kneeling by the block once more, rolling the spindle with renewed vigor. Again an age passed and nothing happened; and then, just as he was on the verge of throwing the spindle down, it began to smoke. Delighted, he stopped and turned to Mata who nodded and urged him on. His weariness forgotten, he rolled the spindle faster and faster until its tip glowed red.

"Now, the tinder. . ." said Mata. "Keep blowing!"

His first attempt was a failure but rolling the spindle until it glowed again he managed the second time to light the tinder, and within a few moments more a small kindling fire crackled at his feet. Finn could not remember ever feeling such triumph —not even when he had caught the great salmon. Nor was his pleasure diminished when Mata said, "Good. Now stamp it out, and try again." His next attempt was more successful and slowly his skill improved, until he could light fires in all weathers. Next he learned to site his fires according to their uses; against a boulder to reflect the heat and keep him warm; in a chamber dug into a bank for smoking meat or fish; in a trench, sheltered from the wind and with spits on either side, for roasting meat.

Then she sent him off into the woods to gather herbs and grasses, teaching him which grasses yielded seeds that could be ground into paste to thicken broths, or allowed to harden and be eaten cold. He learned the many uses of herbs—which could flavor food or heal a wound, which boiled in water could lift the spirits, and which were deadly and at all times to be avoided. Many days were spent at this, during which time Finn hardly noticed, so busy was he, that Hann was hardly to be seen between dawn and dusk.

Yet if he thought that Hann had turned, in his grief, from

matters that properly concerned him he was soon to learn otherwise. On the fourteenth day after the burial he came to Finn as he was helping Mata to hobble over to the fire in the morning, and told him that he was going to see Sanu, the holy man, and that he should come with him. As Hann strode up the well-worn path to Sanu's cave, Finn walked beside him, not caring why he had been brought, content simply to be with the man he loved. Finn's heart was brimful of love, a love that until now had had no object. Often, as a child playing alone by the stream, he had dammed a small rivulet that ran down the valley side below his bolt-hole. The water, held back by the twigs and mud, had risen and gathered strength until it had burst out over the top, roaring as it came. So it was now with his love; he would have died at that moment for the man beside him. Like his love his words came out in a torrent, as a boy who had learned to hold his peace suddenly found himself able to talk.

"I can run and swim faster than any of the others. . . . I can creep up on them and leave them, and no one, not even Gronu hears me . . . and I know the spoor of all the game in the forest. . . ." Hann appeared not to listen as they climbed steadily beneath a canopy of pines, but the boy continued listing his accomplishments. Finn was justly proud of what he had taught himself, but he spoke this way now out of fear, not boastfulness. His fear was that Hann might even now change his mind, see or be made to see how absurd it was to take this ragged creature as his son. Hann seemed to sense this, for after a while he spoke.

"I know you will not let me down," was all he said.

"I would die first . . . father." Finn's voice faltered as he spoke this last word, not knowing if it was proper, but having longed to say it. The earth did not erupt beneath his feet, nor did the sky come crashing about his ears, or the beasts of the forest cry out in protest. More than this, he saw as he glanced timidly sideways that the word had pleased the man whose pleasure was now his only desire.

46

"They think I am out of my mind, taking you for my son," Hann said. "They think my sorrow has robbed me of my wits."

Finn remembered the faces round the fire. "We will prove them wrong," he answered defiantly.

Hann nodded. "With what you have learned for yourself and what I can teach you, we will." He reached over and ruffled the boy's hair. "You and me and the deer."

Finn was puzzled. "The deer?"

"They think I have lost my deer-wisdom too. As though the loss of a boy. . ." Here his voice wavered, and Finn could feel his grief through the outwardly dismissive words. "As though the loss of a boy could take *that* from me. That is what they mutter around the fires, that is what they are laughing at when I leave them and go out onto the scree to be alone. But they will know better soon."

From early childhood Finn had learned to read through the sounds of people's voices what was in their hearts. The slightest change of tone or pitch told him when to back down in argument, when to press his point, when, most importantly, to run for cover; his survival had depended upon it. Now he heard, as only he could have done, the bitterness that lay behind Hann's boast. He felt how heavily the burden of leadership weighed upon his shoulders, and how the carping and mockery of men who should have known better wounded him in his sorrow. For those wounds and for that sorrow he felt rising within him an anger that he had never felt on his own behalf. Burning with all the passion of a boy of thirteen Summers he wanted to march down to the ledge there and then and fight all comers. At that moment he could have killed in his anger, and knew almost at the same moment that such thoughts would appall Hann. Suppressing his anger, he asked in a voice as even as he could muster, "How do you know when the deer will come?"

At once Hann's mood seemed to lift. He liked to talk about the deer. "There's no mystery—the tallies tell me." All the hearth leaders kept tally sticks, marking the movements and

47

numbers of the herds back to the time when the tribe first entered the valley. But only Hann's and those of his forefathers were so highly regarded as to be committed to Sanu's care.

"Others keep tallies," Finn said with as much scorn as he could muster. "But at this time they always turn to you."

Hann smiled at this. He knew, of course, that the boy was flattering him, but what he said was true, and it pleased him to be reminded of it. "There are other signs," he said, "for those who have eyes to see them."

"What signs?" asked Finn.

"When the time is ripe the world is filled with signs. Things you can see and hear, like the geese in the sky, or the gulls and ravens, and things you can feel as the deer feel them."

"Like the wind?"

The question seemed to please Hann, and he nodded. "The wind. And the nights growing longer, and colder. When the deer feel these things at the grazing grounds by the sea, they start to grow restless. For they know that soon Annu will come to lead them over the grasslands."

Despite all that Finn had taught himself, despite the stories he knew, there was still much—things that fathers told their sons or children learned at their mothers' knees—that he understood only imperfectly. Of Annu, Father of men and deer, who dwelt in the dreamlands, Finn knew only scraps, often misheard, often interrupted, that he had gleaned squatting at the edges of other people's campfires. His ignorance frightened him and he spoke hesitantly, afraid to reveal it even to Hann, "And he is summoned by the dance?"

To Finn's relief, Hann nodded. "We dance the Reindeer dance to invoke Annu. We sing His praises, tell Him that His children are hungry, and urge Him to come to earth, take the form of a buck, and lead the deer under our spears."

More confident now, Finn asked, "How do you know when the dance should begin?"

"What happens in this world depends upon the other," said

48

Hann. "That is why I must consult Sanu. My wisdom alone is not enough. He journeys between the worlds, knows when the time is right. Both worlds must be in harmony before the dance begins."

Finn thought about this for a while. "And if we didn't dance? What would happen?"

Hann looked shocked. "Don't even think such thoughts! Dismiss them at once if they come again. And never breathe them to a living soul!"

The vehemence with which Hann spoke surprised Finn; it was as if the idea had genuinely never occurred to him. Finn wished that he had bitten off his tongue rather than upset Hann, who now strode on in silence, but to him the question seemed an obvious one. Surely everybody had thoughts such as these?

They continued in silence until at length they reached the clearing where Sanu's cave was set in a mossy bank among a few stunted pines. There was little to inspire awe, Finn thought, in this low, shallow cleft in the rock, with a deerskin stretched across its entrance, through which curled a wisp of smoke from a fire within. Nor was the frail old creature who sat before it the terrifying figure he remembered from the burial or the yearly rituals. Yet as they drew nearer Hann's reverent mood communicated itself to Finn with such force that he was greatly relieved when, at the edge of the clearing, he was told to sit and wait.

Hann spoke in whispers. "He may wish to speak with you in a moment," he said.

"With me?" Finn was alarmed at the prospect now.

Hann nodded. "I must tell him what I have done, what is between us. He will have the last word." With that he left him.

Finn sat a while, his thoughts in turmoil, hardly aware of Hann crossing the clearing behind him, and the old man's faint greeting. What was he to make of this? Sanu was to him as to most members of the tribe, a remote and mysterious presence.

As well as being the final arbiter in matters of kinship, he was custodian of the rites and customs of the tribe, their lawgiver, healer and intermediary in the dreamlands. He journeyed there often, sometimes of his own volition, sometimes not. His comings and goings between the worlds were a constant source of awe and wonder and the object of much speculation around the fires at night. At times he would wander off into the mountains for days on end, at others he would retreat into the depths of his cave, which some said went down into the center of the mountain. Days later he would return, bringing people news of their ancestors or greetings or warnings from the other world. No great enterprise was considered without his advice, no decision acted upon without his blessing. That was why the path to his cave was beaten hard by the passage of countless feet. Yet Finn had never as a child been brought to him for his blessing, had never been carried to his cave when sick, nor had he been instructed by him in the ways of Annu, or the meanings of the rituals. He doubted whether Sanu was even aware of his existence. Finn had accepted as final Hann's decision to adopt him, confident that the tribe, whatever their misgivings, would eventually do so too. Now for the first time he realized that the old man across the clearing, to whom Hann was talking so animatedly, had the power to put an end, here and now, to his new-found prosperity.

His mind raced as he waited at the edge of the clearing, hardly aware of the hum of Hann's and Sanu's talk. Thoughts and fears crowded into his mind. What if Sanu found out his ignorance and rejected him—what would happen then? To return now to his former state seemed unthinkable; things could never be the same again no matter what happened. How much worse it would be now than it had been before. It would have been better never to have aspired to belong to the tribe, to remain what he had always been, than to have tried and failed. Yet acceptance, too, had its pitfalls, as was now becoming clear.

It had never occurred to anyone, least of all Finn himself, that he would be initiated like the other boys. Yet now, because it was Hann's wish, it was his also. From where he was sitting he could see the sacred mountain where the rituals took place. Even Gronu, for all his bravado, betrayed his fears when he looked to that distant cloud-covered peak.

It seemed to glower at him now from across the valley. No matter where Finn turned his eyes, somehow, slowly, it drew them back, as though saying to him, "There is no turning back, you must come on, I am waiting for you." Finn had never before had time to think of the future, living as he had from day to day, his time taken up with the needs of the present. Life had always been hard, but its patterns and its limits had been set, and there was a kind of safety in that. Suddenly all that had gone. Something new to him, hope, had entered his life, and because of it his world had become a frightening place. Now there was so much to think of, so many things that could put an end at once to his happiness, that he felt an almost irresistible urge to flee to his bolt-hole, to lie looking at the pictures the clouds made in the sky, and return to the simple life he had always known. Yet even as he tried to imagine it his eyes were drawn once more to the mountain, menacing, barring his path, telling him there was no turning back. So engrossed was he in these thoughts that he failed to notice time passing, the sun moving across the sky, and Hann crossing the clearing to stand over him.

"He wishes to speak to you," he said softly. "Go over and sit beside him. Let him speak first, and answer honestly."

Hesitantly, Finn rose, took a few steps toward the hunched figure of the holy man, then stopped and looked back uncertainly to Hann. He nodded and whispered, "Don't be afraid."

Not until Finn was close enough to Sanu to have been able, had he dared, to reach out and grasp his forked white beard, did the old man turn to look at him. Not taking his eyes off Finn for a moment, he beckoned to him to sit down beside him, and continued to look him over appraisingly for some time before he spoke.

"You have a lot to learn before the Spring. Will you be ready?" he asked.

"My father will see that I am," said Finn. Again the word "father" sounded strange coming from his lips, and he wondered with a start whether he had said too much, presumed too much. He had assumed from the man's question that all was settled. Had he been wrong?

The old man merely nodded. "Tell me how we got our name," he demanded, and in that "we" Finn had his answer.

There was cause for joy too in the question. Finn knew this story well; it was the one he had told Venn. Closing his eyes so as not to make the slightest mistake, he recounted the tale of Aela and the theft of fire.

When he had finished, Sanu nodded and beamed at him. "You have learned the story well," he said. "Who taught you?"

"No one taught me." Finn was proud now. "But I have heard it round the fires many times. . . ."

Sanu seemed impressed. "Few, apart from the Elders, have it word for word like that."

Finn flushed at the compliment. "I think perhaps it mattered more to me, because..." and his hand crept unconsciously to cover his tattoo, "because of who I am."

The old man's hand caught his arm halfway, and Finn was surprised at the strength of his grip. "Who you *were*," he said and smiled, an almost toothless smile. Dropping his hand to his side, Finn smiled too, ashamed at being caught.

Still smiling Sanu went on, "It always matters, whoever you are. Without our history and our customs what would we be? Like the leaves that float down the stream in the Autumn, lifeless things coming from nowhere, going nowhere."

The old man lapsed into silence for a while, and Finn was wondering whether he expected some reply. Then he spoke

52

again, this time in an almost casual tone. "I saw your friend last night . . . Hann's son."

"In a dream?" asked Finn, brightening.

Sanu laughed, a curious sort of giggle that made him seem for a moment strangely childlike. "Better than a dream," he said. "I was *there* in the dreamlands."

Finn was torn now, afraid to betray his ignorance of these matters, but eager to know more. His curiosity won. "Was he afraid?"

To his relief Sanu did not seem surprised at the question. "There was no need for him to be afraid, as you might have been. He had been there many times before." He obviously sensed Finn's uncertainty, for he continued, "When a man or woman dies their spirit goes to the dreamland, but when they are sick their spirits go there and their bodies stay here."

"Is that why you go there?" asked Finn.

Sanu nodded. "Sometimes, if it is not their time to die, I can go there and drag their spirits back to our world. Sometimes not. You remember how the boy was?"

Finn thought back to the countless times on the scree by Hann's hearth when he had crouched beside the boy, trying to look in the direction his eyes were gazing, trying to see what he saw. "Like he was not here with us?" he offered.

"That's it!" Sanu slapped his thighs, pleased at the answer. "He was in the dreamland, at least part of him was. What he lacked here, sound limbs and a keen mind, he had there. But his sorrow was that he was neither of this world nor the other. He crossed between the two sometimes by choice, but more often not, and often he wandered in the darkness between."

"And now he is whole?"

Sanu smiled serenely. "He has straight limbs, like yours, and his mind is as agile as yours is. He can talk and sing, run, and dance. Toward the end he was there more and more. . . ."

Finn remembered the end; the sound of Sanu's drum beating, the worried faces of Hann and Mata, and his own lonely vigil at the tent mouth as the little twisted figure tossed and turned and moaned in his thin, piping voice. The old man's voice dispelled the image. "I tried to bring him back, but he liked it there so he stayed."

"He *liked* being dead?" Finn could not help saying it. "Liked it better than the real world?"

"He is in the real world. *This* world is just a shadow of the dreamland. And remember, nothing dies, things just change. His life with us was confusion and suffering. Now he is happy with his ancestors, Hann's people and Mata's, in the dreamland. There they have the sun ever warm on their backs, and the grass ever cool underfoot, and the spirits of the deer run like an endless river under their spears, and die without fear or pain. And in the morning they rise up and run again. There is no sorrow, and the people spend their days hunting, feasting and dancing under the smile of Annu."

At this the old man lapsed into silence once more. Thoughts of the things he had just described seemed to enrapture him, and his eyes took on a faraway look as he stared into the distance. Finn wondered whether he should rise and leave him. But there were so many things that he wanted to know, and he was not sure when, if ever, he would have the opportunity to ask them again.

He cleared his throat nervously, and the old man looked at him. It was clear from his expression that it was all one to him whether Finn chose to speak or not. "When we sleep..." Finn asked hesitantly, "is it the dreamlands that we see?"

Sanu nodded. "Sometimes we see the dreamlands, sometimes we see this world through other eyes." Then, sensing what lay behind the question, he asked in his turn, "What dream have you had?"

"A strange dream. Like nothing I have ever seen or heard of," said Finn eagerly. "I was in a clearing in the forest, and there was a fawn. And it came to me when I called, and was unafraid. And I felt as though... as though I loved it like a

54

brother..." He blurted out these last words in a hurry, as though ashamed of them, but the old man showed no surprise.

"That was a good dream," he announced after a moment's thought. "You should love the deer for they are everything to us, and the more you grow to love them the better the hunter you will be. They too are children of Annu."

Before he could stop himself, Finn said, more to himself than to Sanu, "That's a cruel fate, to love the deer and be forced to kill them."

Far from being angry as Finn had expected, Sanu simply said, "It was our punishment."

"But why?" Finn persisted. "Was the theft so terrible?"

Sanu nodded gravely. "It was forbidden to us; that should have been enough. We tried to set ourselves above the beasts. Annu was angry, but I think perhaps He was proud of us too. He punished us in that way to show us that if we wish to be above the beasts there is a price to be paid, and that price is the blood of the creature we love best." He paused, seemed lost in thought, then suddenly brightened. "And yet, that punishment has brought us many blessings."

Finn's puzzlement must have shown in his face. For Sanu asked him, "Consider us. What is it that sets us apart from everything around us?"

Finn thought for a moment. That "we" still thrilled him, but he tried to find an answer to Sanu's question. The people were different, even from the highest animals, even from the deer. They lived, hunted, ate, slept, bred, and died, did all the things that animals did; and yet he knew there was a difference; something, he felt, but could not express. He opened his mouth to try, but the words would not come, so he merely shrugged instead.

"Custom!" said the old man. "Our songs and pictures, our dances and rituals, the way we see this world, and the world beyond—these things place us apart and keep us together. Wolves fight each other for mastery, does desert their young, but we help each other, share our food in the Winter, struggle and survive together. Why do you think that is?"

"Because of the hunting?" offered Finn.

Sanu clapped his hands and yelled with delight, nodding vigorously. "We must come together to hunt. And from the hunting comes everything else...our songs, our customs... everything that makes us what we are, everything that makes us different. I think that is why Annu made us hunters, to *make* us work together."

Twice now he had said it, and this time Finn could not let it pass. "You *think?*"

If the old man was in any way put out by the boy's tone, he gave no sign of it. "I do not know, or see everything," he said. "Even on my journeys, the things I see in the dreamlands are only a reflection of what is really there." He paused, seeing the boy's confusion, then concluded, "No doubt we shall all know everything at the proper time. In the meantime, some things are given to us as mysteries, and we should accept them as such."

By the time Finn had considered this, Hann had joined them once more, presumably at Sanu's beckoning, and was standing above them. Sanu smiled up at him. "He asks good questions," he said. "And has good dreams." A look passed between the two men, the meaning of which was not entirely clear to Finn. It looked rather as if Hann was saying, "See, it's as I told you," and the old man was agreeing. Before he had time to read any more in their faces Sanu had turned to him and said, "Now I must talk with your father." And Hann had nodded in the direction of the track by which they had come. As he left the clearing and began to descend by the track, Finn glanced over his shoulder and saw the other two deep in earnest conversation.

CHAPTER
FOUR

▲ ▲ ▲
▲ ▲

AFTER THE THINGS Sanu had spoken of and the glories he had
hinted at, the camp seemed a poor and mean sort of place when
Finn returned to it alone some time later. It was past midday,
and that languor had settled on the ledge that was a feature of
those late summer afternoons before the Autumn kill. On any
such afternoon in the countless generations past a watcher
might have stood where Finn now stood, and looked down
upon the same scene. Hunters sat or lay around in groups,
chatting idly or not at all; some, having eaten, slept. Most of
the women, their day's work done, had gone down to bathe,
and the sounds of their play and the cries of the children
echoed up from below. Those who remained sat or squatted on
the scree and talked with little animation, the buzz of their
conversation barely stirring the silence. Even the smoke from
the few sultry fires rose reluctantly, and hung below the rock
face that overhung the cave, as though uncertain where to go
next.

Yet, in his present mood, even this was not quiet enough for
Finn, and he picked his way across the camp, ignoring the few

incurious looks he drew, and made his way down the scree and into the trees on the far side. He told himself he was wandering aimlessly but his feet took him straight toward the valley mouth along the hillside to his bolt-hole. He had somehow imagined, after all that had happened, that he would have no further need of this place, but the feeling of relief with which he settled himself in his accustomed place told him otherwise. For most of the Burnt Shins, brought up in the communal atmosphere of the camp, solitude was something to be avoided at all costs; to Finn it had always been his consolation and refuge. While others had laughed and played in company, his happiest times had been spent alone. When they, in fear or pain, had run to their mothers, he had fled here. Now he knew that whatever might happen, however much he became a part of the life of the tribe, his instinct in times of trouble would always be to find some lonely place.

He was troubled now as he settled in his niche, closed his eyes, and tried to think of the future. The future! To him the future had concerned that evening's meal, or his chances of securing a halfway decent skin at the Autumn kill. All life had had to offer him in the future was more of what he had: bare existence on the fringe of the camp. If he had hoped at all it was that somehow he might be able, as he grew older, to find some way of making himself useful to the tribe, though he had always known that any knowledge, any skill he could acquire, would have to be self-taught. Now suddenly he was forced to consider all sorts of matters that had meant little to him only days before. The things he must learn in order to become a hunter, the initiation that was to come, the trials he must undergo, the mysteries of which Sanu had spoken; all these seemed to oppress him now, to loom threateningly before him as the mountain had done. Although he could not turn back, nor would if he could, he knew that life would never again be as simple as it had been, and that some small part of him was already wishing that it could.

"I thought you'd come here!" Shani's voice interrupted his thoughts. Finn sat up sharply, almost striking his head as he did so. She was staring down at him as she had done the last time she had found him here. But now she looked quite different. For one thing she was not surprised to see him; this meeting was no accident. Perhaps she read this thought in his face, for as at her beckoning he climbed from the cleft and sat down near her, she said, "I followed you up from the camp. I wasn't sure I could remember the way."

"I didn't see you," said Finn, "or hear you."

Shani laughed. "You boys! You all think you are the only ones who can do anything."

Finn's irritation at being disturbed melted under her smile. He had not liked the turn his thoughts had taken and now, gazing up to where she sat on a grassy rise, he was grateful to Shani for interrupting them. Where his world had grown bleak and forbidding she had suddenly brought warmth and color once more. In her cloak, smock and leggings of pure white fur she cut a striking figure against the blue-gray sky. A pale watery sun had broken through, turning to gold the flesh of her face, arms and thighs. Finn could tell, as she smiled down at him, that she was well aware of the effect she made.

"Why did you follow me?" he finally found himself able to ask.

She tossed her head and her hair fell, dark, across the white fur of her cloak. "I'll go if you want," she said, and made to rise.

"No!" he said too quickly, betraying his feelings. Her face registered her triumph as she sat down once more.

"But why?" persisted Finn.

She shrugged. "No real reason. I was bored. I didn't want to swim. And the women were all talking about Mata."

Finn hung his head. That Mata's recovery was taking so long had been preying on his mind. Shani edged nearer to him, and there was real concern in her voice as she said, "She'll be all right. The old women say it often goes that way."

Finn looked at her with new hope. She gave him a little smile, and nodded in confirmation of what she had said, so that he was reassured.

After a pause Shani went on, "It was *awful* when they did it, though. We were all gathered in a ring, well, three rings really, the youngest of us at the back, so they couldn't see probably, and..."

"I don't want to hear about it!" Finn spoke firmly, but if he surprised himself by his tone, Shani seemed unperturbed. "I know," she cooed, "you're fond of her."

"It's not that," said Finn. "Though I am," he added quickly. "It's just not right for me to hear it. It's a women's affair, no business of mine, and none of yours to be telling me."

Shani laughed and even when, in response to his face, her face took on a sober expression once more, her eyes laughed on. "You mean you've never wondered about it? Not once?"

Finn blushed and cursed himself for doing so. "Of course I have."

"Well then, I'll tell you—" He shook his head, and she moved even closer to him. "But first you must tell me what Sanu said."

So that was it! That was why she had come; not out of concern for him nor any desire to talk to him, but out of curiosity. Finn doubted if he had learned anything so far that she did not already know. That she should have come to him of all people for enlightenment was laughable, yet he did not feel like laughing. Rather he felt disappointed and resentful.

"Sanu said many things," was all he said, sullenly. She was looking at him expectantly, so he went on, "He said there are things that are given to us as mysteries, and that we should accept them as such."

Shani pouted and pushed him away. Finn took bitter consolation in her anger but almost at once she turned, smiled, and drew herself close to him once more. "Don't tease me," she chided him softly. "What about the initiation? What did he say about that?" Her breath in his ear sent a shiver down his back.

"It's forbidden!" he cried, exasperated. "Death for you to know, or for me to tell."

She was unmoved by his outburst. "Who would know? You tell me what you have learned and I'll tell you of the women's rituals. It will be our secret." Then in a softer voice she whispered, "Secrets bind people, bring them closer."

To be closer to her of all people, Finn would have taken any risk but this one. To reveal such things, to break such ancient laws, would be to invite disaster, bring retribution not only on their own heads, but on the whole tribe. How could she not know this, or if she knew, not care? Even so, had Finn known anything worth telling, he might at that moment, with Shani gazing so trustingly into his eyes and leaning upon his shoulder, have told it all. As it was he was as ignorant as a child of two, and for the first time in his life, he was glad of it.

"Why didn't you ask Venn, or Gronu?" he asked miserably, after a while.

"They wouldn't have told me." She turned away from him now.

"And you thought I would?"

Shani failed to notice the rising anger in his voice. "I thought you might," she said.

Finn threw back his cloak to reveal his tattooed forearm. "Because it wouldn't matter to me? Because of this!" He spat the words out bitterly.

She looked truly shocked. "No. Because you know you can trust me." Her voice was pleading now. "I never told them about this place. You remember... the day we caught the salmon..."

"I don't need reminding. I carry the reminders." He threw the ragged cloak back further to reveal on his shoulder the fading marks left by the beating he had received. The vague, ill-directed anger he had felt on Hann's behalf, his bitterness at learning Shani's real reason for coming here, and something more—the memories of past humiliations that she had accidentally revived—all now welled up within him with a force that frightened him. He had never felt this way before, and his whole body shook as he spoke.

"Never again," he said fighting back tears of suppressed rage. "Never again shall I be beaten like a child, or chased from the firelight like a scavenging wolf. I am Burnt Shin now, as much as you, Gronu or any of them. I am Hann's son, and those who doubt it will soon know better."

Finn braced himself for another petulant outburst, and was surprised to feel her hand soft upon the shoulder he had just exposed. Her touch disturbed him as it always did, but her words disturbed him more.

"So the cub has learned to use his teeth," she said softly. "I am glad of it. Now he must learn not to use them on his friends." With that she left him, slipping away so softly that it was a moment before Finn realized she had gone. Before he could call to her, she had disappeared into the trees, leaving him to reflect on the changes that had taken place not only in his life but in himself.

▲ ▲ ▲

Preoccupied with Shani's words, Finn failed to notice, on entering the camp, an atmosphere of suppressed excitement. He found Hann seated at the entrance to his tent, chewing contentedly on a piece of dried meat, and looking happier than he had been for many days. He greeted Finn cheerfully. As though he had been waiting for him, he beckoned him to sit and eat. Now, as his jaws worked at the tough meat, Finn looked around him noticing for the first time a group of hunters seated close by, unwilling to approach, and beyond them a continual passing back and forth of young men and women. He looked back to Hann, who smiled.

"I have told them I have news," he said, "but that I must eat first." He leaned forward, beckoning to Finn to do the same. As he did so Finn saw, not without satisfaction, that the hunters in the distance leaned forward in hope of hearing what was said.

"It is time for the dance," he breathed in Finn's ear. "It starts at dawn."

Finn's jaw dropped and he turned in the direction of the hunters. Hann shook his head. "They can wait, until the Elders have assembled, and we have eaten."

As was proper, Hann first made the announcement to a select group of the Elders, but there was no keeping a secret such as this. As soon as the Elders had followed Hann into the depths of the great cave, the word traveled like fire through bracken down the line of the camp. Finn watched with a thrill as the news, news he had been the first to hear, passed from fireside to fireside. He followed its progress with his eyes as one after another the hearths sprang to life. The crowd that had gathered at the mouth of the cave almost as soon as Hann had returned from his talk with Sanu grew moment by moment as young and old abandoned their tasks or rose from their rest to hear the news at firsthand. The older and wiser, particularly among the women, not waiting for the announcement that could mean only one thing, had already started preparations for the long night's work that lay ahead.

By the time the chief Elder had emerged from the cave the four youngest hunters had gathered their weapons and provisions and were standing expectantly at the edge of the camp. He had barely uttered the words, "The time of the dance is upon us," before they had set off, climbing high to the hilltops at the mouth of the valley to scan the horizon for the first signs of the deer. In an instant the crowd at the cave mouth had scattered, each to their allotted tasks. Children, who at the first signs of change on the ledge had gathered anxiously at their mothers' knees, now jumped and sang, running about on fat little legs, searching for someone, anyone, who had not yet heard the news. The men who were to dance dived into the half dark of their tents, dragging robes and masks out into the light. Robes were shaken out, masks examined with approving nods or curses at some missed loose stitching or accidental damage from a careless foot in the night. Women gathered their families, sons and daughters, at firesides and issued orders. "The deer are running," went the cry. "So too must we." The dance would begin at dawn, and would continue day and night until the lookouts on the hills sighted the herds. From that moment it would take less than a day for the deer to reach the river, so all must be prepared in advance. The men were all resting ready for the dance, preparing the dancing ring, or taking to the hills; it fell to the women to supervise the tribe's own migration. In one night every tent on the ledge had to be collapsed, loaded onto sleds, and hauled from the ledge down to the Autumn campsites by the river. Then there were bedding, clothes, hearth and boiling stones, weapons and cooking implements to pack—everything, in short, that the tribe would need for the three-day orgy of slaughter and feasting that was the Autumn kill. Through days and nights to come, as the dance progressed, the young men and women of the tribe would toil back and forth between the ledge and the encampment burdened like an army of ants; but this first night was crucial and, but for the dancers, few would sleep.

Well before the following dawn all was ready at the dancing ground. Almost as soon as the announcement had been made, a party of the younger men had started down the hillside to the stone circle at the valley's mouth. All through the night they had worked by firelight, clearing the long grass, and leveling the ground within the ring of low flat stones. At the same time the two pairs of young hunters, having reached the heights, settled down to begin their vigil, staring out across the grasslands for the first sign of the approaching herds. Not until their

64

beacon fires flared would the dancing stop. Up on the ledge the activity sparked by Hann's announcement had continued through the night. By dawn, when the dancers descended to the ring, the tribe was almost equally split between the ledge and the encampment by the river; it was a weary rump of the tribe that Sanu led in procession down the hill.

Finn was among the young of Hann's hearth following behind the Elders and the women. As they cleared the scree and entered the trees, they could hear the drum summoning the dancers. The simple, insistent beat gradually gathered speed, and Finn could sense, as his own heart quickened in response, what the dancers must be feeling as they hoisted the great Reindeer masks onto their shoulders and rehearsed the steps of the dance. The small procession gradually debouched onto the level ground and filled the space around the ring. Finn could see the dancers among the trees by the water's edge, dressed in their finest smocks, leggings, and Reindeer masks. In their hands were their ritual spears, specially crafted and with heads of such delicate manufacture that a man could have, had he dared, snapped one with his bare hands. Their bodies, oiled with deer fat, glistened as they strode restlessly back and forth among the trees. Their restlessness, urged on as they were by the drum's insistent beat, grew with every passing moment and spread through the crowd. Notwithstanding their mostly sleepless night, some were already swaying to the drum's rhythm or shuffling their feet in improvised dances of their own. Tired as they were, few could keep still at a time like this, with the year on the turn, the deer on the move, and the prospect of action at last after the long, languid Summer. Impatiently, they turned to Sanu where he exchanged a few last words with a masked figure who Finn knew with a thrill of pride to be Hann. From all sides voices called upon him to begin, but conscious of his position, he paid them no need.

At last a hush descended on the crowd, the masked dancer disappeared into the trees, and Sanu marched to the center of the ring to set the dance in motion. As he raised his arms to the sky and moved his lips in silent prayer, oblivious to all around him, the only sound that could be heard was the muted beating of the drum. Then, turning toward the grove where the dancers crouched concealed, he opened his arms as though in invitation, then wrapped himself in his cloak, striding from the ring looking neither left nor right. He passed through the crowd without a backward glance, the drumming growing louder, and to a shout of acclaim the dancers broke from the cover of the trees and bounded into the center of the arena. Finn watched transfixed as they passed in file back and forth across the leveled ground of the ring. On the first pass—crouched, antlers tossing, coughing and grunting—they were Reindeer, lumbering across the boundless grasslands. Then they stamped, turned as one and became hunters, spear arms raised, tongues clicking, stalking forward to the kill. So they turned and turned again, man and deer, hunter and hunted, invoking their God, in whom was all that was man and all that was deer, and something else, something greater, that was neither.

Time and again they crossed and recrossed the ring, their feet pounding the hard earth to dust. Time passed; the crowd began to shift and stir and gradually to melt away. Sanu had long since retired to the innermost depths of his cave to add his potent prayers to the exhortations of the dancers, but for the rest of the tribe there was still much to be done. The tents that had been dragged down to the encampment had to be erected, hearth stones laid out, fires built. The women who would lead the beaters, driving the herds onto the spears of the hunters, had to walk the ground beyond the river where the deer would come. They alone knew the routes they would take down to the water's edge, on them alone rested the responsibility for ensuring that the greatest number of deer entered their hearth's killing ground. Along with all that, there was broth to be boiled, the very young and the very old to be fed, food to be brought for those who danced and those who watched—life and ritual had to go on side by side.

Thus it was that by the time the first dancer had sunk exhausted to one knee only a few, among whom was Finn, remained. Not checking its pace for an instant the dancing group passed on, as a fresh dancer emerged from the shelter of the trees. Raising his spear as though to strike, he stalked toward the slumped figure. His spear flashed in a symbolic slaying stroke, the antlers dropped, and the new dancer took his place in the group, leaving the former one to stagger to the trees, there to be revived and rubbed down by friends and relatives.

As evening drew on more dancers drooped and fell, to be replaced by fresh men, until all of the original twenty were stretched out on the grass. As night drew on some returned to the dance, as the replacements in their turn fell, and drummers changed over without once causing the monotonous rhythm to falter. Bonfires were lit; by their light the dance continued, watched by a crowd that swelled and thinned by turns as people retired to the ledge or the camp to eat or sleep, and then, refreshed, wandered back. Only Finn stayed, although he had singlehandedly dragged Hann's tent down to the encampment during the night, and had long since lost track of which of the dancers was his father.

Dawn warmed the hilltops, and the lookouts who shivered there. Conscious that all eyes below were turned to them once more, they anxiously scanned the distant horizon. Yet the watchers by the ring looked in vain for the glimmer of beacon fires, and the dance maintained its relentless pace through the second day. Not even Venn's offer of food—broth and dried meat brought up from the camp by Laela—could tempt Finn from his place at the ring's edge. He remained, seated now where he had stood at the start of the dance. It was impossible to tell where Hann was now, whether dancing in the ring or stretched out in the trees beyond, but Finn was determined that, wherever he was, should he glance out at the faces that ringed the stone circle, he would see foremost among them the face of his son. This dance was Hann's affair more than any man's and the tribe now knew that even in his grief he had not neglected it. Now they would see that he had chosen a son who was worthy of him. Whoever else came and went, Finn would see the dance out to its end.

It was late afternoon when Finn, his senses numbed by the incessant pounding of the drum, became aware that all around him the crowd was stirring. Across the ring people were looking not at the dancers but beyond them to the distant hilltops. Over his head and in the growing throng behind him he could hear voices raised.

"There, see!" cried one.

"It's nothing! You're seeing things," said another.

"I saw it too!" said a younger voice, only to be angrily hushed by its elders.

Hauling himself to his feet—staggering a little as feeling returned to his cramped legs—Finn too turned his eyes to the heights. Almost as he did so the voices fell silent; from the lookout post on the far side of the valley a thin plume of smoke spiraled slowly into the sky. Moving in mass, as if at a command, the crowd turned to the other hilltop, not daring to believe until it was confirmed by the lookouts there that the herds had actually been sighted. An agonizing wait followed. No word was spoken as a hundred necks craned into the distance, and the drumming and dancing went unregarded. Already one or two dissenting voices were crying that the smoke was a mistake, pouring scorn on the men on the hilltops. Then in support of the first signal, a second column of smoke appeared on the other side of the valley. With one spontaneous shout of joy the crowd scattered; some, the younger element, racing to the hilltops to see the signs for themselves, some to cry the news at the mouth of Sanu's cave, and some to carry the message to whoever, deep in the woods, in the camp, or on the ledge, might not yet have heard it.

Now the dance could finish and already, as the dancers completed their final pass toward the trees, their friends and families gathered to greet them. There was little enough time for celebration; the herds would be on them shortly after dawn. In times past the dance had gone on for many days and dancers had had to be carried down to the killing grounds to recover as best they could before the deer arrived. This time, though, the dance having had its due effect after only two days, the hunters would be fresh when the herds reached the river. But as the dancers left the ring, flopping to the ground, one remained. Turning once more to the center of the ring he continued to dance, not the Reindeer dance now but a fast, frenzied dance of his own making. The drummer faltered, caught by surprise, but recovered after an instant; quickening his pace to match the dance, he played on. It was not unknown for individual dancers to carry on when the dance had stopped, if they were caught up in the joy of the moment or for some purpose of their own. It was accepted by all as being his own affair. Most were too busy attending to their own fathers, brothers, or husbands to pay much attention to the lone dancer, or even wonder about his identity.

Finn, however, knew at once who it was. He knew without needing even to wander among the prostrate figures who lay in the grass; he also knew, instinctively, the meaning of the dance. Time passed, the exhausted dancers, relieved of their masks, slowly recovered and hobbled off toward the camp for food and rest before the further exertions of the hunt. But the lone dancer showed no sign of slowing his pace. The sun was sinking now, throwing the valley into gloom. Soon the dancing ring was all but deserted. Only the drummer, the dancer and Finn, his son, remained. At the edge of the trees, on the track leading down to the camp, a few stragglers stopped and looked back in disbelief. Finn heard Hann's name on their lips, heard them whispering that this was no time for such things, and he knew that only he understood. The drummer too, tiring now, turned to Finn as he approached, a question in his eyes. Taking up another antler, Finn began to beat the drum in time to the dance. Then, having caught the rhythm, he nodded to the drummer who gratefully retired, massaging his aching arm.

Sometime later, as he watched the dancer cast his spear aside, Finn recognized Venn's voice at his shoulder. "What is he doing?" he was saying. "The beacon fires are lit. The deer will be here with the dawn. He should rest!"

Finn heard in Venn's voice the concern that had brought him back up the trail from the camp. "He is dancing out his grief," he said. "He'll never rest until it's done, and nor shall I." His voice did not invite a reply, nor was there any. It seemed that Venn understood for he said no more. When, later, Finn glanced back, he had gone.

Faster and faster the dancer spun, thrashing the air with his arms, beating the ground in fury with his feet, his sweat staining the dust beneath him. The sun sank to the earth, casting its beams over the waters and through the trees, like the fingers of a great golden hand reaching out gently to touch both dancer and drummer. Its touch was healing, seemed to soothe them, for the drumming slowed as the dancer's fever passed. At length Finn saw the antlers dip, the figure crumple and fall to one knee, and he knew that it was over. As he ran to Hann's side he saw salt drops that were not sweat fall from under the mask and splash the dust. There was nothing to be said. He fell to his knees beside him and remained there, silent, as the sun set for the last time on their sorrow.

FIVE

FINN HAD NEVER SEEN the salt river but the Autumn winds brought its taste and smell and the deer brought its sounds. He heard them again now, the cries of the gulls, and a roar like surf upon a distant shore. Only the black specks of the ravens among the wheeling gulls told him that it was not water that rushed toward him over the grasslands, but a living sea of flesh and bone, fur and antlers. Tucked into every fold of the ground, molding themselves to its shape, Finn and his companions sheltered as best they could from the knifing wind, and strained their eyes to the horizon. They had not far to look—a bare hillside not more than three spear-casts away from which the ground fell away to where they lay.

He glanced over his shoulder down the slope, following the line of stakes each as high as a man that led down to the river. Another line, so distant that they seemed no higher than his thumbnail, followed the same route, the two lines converging as they reached the level ground at the water's edge. At the top of each stake, blown by the wind, ravens' feathers fluttered and bone toggles rattled against the stave. Once having entered the mouth of the funnel the deer would be driven by the stir and clatter on either side and with increasing urgency down to the flat ground and the ring of turf butts that lay between them and the river. There Hann and the hunters lay concealed, their spears laid out in rows behind them. This was Hann's killing ground, and there were ten others, one for each hearth, along the level ground beyond the river, upstream from the Autumn encampment.

Downstream at the camp the old and the very young prepared for the feasting that would start that night and last for many days and nights. There, among the skin tents that had been painfully dragged down from the mouth of the cave, they tended the ten great fires and the countless others that circled them like stars about the moon. Occasionally someone, smoothing out deerskin rugs at a fireside, laying bowls within the stone hearths, or sharpening birchwood skewers, would suddenly stop and be still, look up and cock an ear toward the river. Then a silence would gradually settle on the whole camp as all held their breaths, listening for some sound from the killing grounds that would tell that the herds were upon them. Finally, hearing nothing, they would return to their labors but the tension remained and communicated itself even to the infants who grew more restless and fractious as time passed.

It was the young women and the older children who first saw that which all had longed and prayed for through the endless Summer. They lay scattered in small groups far beyond the river, the killing grounds, and the lines of stakes in patterns that looked random but had been the subject of fierce debate between women and hunters. These groups, each led by a mature woman, would be the first to see the glorious onrush of the herds, the first to smell that smell, thick and rank but sweet after many months without fresh meat. As the deer rushed by, intent on the river and the forests beyond, they would lie low to spring up shouting and waving once the deer had passed, spreading out in a straggling line and driving them toward their husbands' and fathers' spears. There was fierce competition among the women of different hearths to ensure that the greatest number of deer passed through *their* killing ground. For hours before dawn the hunters and the women had walked the ground, discussing the tactics of the kill, the lie of the land, and the routes the herds had taken in previous years, which only the women knew. Once chosen, the routes and hiding places had been marked with piles of stones. In the absence of Mata, recovering now but still weak, it fell to Laela, Venn's sister, to lead the beaters of Hann's hearth. The strain had been showing when she had led the women and children across the river to their allotted places. She had been tense and irritable, and had even struck an unruly boy in her group, something she had never done before.

Finn shifted his position slightly, sliding his forearm under his chin. It was his right forearm—he would probably never lose the habit of hiding his tattooed left within his cloak. The grass beneath him was warm. With the added warmth of Venn beside him and another boy to his right, he grew sleepy, as they all did, and his eyelids drooped. It was difficult to stay asleep for long, though, as the rattling of the staves soon intruded into his dreams and jerked him back to wakefulness. Then, too, there was the anticipation of what was to come. When the beaters arrived, driving whatever portion of the main herd they had managed to divert into the mouth of the funnel, it was the job of the oldest boys to close the mouth of the trap, and drive in stragglers. Once the deer had passed they were free to sprint after them and show their skill in the killing ground. Others, scattered down the line of staves to drive in any strays, could follow too in due course. But the mouth of the trap was the place of honor, and this year Finn's by right.

The gulls and ravens were above them now circling on the wind while below, borne on that same wind, Finn could hear the muffled drum of countless hooves, the clack of antlers, and fainter still, the cries of the women and children. As the sounds grew nearer, the boys became alert; they drew themselves up onto all fours, not taking their eyes off the horizon and un-clasped their cloaks, letting them slide off their shoulders onto the grass. Almost as they did so, the grassy skyline opposite became forest: a living forest of antlers that gathered and grew and spilled down the hillside toward them. The herd seemed to cover the earth with brown and white and gray until not a patch of green could be seen. A stone tossed into their midst would not have touched the earth, Finn thought. It was as if the hillside had turned in an instant to brown muddy water and was now tumbling down to join with the waters of the river below.

For a moment the boys froze, halfway between crouching and standing, mesmerized by the power and majesty of the spectacle before them. This torrent of flesh and bone seemed unstoppable—surely it would sweep them all into the river or trample them to dust, surely even the greatest pines in the forest would be forced to bend before this awesome primal force. For a moment it seemed as if all creation were on the march, winds, clouds, herds, all moving as one in one direction, with only a few puny men and boys in its way. The leaders of the herd, strong, fat bucks, were within spear range already, and Finn could see the alarm in their eyes and the steam of fear rising from the backs of the herd close on their heels. Realizing all at once that another moment's delay would mean disaster for the whole hearth, the boys sprang into action, fanning out well to the left of the approaching mass, waving their cloaks, howling like wolves.

The effect was instantaneous; the leading bucks swerved to the right, the herd following them as one, and dashed past Finn into the mouth of the funnel. Finn and Venn stood by the foremost stave as the herd thundered by, close enough for them to reach out and touch them. The rank stench hit them like a wall. Vern laughed and turned to Finn. He shouted something that was lost in the tumult and carried away on the wind, but

Finn knew what he was saying. No words were necessary. This was the moment longed for by every man, woman and child in the tribe; the time when they felt more truly alive than any other. The return of the herds meant survival through the Winter, brought the promise of Annu's continued favor, but it meant even more than that. The creature whose ranks were now filling the whole length of the funnel was more than just their walking larder; it clothed them and sheltered them, gave them every single thing their lives depended on. It was the object of their dances and rituals, the subject of their songs and paintings; it was at once the hub of their universe, their ideal of beauty, and the image of their God. It was impossible to think of a world without the Reindeer, who were as fundamental to their existence as the earth that now shook beneath their feet.

Over the backs of the herd Finn could just see, through the dust, their companions at the other side of the funnel entrance. They were still waving their cloaks, but their cries were drowned by the sound of the hooves, the clicking of ankle bones, and the incessant grunting and coughing of the frenzied deer. Those others too had done their job; now the whole of that portion of the herd that Laela and the women had driven toward them was racing down the narrowing lane toward Hann and his companions. At intervals down the line the remainder of the youths waited, crouched on all fours, draped in skins and howling like wolves. It was their job to discourage any beasts who might be tempted to stray. But, as frightened deer press together and follow in the steps of those ahead, there was little to do as they raced by but assess, with expert eyes, the state of the herd. They were in prime condition, ready for the rut, and though at the shoulder they were no higher than Finn's waist, their antlers at this season overtopped his head. They were fat too, from Summer grazing, and their coats were sleek and shiny. The scars from last year's flies were healed and the new larvae buried below the skin had not yet started to burrow through. This kill was for skins as well as meat.

Although they had seen the sight many times before, Finn and his companions stood and stared as though entranced. At times the herd seemed as if it was one vast beast, or a never-ending river roaring its way down to some unknown lake. Then suddenly it would dissolve into its constituent parts, broad feet, blunt muzzles, staring eyes, the tossing antlers of the bucks and does and the black buds on the calves' heads.

Then suddenly they were past. Silence fell, and almost at the same moment the women and children appeared, laughing and tumbling down the hillside. Needing no further signal, Finn and the others snatched up their spears, ran across into the mouth of the funnel, meeting their colleagues from the other side, and followed in the wake of the herd. Finn was well in the lead, flinging his cloak over his left shoulder as he sprinted through the churned muddy lane that led down to the killing ground. As the ground leveled out he saw before him all the horror of the slaughter. The awe that had come over the boys at the mouth of the trap at the first long-awaited sight of the deer had stilled the hunters' arms too, at first. As was the custom, the leading bucks had been allowed through—every hunter knew that Annu led the deer in the form of a buck and none would risk injuring him in his Earthly form. They had passed unmolested, swimming the river easily with their broad feet, climbing the far bank and forging on with renewed vigor as they smelled the pine forests ahead. Once they had passed, however, the killing began. As the herd spread out into the open space along the riverbank, searching for crossing places, the men abandoned their hiding places, climbing up onto the butts, hurling spear after spear into the throng below. They threw until their arms ached, then dropped to the ground, to be replaced at once by a brother or son. Others passed up spears from the seemingly inexhaustible supply to the men on the butts; each spear shaft being marked with the family's distinguishing notch to avoid disputes over carcasses. As the supply of spears dwindled, the hunters would rush out into the killing ground whenever gaps appeared in the herd, hurriedly wrench-ing spears from carcasses, finishing off wounded animals, and ear-marking kills before racing back to the butts to kill again. Around the edges of the herd the carcasses were piled high, and even in the middle where the press was thickest the spears of the strongest, men like Hann, had found their mark.

By the time Finn reached the level ground dead and wounded deer covered the visible earth. Some, sunk to their bellies in the earth, struggled to rise, hampered by spears jutting from their sides, staring around them with blank, sightless eyes. Others stood at bay, legs splayed, chests heaving, turning this way and that to try to face the threat or to escape back the way they had come. Most, however, bunched up in the center and pressed on down to the riverbank, where they could see the head of the column swimming to safety. Even in his excitement Finn, confronted by this sight, felt the sorrow of it, the cruel irony that to live they must slaughter that which they loved. He knew that Annu willed it, that the bodies of the deer were a sacrifice to Him, and that their spirits were released at once to roam the dreamlands forever. He knew too, that without this carnage the tribe would not survive the Winter, that they would die out, and the world would end. Yet as he looked about him all he could see was bloodshed, chaos, and terror. He turned away from the mass of slaughtered deer to look at the men on the butts. Most were laughing, some snarled as they pitched spear after spear into the heaving masses below. Their faces, contorted by blood lust, were the more horrifying for being known to him. Here were men he had known all his life suddenly become like wolves. "If we wish to be above the beasts," he heard Sanu saying, "there is a price to be paid, and that price is the blood of the creature we love the best." Now he saw the full meaning of these words: not only their lives, but their *way* of life depended on this moment, this transformation. They must become like beasts so that they could continue to live like men. There was no time now for pity or for love; that time would come again. Now was the time for butchery and, as he ran forward to it, Finn heard himself singing.

Over to Finn's left a group of twenty or thirty deer had broken from the main herd and were circling back from the river in a panic-stricken attempt to escape the darting spears of the hunters on that side. They were coming in Finn's direction. Raising his spear arm to shoulder height he advanced to meet them. Venn and the others had caught up with him now and, seeing the approaching mass, they fanned out to his left, eager to take whatever kills they could at this late stage. At once, becoming aware of this new threat, the herd changed direction again, passing across Finn's front from left to right. The bucks were not the best—the strongest would be down by the river by now—but he could see, in the midst of the group, one fine doe with that almost unblemished white fur that was so highly prized.

Finn set his feet apart and turned to follow the progress of the group; they were now changing direction again to rejoin the tail of the column that pushed and butted its way down to the river. Narrowing his eyes, he drew back his spear arm until he could just see, at his far right, the tip of the flint spearhead that bore the unmistakable sign of Hann's work. Finn's own spear-manship had been self-taught, and would have to suffice until the Winter when Hann would have time to teach him. Above all he must not let Hann down, not here in the ring before all the men of the hearth. The doe drew level with him; there were two others between Finn and her, and she dipped her head as she passed. Finn was about to lower his spear and take up a new stance when the antlers rose once more; just before she passed beyond range she exposed her strong white neck for the briefest moment. It was not an easy shot, but Finn was intent on winning that pelt. He cast; the spear struck home, slightly high but firm, and to his joy he saw the herd split and pass around the doe as she sank to her belly, then fell over on her side. As he raced forward shouting his delight, he was aware of

Venn on his left rushing forward too. By the time he reached his kill the deer had passed on, making for the river. His beast was still kicking—the spear had hit the main neck muscle but it was not a clean kill.

Leaping over the body and heaving out the spear in one movement, he plunged it with both hands into the back of the animal's neck. The bone cracked beneath his spearhead and the creature kicked once, then was still. As he removed the bone scraper from the top of his legging and earmarked the deer with the single oblique stroke that was Hann's, he saw that the men had abandoned the butts. Rushing on the last remnants of the herd, they were thrusting at close quarters now. Most had made and marked their own kills, and were spearing indiscriminately now to swell the communal larder of Hann's hearth. Finn raced among them, fighting his way through the laughing hunters down toward the river. There was scarcely room upon the earth to plant his feet and twice he stumbled over carcasses on his way to the clear ground beyond the butts.

There were still good kills to be made, Finn knew. Most of his companions were making for the tail of the herd that clustered on the last bare stretch of ground that sloped down to the water's edge. But Finn had a plan of his own. The river was alive with deer swimming steadily across to the far bank where there were no men. It was generally agreed that deer that reached the far bank should be allowed to go their way unharmed, so along the bank by the killing ground groups of hunters now gathered, eager to take a last few kills from the main body of the herd.

Finn knew, as they did, that the best and strongest bucks would be well to the fore of any column, either climbing the far bank by now, or well out in midstream. Some of the men were already waist deep in the fast-flowing water, accepting, for the chance of one last good kill, the risk of being swept into the midst of the herd and borne under by the heaving bodies and thrashing hooves. Finn was a good swimmer, but he lacked the strength of these men, for a boy of his age to venture into the water was a grave risk. No one expected the boys to come home with fine pelts or a good prime carcass; their position at the mouth of the trap, and their necessarily late arrival on the killing ground precluded this. But Finn meant to make his mark. He would present his father with a fine buck for the feast so that neither Hann nor any other would be in any doubt that he was worthy of him.

The deer in midstream were so tightly packed that Finn felt he could have crossed to the far bank on their backs without once getting his feet wet. Here and there a carcass bobbed in the water; a buck or a doe with a spear in its side or a fawn pulled under by the press and drowned. Beyond the herd bodies floated downstream, silent witnesses to any in the encampment who had not already heard that the kill was on in earnest. Discarding his clothes at the water's edge Finn stepped into the icy water, feeling his way on the pebbly bed with his bare feet. As the water reached his waist and lapped over his stomach he gasped with the shock of its cold. He could feel the current tugging at his legs, trying to drag him away, pull him under or carry him down to a brutal, bloody death in the churning water where the herd crossed.

Finn had carefully explored the river below the killing ground some days before, in readiness for this moment. He knew that where he now stood the bed of the river formed a kind of shelf that reached out into the middle of the river, but how far it went, or whether he would be able to stand in the strong current remained to be seen. Feeling his way with his feet, and holding his spear shaft over his head he began to edge forward, all the time scanning the ranks of the herd for a suitable mark. They were already at the extreme range of his cast. A full-grown man could easily have lobbed a spear into the midst of those brown and white backs, but Finn would have to take his prey, if at all, from the edge. He stood and watched; his spear arm began to ache, and his legs grew numb beneath him. It began to seem a hopeless task as time after time he first chose then rejected a target. Then too, he began to feel ridiculous, and to think how much more foolish he would look emerging from the water with his spear unblooded, while his companions up on the killing ground were already skinning their no doubt impressive tally of lesser kills.

He watched with mounting despair as the bulk of the herd passed before him, the few that suited his purpose hopelessly out of reach. Then, just as he was in the act of slowly turning back, still fighting the drag of the current, a movement in the herd caught the corner of his eye and he turned once more. A single buck had detached itself from the herd and was striking out to the far bank on its own. It was heading for a point directly opposite to the shelf on which Finn stood, and its prog-ress there would bring it at just one point within range of his spear. At this distance and with most of its body underwater, it was difficult to assess its size, but judging by its antlers alone it was a kill of which Hann himself would be proud. Finn was already farther out in the water than any of the hunters, and being upstream, he and his buck—he already felt it to be *his* buck—were out of their sight. None of this mattered to Finn; his whole world at that moment contained only himself and the buck. How he would catch or mark his kill, the risk he ran of losing his spear, and the even greater risk that in the act of casting he would lose his balance and be swept away—all mat-tered less to him now than the glory that would be his when he presented such a kill to his father. It was a long cast, and the dull ache as he raised his spear arm told him that this throw would not be his best. He considered edging out farther along the shelf, but he could already feel the pebbles sloping away under his feet, and the buck was rapidly approaching the only point at which it would be in range. Assessing at a glance the current, the wind direction, and the speed of the deer in the water, he threw. He saw the spear skimming above the water; then his feet were no longer beneath him, and the daylight was extinguished as the water devoured him.

Here was yet another world, devoid of light or air or any sound except for the roaring in his ears. In this world he had no power of his own, his limbs went where they were forced, and his body was tossed about and twisted like a leaf in the wind. All sense of direction gone, he felt rocks and, once, a bank of pebbles maul his body. The buck, the hunters on the bank, his friends on the killing ground, all were forgotten now as though they had never been, as this world and everything in it hurried him on to his imminent and certain end. Then they were back. For an instant his head cleared the water. He was facing downstream, and as he sucked watery air into his lungs he saw, frozen as though in a wall painting, the hunters unaware of his plight still spearing the last of the herd, the buck, dead, circling slowly toward him, and, over on the bank to his right, someone running and waving. He was sucked under once more. It could only be a moment now before the water bore him under the hooves of the herd that would churn his flesh to a bloody pulp, like the level ground he had run down only minutes before. In less time than it took to skin a buck there would be one pale body among the brown and gray that floated at the ford by the camp, one piece of white and bloody flesh among the fur and antlers, one more son for Hann to bury.

His side rasped against a pebble bank and he grabbed for the stones with arms and hands as cold and unresponsive as stone. His fingers skeetered over the surface, finding no purchase. The current took him and spun him round and round. Across his mind flashed the memory of the times as a child when he had rolled down the grassy banks by the bolt-hole. At each turn the roaring grew louder, and his lungs seemed to scream in agony. Then he struck something hard, a pole or some tree that had mysteriously taken root in the riverbed. It arrested his flight just long enough for him to reach out one last time to his right, where he guessed the bank must be. His fingers clutched at nothing but water, and he felt himself slide once more when a hand from above grasped his wrist, drawing him upward and out. As his head broke the surface in the middle of the stream he saw that the water had turned him round, that he was facing upstream, and that it was Venn's hand that was dragging him toward the bank. It was Venn's spear thrust into the shingle that had held him just long enough to get hold of; Venn who was thigh deep in the water, himself in danger of being carried off. By now, though, Finn's feet had struck hard ground, and with a little help he was able to drag himself free of the water onto the bank where he lay, gasping like a salmon. Venn ran his hands over Finn's body feeling for broken bones as Finn coughed up water. It felt as though it had bruised his insides as much as the stones had damaged his body. Satisfied that all was well, Venn finally got to his feet.

"Nothing broken," was all he said. "Your buck's floating down to the ford. I'll try and catch it before it's too late." Finn nodded feebly. He tried to utter his thanks, but dissolved into a coughing fit. Before he could say a word Venn went on, "Your spear's gone. . . ." He turned for an instant to see his own spear shaft disappear beneath the water. "So's mine." With that he was gone, racing down the riverbank in pursuit of the dead buck.

Slowly Finn hauled himself to his feet and hobbled upstream to where his clothes lay. It was not until he had struggled back into them, and begun his painful progress downstream once more, that the full enormity of what had nearly happened dawned on him. Still occupied with their kills, only one or two of the hunters spared him a curious glance as he limped past. Mercifully none of them had seen what had happened upstream, and if Venn kept quiet about it no one would ever know. No one would understand why he had taken such a risk. Hunting the deer was not dangerous; no one had ever been known to die at it, not even hunting after buck in the rutting season. To risk one's life for one buck, however fine, at the time of the Autumn kill, when they covered the earth from one horizon to the other, would have been laughable to them. So it would have been to anyone but Finn. If only his buck had not filled with water and sunk, if only he could have something to show for it all, something to present to his father, something with which to bargain for a new spear for his friend, who had thought his life worth saving.

Venn was sitting exhausted on the bank by the time Finn caught up with him. His race down the riverbank and the shock of what had happened seemed to have hit him too, for he was white-faced now and breathing hard.

"I lost him, he went downstream," he managed to gasp out between tired sobs. Finn flopped down beside him and threw his arm round his shoulders. They said nothing more as they sat and gazed out over the water. Venn would have a new spear, of Hann's making. Finn would see to it, however much he had to beg his father, however much he had to tell him, even if he had to tell him the truth. Only a gift like that, which many a grown man would prize, would serve to proclaim his gratitude and his love. As they looked far across the river they could see in the distance the last of the deer entering the fringes of the forest and comparative safety. Finn sighed. If he had had to lose the buck he would rather it had been that way. He would rather have seen it vanish into the tree-line than fill with water and sink or float down, unmarked, to be dragged from the water and laid claim to by whoever saw it first. Although any hunter could recognize at a glance the carcass of a beast he had killed himself, his claim to an unmarked beast would only succeed in making Finn ridiculous. Since he had no intention of bickering over the carcass with some old woman or child, he had to hope that at best his buck would feed *somebody* that night if not, as he had hoped, his father's hearth. He was thankful, at least, as he looked at his friend slowly recovering his breath beside him, that the cost of his folly had not been higher.

Venn's breathing gradually steadied, and at last he was able to gasp, "I hooked him and marked him, mind, before he floated off." He fell back into the grass, laughing weakly. Finn gaped at him for a moment, then he too began to laugh. With its foreleg hooked over an antler, lifting its nostrils clear of the water, the buck would float down to the ford by the camp, where everyone knew Hann's mark. Hann's hearth would feed on his buck after all. Venn would have a new spear, he would see to it. Upstream the hunters, having dragged ashore what carcasses they could, were heading back up toward the killing ground. They looked up at the shouts of laughter from the riverbank, shook their heads, then went their way muttering that the world was changing. They had taken their hunting seriously; it seemed to mean nothing to some of these boys.

Back on the killing ground hunters and women were already at work on the slaughtered deer that lay strewn about the ring, choking the exit that led down to the river. Hanging from trestles that had been thrown up the moment the slaughter had ceased, many were already unrecognizable as the creatures who had dashed for the river but a short while before. Women bled the bodies, plugging wounds with their fingers to let the blood drain into the chest cavity, then ladling it into wooden bowls. The men were busy with the skinning, rolling fur off legs and backs like bark off a birch tree. Nothing was wasted—hides, antlers, offal, bone, flesh, eyes, heads, and hooves, all were collected. What little remained was left where it fell to attract the wolves and carrion eaters, many of whom would themselves fall prey to the hunters in days to come.

When Finn came upon Hann he was skinning his own doe for him. He nodded a greeting at Finn, not noticing his hesitant manner. Finn watched him for a few moments working his blade down the beast's belly, his fingers separating fur from flesh. He was wondering how to tell him of the loss of his spear, and how much he would be forced to confess, when Hann spoke.

"It was a good choice," he said, stopping for a moment and nodding down at the doe.

Finn flushed. "I killed a buck, too. A big one, in the river. It's marked and floating down to the ford."

Hann looked pleased. "I'll look him over when we get down there," he said. "And if he's good enough..." Then, noticing that Finn's hands were empty, looked around and behind him for his spear, and then into his eyes.

Finn reddened even more. "I caught him in the neck...it fell out," he explained awkwardly.

Hann clicked his tongue, and his expression changed as he turned away. "It must have been a feeble throw," was all he said as he went back to the skinning.

Finn hung his head. He had wanted to impress Hann and had failed. More than that, he had lost a valuable spear, and almost thrown away his life and Venn's. His disappointment must have shown on his face for when Hann looked up again he added, "Even so, the best of us lose spears sometimes."

Finn doubted if Hann had ever lost a spear in his life but he knew the words were kindly meant. Far from putting his mind at rest, though, it simply made it harder to say what he had to say next. And there was the debt he owed Venn, and the fact that he did not want to keep secrets from Hann.

"Venn lost his spear, too." Still working, Hann looked up. His face was a mask in which Finn could read nothing, but Finn knew at once that for his own peace of mind he would have to tell him everything. It came out in a flood of words. "It was in the river. I had to go out into the middle to get the buck. I lost my footing and Venn had to use his spear to fish me out. I'd have died if he hadn't." Just as he finished Hann peeled off the last of the pelt and unrolled it. It was not as good as it had seemed at first sight—unscarred, but blemished in places. It lay there between them like an unspoken comment on what Hann had just heard. Finn's misery was complete. He turned away, angrily shaking away the burning tears that started in his eyes.

"I wanted to show you what I could do," he protested as he felt Hann's hand upon his shoulder. "Show you I was worthy of you. Make you proud of me." His voice trailed away.

"And you have." Hann was beside him now. "It takes courage to go out into the river, and it takes courage to tell the truth. Now let it end there. All the deer that ever roamed the earth aren't worth your life, or any man's. I have buried one son, I want the other to bury me when the time comes." Finn nodded, but it was a while before he could look up again. By this time Hann had rolled up the pelt once more.

"I wanted to give it to Mata," Finn muttered. "But I don't think it's good enough."

Hann smiled and handed it to him. "If *you* give it to her, she will wear no other," he said. "Now follow me, there is work to be done."

Without another word Hann strode off. He knew in his heart that he had been too harsh at first. Finn was still a child in many ways, more vulnerable, despite his hard life, than others of his age. He had a way of following him around, worshiping him the way a child does, no doubt because it was all new to him. Yet within less than a year he must turn him out into the tribe as a man. It would take years to teach the boy all he needed to know, and all he had was one Winter. Still, the boy was brave and great-hearted and truthful. If he had wanted to make him proud he had succeeded better than he knew.

▲ ▲ ▲

By the light of the fire all Finn could see were cheery faces glistening with fat, cheeks bulging as they devoured great gobbets of meat. Chunks of his buck hissed and bubbled on a dozen skewers, the fat turning clear and running down the sides to drop into collecting pans or spatter onto the hot stones. This first meal of fresh meat after the kill was the sweetest moment of the year, and even now, though his belly was taut as a drumskin, Finn had not had enough. Alternating as they did between feast and famine, the Burnt Shins were blessed with elastic stomachs; tonight they would gorge like wolves. Wiping his fingers in his hair Finn lay back, looked at the sky and belched contentedly. His former cares were forgotten now. This night Hann had honored him in front of the whole hearth. The great feast was a time of speeches and boasts and the faces round the fire had gazed up eagerly at Hann as he sang Finn's praises and his own. When he had finished, they had linked their names together and shouted their praises to the skies— the man who had led them in the hunt, and his son, who had killed his first buck.

Still lying on his back, but lifting his head slightly, Finn glanced around the fire. Beside him, still upright, Hann was cramming home a huge mouthful of meat and chewing happily, while another hunter told him a long and improbable story he had heard and enjoyed many times before. Beyond them lay Mata, propped up on a cushion of fawnskin. Too weak as yet to eat fresh meat, she was sucking at the sweet fat from around the beast's eyes. Across the fire, Laela laughingly fought with Venn for a choice cut that he had tried to steal from her. They were both in good spirits; she because she had acquitted herself well at the drive; he at the promise of the best spear from Hann's next batch. Indeed it would have been impossible at that moment to find a glum face at any of the ten hearths. The tribe's mood perceptibly improved as their stomachs filled, and everywhere Finn looked he saw merriment, love, and laughter. All ages and both sexes ate to their hearts' content, falling back when replete to gasp for air and gape at the stars or stagger, heads swimming, into the night to visit other hearths or sleep where they fell, before returning to eat again.

Finn became aware that Hann was nudging him and he sat up, taking care not to show the pain that seared through him. He had begun to stiffen up from the battering he had received earlier. Hann gestured toward the wooden pot beside the fire where the leg bones and the tongue lay, boiled, but as yet untouched. It was his buck and the choicest of the marrow was his by right. Marrow was a luxury Finn had seldom tasted, but once tasted it was never forgotten. He already knew, as he gingerly fished out a leg bone and cracked it on a hearth stone, who was to have the first of it. Crawling over to where Mata lay he held the opened bone to her. A murmur of approval ran around the fire. Smoothing his hair with her fatty fingers, she smiled at him. "For me, little wolf? Come, we shall share it." Sitting close to her for warmth, they took turns to suck noisily at the ends of the bone, reveling in the piquancy of the hot, oily stuff that lay within. At last he lay and dozed intermittently, his head on her shoulder. Mata was recovering her strength slowly; her hand was healing and she had declared herself ready for work in the days to come. There was meat to be smoked, blood and bones to be cooked, skins to be scraped and sinews to be made into thread. The first skin she would work would be her own, given to her by her son. It had been received with all the rapture that Hann had predicted; this woman had waited many years for a son's gift.

Almost as soon as Finn's eyes had closed he felt a foot prodding his stomach, and he opened his eyes to see Venn, his face reflected in the flames, golden against the night sky, smiling down at him. He had eaten his fill for the moment and was off to visit other hearths. All around them in the great encampment there was a constant coming and going as visits were made and almost immediately returned. Even the smallest children were allowed to wander without fear from hearth to hearth.

"I'm off to see Gronu," said Venn. "Come with me."

Finn looked unsure. To tell the truth he was afraid of Gronu. He had had little or no contact with him since that meeting by the stream, and of that encounter he still bore the marks.

89

It was Mata who persuaded him. "Go on, little wolf," she whispered in his ear so that even Venn could not hear. "You cannot lie by me all night. You have killed your first buck— strut about the camp, make a show." In fact Finn would gladly have lain beside her all night, and he still felt slightly ashamed about the buck; to be dragged from the river half drowned seemed little enough to boast about. Yet Venn seemed keen, and all at Hann's hearth had agreed that it was a fine buck. It occurred to him, too, that he had promised himself that he had done with running and hiding. He grasped Venn's outstretched hand that hauled him to his feet, and arm in arm they wandered through the camp.

Gronu was seated at a hearth of his own with three or four of his hearth companions and, though she was of a different hearth, Shani. As they approached out of the darkness Gronu was in the middle of a story. It was a gross breach of Burnt Shins etiquette to interrupt a speech or a story, so the two boys waited politely in the shadows.

"I had been told that Sanu had gone on a journey to the dreamlands," Gronu was saying, "so I crept up to his cave mouth and twitched the curtain . . . and that was how I learned how the spirit leaves the body!"

He had his listeners spellbound, and looked around the circle of faces to confirm the fact. It was Shani who broke the silence.

"How then?" she cried impatiently.

"Through the mouth," said Gronu. "His body was still there, propped against the cave wall, and his spirit had gone but had left his mouth open so it could re-enter when it returned."

The others looked to one another in amazement, unsure how to take this. He went on. "And though his body was as still as death it was pining for him, for it kept calling to him all the time."

"What did it say?" This was Shani again, biting into a piece of meat with her even white teeth as she did so.

Gronu looked pained, as though trying to remember exactly. "Not words exactly, but a strange, sad cry like this . . ." He lowered his head, let his mouth sag open, and made the noise of an old man snoring.

Laughter among the Burnt Shins was infectious, and on full stomachs, hysterical. The smallest jest at the right moment could leave an entire hearth helpless on their backs, drumming their heels and clutching at aching sides. So it was now, and it was some time before silence fell. When it finally did, Shani dug him sharply in the ribs. "You should not joke about such things!"

Gronu had not once smiled, and now looked around him with wide-eyed innocence. "I see nothing funny in this," he protested, and once again all, including Shani, laughed. Standing, grim-faced, in the shadows Finn felt even Venn beside him shaking with mirth.

"A less pious man than myself . . ." Gronu went on, and Finn noticed how he referred to himself as a man, though he was no older than the others around him, ". . . would have simply said 'Aha! So the old fool's asleep, that's it!' But I knew better . . ." At that moment he became aware of the two waiting for him to finish, and stood up at once.

"Venn!" he called out, obviously pleased to see his friend. "Come and join us!" Venn strode forward, exchanged greetings with all present, and sat himself beside Shani. Finn, who had only reluctantly been dragged along, who had not laughed at Gronu's story and feared that this had been noticed, and who was in any case not even sure that the invitation extended to him, came forward hesitantly, and sat across the fire from the three of them.

"He's been telling his stupid tales again," complained Shani cheerfully, and Venn and Gronu exchanged a laugh that spoke of the intimacy between them. Back from the fire, half in the shadows, Finn envied them this closeness and their closeness to the lovely creature who sat between them laughing, teasing, flirting with each in turn and clearly enjoying their presence on either side. There followed a lot of good-natured banter that centered on the question of which of them she would marry. She seemed to take this as her due, it being generally assumed by all the tribe that it would be one of the two. For some time she allowed them to score points off each other, not neglecting to score a few on her own account. At last she grew tired of this, and after claiming that they were all too childish for her at present, declared that she did not think she would marry at all.

During all this Finn sat quietly, taking a bite from the leg joint each time it was passed round the fire, grateful not to be noticed and hoping for a chance to slip away before too long. The talk turned to the day's kills, and after a little boasting on his own account, Venn ended this hope by announcing, "Finn killed the biggest buck."

At once everyone, Gronu and Shani included, turned to Finn. He had not even been sure if they could see him; indeed he had rather hoped that they could not, being unsure how this announcement would be greeted.

"It was the biggest that came into our killing ground!" exaggerated Venn. "Hann himself would have been proud to take it." Finn shifted uneasily in his place, though he knew this praise was kindly meant.

To his surprise and immense relief Gronu merely nodded. "So I had heard."

Finn need not have been so surprised. It *had* been a fine specimen, and in the immediate aftermath of the hunters' return, while the fires were being banked, among the hearths all the hunters compared skills and passed comment.

"So, Finn, you put us to shame again," said Gronu, reaching into a wooden bowl. "First with the salmon, and now with the deer."

Any hint of menace that might have lurked in such a remark was dispelled by the fact that Gronu had used his name for the first time ever. As Gronu rose and came to sit by him,

Finn saw that he had produced from the pot a boiled deer tongue, which he now offered him. He bit into the proffered delicacy, seeing Gronu's companions nudging each other, noting this mark of favor. Now with Gronu beside him, his arm across his shoulder as they shared the tongue, he felt himself falling as all others fell under Gronu's spell. When he saw that Shani too was smiling at him, a smile that came from the heart and told him he was forgiven, gratitude and love for the boy at his side flooded through him.

Across the fire Shani had taken up a fragment of bone and was picking her teeth with it. Suddenly she paused, frowned, and stared into the fire as if deep in thought, continuing that way until she was sure all eyes were upon her before announcing, "I think I shall marry Finn!"

A chorus of protest followed this statement, not least from Venn, who by now was all but resting his head upon her shoulder.

"Well..." she protested as Finn blushed, grateful for the fire's glow, "he doesn't stamp and strut all the time like the rest of you. And he doesn't keep crowding me like a rutting buck." So saying she shoved Venn sprawling into the darkness, and in the laughter that followed none joined more loudly than Finn. As it subsided they heard at a nearby hearth the strains of a familiar song. It had started at one of the great hearths upstream and was now traveling down the line of the river as fireside after fireside added their voices to the swelling chorus. It was the simplest and most ancient of their songs, the one most favored by the old. The young had their own songs, songs of hunting and of love, songs in praise of Reindeer, friends, favorite weapons, songs that came and went within a day as moods and fancies changed. This remained though, and wild and primitive though they thought it, the youth at Gronu's fireside took it up at once; at times like this it still thrilled them like no other song, no other *sound* on earth. It spoke of the love of their God, the glory and beauty of their world, and their sheer joy at living. But more than that it proclaimed to the world and the heavens who they were. The whole tribe was singing now, countless hands beating, countless voices chanting, countless faces shiny with fat shouting their defiance to the stars—they were the Children of Annu, they were the Burnt-Shinned People, they were the Reindeer People.

CHAPTER
SIX

▲ ▲ ▲
▲ ▲

EVEN AMID THE NOISE and bustle of the camp in the wake of the Autumn kill, while carcasses were still being dragged up from the river, Finn could not take his eyes from what his father was doing. Hann sat before him, a flat stone anvil gripped between his knees, patiently working at an oblong of flint. It had been hacked many months before from his own small quarry in the mountainside whose location was a jealously guarded secret. Originally the size of a man's head, it now bore the marks of Hann's work, as though some enormous blade had sliced off about a quarter of it. Finn watched, fascinated, as Hann turned it over and over in his big capable hands, narrowing his eyes as he examined the zigzag ridges down the exposed core. He knew what his father was making, could see in his mind's eye what it would look like. But unlike Hann, he could not discern its outlines in the stone before him. Almost before he could try Hann had judged where to strike and, holding the point of his old bone chisel at the flint's top edge, he raised the round stone that served him for a hammer and struck once. A flake the length of a man's hand from wrist to fingertip fell onto the anvil with a clatter. Laying aside his tools and material Hann took up the flake and looked it over. To Finn's eyes it was perfect; though not yet the perfect laurel leaf shape that marked Hann's spearheads, it could have been bound into a spear shaft there and then and not have disgraced its owner. Hann's face gave nothing away, but seeing Finn's eyes on him he at last thrust out his lower lip, nodded reluctantly, and smiled.

Taking up his tools he placed the chisel, raised the stone, and struck again; another perfect flake rattled onto the anvil. Again he struck, and again, and as Finn watched, spellbound, tapped off six such flakes before turning the flint round and beginning again from the other side. Each blow was carefully considered; not one was wasted. By the time he had finished a dozen spearheads were laid out on the ground beside him, as well as the remainder of the core whose rounded back and single cutting edge he would fashion into a chopper capable of quartering a carcass. Finn knew better than to think that what he had just witnessed was as easy as it looked. Hann's craftsmanship was respected throughout the tribe, and Finn still bore the cuts and calluses that had been the only products of his own first efforts. Still Hann showed no emotion. Simply laying aside his chisel and taking up another with a finer tip, he took up the first spearhead and began painstakingly to nibble away at its edge.

Again no effort was wasted, no placing of the chisel or tap of the hammer ill-considered, and nothing distracted him. Finn watched for some time but at last began to fidget, began to find such faultlessness tiresome. There was so much going on around him. He shifted in his seat, screwed his head around to watch some hunters of Finn's hearth arriving from the river dragging a sled load of jointed meat up over the edge of the scree. They sweated under their load. A group of idlers, who had arrived in the night and lounged about ever since, offered useless advice that was angrily rejected. Finn laughed, and turned to find Hann looking at him, his hammer poised in mid-stroke. Although Hann was the mildest of men, Finn dreaded his rebuke more than death itself; now he saw to his relief that he too was smiling. Finn blushed and tried to justify his inattention. "It all takes so long!" he complained.

"You must have patience," Hann chided him gently.

"Everything needs patience!" mumbled Finn, examining his bruised fingers.

Hann nodded solemnly. "Most wise!" he intoned, then laughed out loud as the boy slapped the ground in frustration.

"It's easier for me," he said comfortingly. "When you are my age you will have seen all of this you ever want to see. . . ." He gestured to the teeming camp. "Then you'll be glad of something to occupy you. Go, come back when you're bored, and make your choice." He nodded to where the spearheads lay.

Finn needed no further urging but scrambled to his feet and, leaving his father to his work, set off to wander through the camp. This was the busiest time of the year; almost as soon as the bulk of the tribe had returned from the river, cone-shaped timber frames began to be covered with deerskins. Children had been dispatched, under escort now because of wolves, to fetch wet wood. The first of these smoke-tents was already at work, packed with fresh lean deer meat, belching stinging smoke through the gap at the top where the poles were lashed. Others identical were being thrown up all along the scree as the meat began to arrive. There were all the usual squabbles over the erection of the tents, disputes over space on the scree, shouted instructions, advice, threats, jokes, laughter, and singing. It would be only a matter of time before one of the tents caught fire, and Finn did not want to miss the fun.

The smoke-houses were only a part of it all. Most of the men were engaged in dragging the meat up from the river, resting overnight, and then setting off again before dawn. Everyone was busy at something, and in times gone by Finn had been the busiest of all. Help offered at this time had often stood him in good stead later in the year, and with so much going on, there had always been good pickings for an active scavenger. There was food everywhere; heads and feet being boiled into stews; marrow and jelly; dried intestines stuffed with dried blood, boiled meat, fried meat, cold meat, dried meat. Even at this time, stuffed from the feasting, Finn had never refused what was offered him. This was the time, too, when he would clothe himself for the Winter. Pelts that had lain in the stream for two or three days were now ready for working—women pulling the hair out in tufts and scraping the skins with a mixture of fat and brains. Elsewhere the best furs were being sorted and scraped. At every hearth would be a pile of discarded skins or furs and from these he had used to take his pick. All that was behind him now. Now he walked the camp in furs as fine as anyone's. Where before he had been all but invisible, now he could expect greetings and kind words wherever he chose to go. Even so, he was glad to discover that this time had not lost its magic for him.

By the time Finn had failed to find Venn, been shouted at by Laela for standing in her light, considered looking for Gronu then decided against it, and returned to Hann's tent, a transformation had taken place. It was the transformation that he knew must take place; but it had seemed when he left to be a lifetime away. Now he was sorry to have missed it. Hann smiled at the expression on his face as he looked down at the smooth, finely boned, finished products. They lay in a row where there had formerly lain a dozen flints, that Finn if asked would have declared beyond improvement.

"You left just as I was about to finish them off," Hann said, "or you would have seen how it was done. Now you must choose one for Venn."

Finn knelt down to examine them more closely. He picked one up and held it high to see the light play over its surface, as he had seen Hann do. All of them bore the distinctive marks of Hann's craftsmanship. The difference between them and the other men's work lay in more than just that lightness of touch and keenness of edge that were themselves undeniable. Where other men stopped and laid the thing down as finished, Hann went on. It was not enough that they served their purpose—they had to be beautiful too, and so they were. As Finn picked up each in turn he thought, as had others before him, that to put such finely crafted objects as these to any practical use was almost a blasphemy. They should be kept as things apart, to be admired for their own sake. Yet as far as Hann was concerned the use to which they would be put was sacred in itself, and into their manufacture he put all the love he felt for the deer and for Annu.

"I can't choose, which do *you* think is the best?" Finn looked to Hann hoping for an answer, but getting none. Hann shook his head.

"It is for you to choose. Which would you choose if it was for you?"

Finn looked them all over once more, trying hard to seem knowledgeable. At length he chose one, he knew not why, and held it out. To his relief Hann seemed satisfied.

"A good choice," he declared solemnly, then nodding past him, "The shaft is behind you." Finn felt the shaft as he passed over it. It was of ash, smooth and hard and straight, chosen by Hann from the best of his stock. A hand's span below its end it was tightly bound with sinew; above the sinew it was split ready to receive the head. This spear, one of the finest he had ever made, was a gift for the boy who had saved his son's life. The care that had gone into it said more than any words could have done how much he valued that life. That fact was not lost on Finn as he watched Hann set the spearhead in its place and bind it firmly home with sinew.

When it was finished Finn took it up and held it by its mid-point, marveling at its perfect balance. Then, oblivious of Hann's watching eye, he ran his hand over the smooth shaft, sighted down its length, admiring its faultless line, and finally tested the fit of the head into the shaft. It was as firm as though shaft and head were one—the head of ash wood or the shaft of stone.

"It's the finest spear ever made," he announced with the assurance of an expert, an assurance that was based on knowledge of Hann's skill rather than any real understanding. Nevertheless Hann accepted the compliment. "I must take it to Venn at once." Finn was already setting out spear in hand.

Hann smiled. "I thought you couldn't find him."

"When he hears what I have for him, he'll find me!" Finn shouted back at him, dodging among the tents.

Hann stood up the better to see the retreating figure, and cupped his hands to his lips. "Tell him the next time some fool falls in the river, to save his spear first," and the answering laugh showed how close they had already become since that day at the killing ground.

Finn found Venn by one of the smoke-houses. He had been helping Laela feed wood onto the fire and was washing the smoke from his eyes with water from a skin bag. Drying his face on his arm he followed Finn farther down the scree to where they could talk alone.

"My father sends you this," said Finn, holding out the spear with both hands.

Even though he had known the gift was coming, there was no disguising Venn's joy as he ran his hands along the shaft.

"Your father places great value on your life!" he said, still unable to take his eyes from the finely crafted spear point.

Finn smiled and looked down. "He says next time you should save the spear first!"

"For a spear like this I would cast away a dozen!" Venn looked his friend in the eyes. "And for your life I would give up even this!"

Given the value of such a spear, the more so to a boy of Venn's age, it was no small tribute, but Finn knew it to be true and for a moment it shamed him.

"You have given me much already..." he muttered. "You gave me friendship when I had none, and though others mocked you for it. What they learned from fathers or brothers I learned from you. *I* have nothing to give you. Had I my father's skill..."

Venn cut him short. "Soon you will have your father's deer luck. Share that with me, and be my brother, and I shall be well rewarded!"

Finn's eyes misted. His heart was so full it was all he could do to blurt out, "Everything. Everything I have, everything I know, I shall share with you!"

Venn held out the spear to him. "And when we are men and hunters, shall we hunt together always?"

"Always!" cried Finn. Each grasping the spear shaft with both hands they called upon the earth and the air, the river and the forest to bear witness to their pact, and then climbed arm-in-arm to the camp.

▲ ▲ ▲

Early next morning before the sun had risen, Hann and Finn were up beyond Sanu's cave where the trees thinned out and the forest gave way to bare mountain. Creeping through the trees with spears raised they signaled to each other with the hunting language of tongue-clicks that Hann was already teaching his son. Emerging from the trees, Finn could already see his quarry, knew that it would not scent, hear or see him, would not run for the safety of the trees. Even so, what took place in the next few moments would affect their hunting in the coming weeks. Behind him the sun was creeping over the skyline, and by its light he could see where their prey nestled between two rocks half a cast away. As they drew closer, approaching from two directions, Finn saw it at close quarters for the first time. The image, molded in clay, was less than a quarter of the size of a real deer; easier to stalk perhaps, but harder to hit, especially in the manner required by the rules of the ritual. Hann was close beyond the target, poised, waiting. Finn raised himself up on the balls of his feet, not taking his eyes off the image for a moment, *willing* the point of his spear to strike true. The sun rose behind him and he felt its warmth on his back, and at the same moment its first beam darted across the valley and struck the image, bathing it in red, the color of blood, the color of life and death. Sensing Hann's movement he also cast and held his position, as the two spears bit into the neck and flank of the image. The signs were good; the clay image had known birth, life, and sacrifice in the same instant, and Annu had blessed their enterprise. Neither of them spoke or moved, and in those moments all of home and hearth, all of friends and kin, past, present and future, fell from Finn, and only the hunter remained.

Later, well wrapped against the wind, each carrying a spear and a few belongings slung in skin bags over their shoulders, Hann and Finn threaded their way through the tents and down the scree toward the trees. Finn had looked forward to this moment since the day when Hann had first promised to take him on an expedition deep into the forests once the Autumn kill was over. Yet it was not without a twinge of regret that he left the camp and the company of the youths of Hann's hearth; now at last the camp had become a friendly, warm place to him, and he could not resist looking back over his shoulder from time to time as they made their way down to the cold, uninviting forest below. The last thing he saw was Shani. She was seated on the scree before her father's tents, spinning thread, rolling the wet sinew on her thigh. The sight of her sent a sharp pang like a physical pain through his body; he could not stop himself from looking back one more time as they entered the trees. She was a long way off now, but she seemed to be looking in his direction, and her hand rose from her work for an instant in what looked like a wave. Finn was not sure whether she had even seen him. For an instant he considered waving back, but, conscious of his dignity and of Hann increasing his pace ahead of him, he simply turned and descended into the gloom of the forest.

Hann's pace continued to increase as they descended until, as the ground leveled out and they began to follow the path of the stream upstream, away from the valley mouth, he had fallen into a steady trot. Finn jogged alongside him with ease; he knew he was as strong as any youth in the hearth and felt sure he could keep this up for as long as Hann. As time passed, though, and Hann showed no sign of slackening his pace, he began to lag. By the time they had gone deeper into the forest than Finn had ever been he could only just see his father through the trees ahead. At last Hann stopped and allowed him to rest. Before they started off once more he showed Finn how to run as a man might run over stepping stones—a slouching, muscle-saving lope that would see him through the many days' journey that lay ahead. They passed countless small herds stopping to browse, and were passed by countless more pressing deep into the forest—a sure sign of a fierce Winter to come. The rut had commenced; every herd was patrolled or shadowed by strutting bucks and the rattling of hooves and the clashing of antlers echoed through the forest from all sides. Before darkness fell they set up camp. Exhausted, Finn would happily have rolled himself in his cloak, thrown himself on the ground and slept there and then. But Hann would have none of it. Years of hunting through the bitterest Winters had taught him that those who gave way to fatigue on first stopping suffered for it later; a little effort now meant a comfortable night and a fresh start on the morrow. Dragging the weary boy to his feet he showed him first how to fashion his cloak into a shelter, choosing a site where the rain wouldn't run, by a boulder that would bounce back the heat from their fire. He made him gather moss to cushion his sleep, and pliant willow saplings to sleep on, to keep the earth from sucking the warmth out of him.

After they had eaten, Hann talked of the days of his youth, of great hunts of the past, but mostly, as always, of the deer. Though Finn grew drowsier by the moment, and simply to stay awake took all his concentration, he was as keen to learn as his father was to teach. This family time, taken for granted by so many fathers and sons, was for both of them the fulfillment of the dreams of years. Hann lay back with his eyes closed, enjoying the warmth of the fire, his full stomach, and the joy of discoursing on his favorite subject.

"You see those bucks as they are now..." he began, "strong and fat, with their antlers at their highest? In a month's time you wouldn't know them for the same beasts. The oldest will already have shed their antlers and you'll be able to count their ribs."

"How do they get like that?" Finn's question was muffled as he snuggled down under his smock.

"During the rut they think with their loins. And a buck with does has to be on his guard if he means to keep them. If he isn't mating with them he's warding off challengers or patrolling the edges of his herd—there's no time for anything else, not even to eat or rest. They've been preparing for this all Summer, feeding themselves up. When it's over they're worn out, some won't even survive the Winter."

"What about the does?" Hann could just make out the question, and glanced to where the boy lay curled with his back to him.

"They just want to mate with the strongest bucks, the ones who can give them the healthiest fawns. When it's all over and the bucks have shed their antlers the does keep theirs. They still have last year's fawns at their sides, and when the snows come they have to fight for the best grazing. They sniff the snow; when they smell lichen they scrape away to clear a patch. She needs those antlers to keep the bucks at bay and make sure her fawn gets it." Hann sat up again warming to his subject. "When the snows come, we'll..." The deep, regular breathing from under the skins beside him told him that his last words had been wasted. He smiled to himself and settled down to sleep, listening, until sleep overtook him, to the howling of the wolves and the sounds of antlers clashing as the bucks fought on in the darkness.

On the second day when the sun was at its highest they climbed up the side of the valley and followed a tree-covered ridge-line that overlooked the level ground below. There they could see among the trees by the stream's edge a small herd of some thirty does and yearlings grazing on lichens and birch bark. An old buck restlessly circled the herd, driving in stragglers and watching for rivals, never resting, never browsing, living off the fat built up during the long Summer grazing. Even as Finn watched a challenger approached, a young buck in his fourth or fifth Winter. He came on in that stiff-legged gait characteristic of bucks in the rut: his head raised so his antlers lay across his back, nose curled, sniffing the air. The old buck trotted forward so as to place himself between his rival and his does. There was no noise, no obvious challenge; they lowered their heads and charged. The peace of the valley was broken by the furious clicking of their hooves and the fearsome crack of their antlers as they collided, yet scarcely a doe even looked up as the beasts strained and shoved. Finn knew that the fight could continue until long after nightfall before one or the other gave way. It was a sight they had passed many times already on their journey, so it was with some surprise that he saw Hann ahead of him squat down to watch, then lay down his spears and sit cross-legged with his chin on his arms. Finn settled down beside him, gazing across the valley to where the two bucks charged and counter-charged. The younger beast was the faster of the two and ran in hard for each clash. The other, older and heavier, would wait until the last moment before counter-charging, conserving energy and relying on his superior weight to drive his opponent back. Such fights, Finn knew, seldom ended in death or even serious injury although it was

105

not unknown for two bucks, antlers locked inextricably, to starve to death. In two years' time the older buck would probably be impotent, and would not even bother to dispute the issue. In the meantime the younger had a long, hard fight ahead if he meant to enjoy the willing, if less than eager, does.

It was only when he turned to his father to ask his opinion of the likely outcome that Finn realized that Hann had been watching something quite different. Apparently unmoved by the combat at the stream he was looking toward the tree-line where the does and yearlings grazed. It was a peaceful scene, in stark contrast to the struggle in the background. In the silences when the bucks grappled or drew back before charging again the contented grunts the does always made when feeding could clearly be heard. Pleasing though the sight was, there seemed at first to be nothing there that could distract Hann from his hitherto ceaseless drive deeper into the forest. Then Finn saw the wolves. He counted six, belly-down in the long grass downwind of the herd, crawling forward, tongues lolling. Hann, who had waited patiently for Finn to notice them, whispered, "The ravens drew them here." Finn looked up and noticed, for the first time, the black dots circling patiently overhead.

"The wolves follow the ravens, and you should follow the wolves if it's deer you're after. Now watch how they attack."

Their approach was painfully slow, and Finn found his attention wandering back to the fight in the distance that never slackened. Then all of a sudden the wolves were up and running. The object of their first rush was a solitary doe who had strayed too far from the tree-line. Startled, she ran back to the nearest cluster of deer, easily outdistancing the wolves, and the whole herd lumbered off a short distance, then stopped and began to graze as before.

Finn shook his head. "Why don't the deer run?" he asked.

"Where to?" said Hann. "They could run to the end of the earth and the wolves would run with them. They can go as fast and as far as the herds, so there's no escape, Summer or Winter.

106

Even in the deepest snow, where the wolves would sink in up to their chests, they run in the tracks the deer have made. The deer *live* with the wolves the way we live with flies. Many times you'll see a wolf walk through a herd and the deer hardly look up. If his tail's down and his ears are up he's just on his way somewhere, and they ignore him. Now, when his ears are back and his tail's stuck out behind that's different, but even then only threatened deer run."

Still Finn shook his head, so Hann explained further. "It saves them all a lot of running around. They need to conserve their strength. So will you when you're as old as me." Finn shifted uneasily where he sat. That morning he had woken so stiff he could barely rise, and even now, though he had run the stiffness off, he was glad of the rest. He looked to Hann to see if he was smiling. It would not be the first time that Hann had teased him over his inability to keep up. One of the strongest hunters in the tribe, though, he was nevertheless past his thirtieth Summer. Hann would soon see the days when Finn would be able to outpace him. In the meantime the older man took an almost childlike pride in his greater strength and speed. Finn did not mind; that Hann should take pride in besting him was itself something to be proud of.

While they had been talking, the wolves had circled round to conform with a change in the wind. They had moved down to a position almost directly below where Hann and Finn sat, and were stalking a doe and a yearling at the bottom edge of the herd. The grass was longer here; the wolves were able to creep to within a stone's throw of the pair before they were forced to show themselves. The doe saw them first, and dashed toward the main herd. The yearling was slower, and before it could join her a young wolf had dashed in from the right, diverting the prey from the safety of its fellows. The deer raced into the open ground, the young wolf snapping at its neck.

Hann shook his head. "They're both young. The yearling was too slow taking to his heels, and the wolf hasn't yet learned what he can kill with a neck bite. The deer's too big for that. The wolf has time to learn, but the deer's time is running out..." He pointed with his chin to where two older wolves were gaining on the fleeing deer. "*They* know what they're about." Even as he spoke the lead wolf sank its teeth into the beast's rump and, as it slowed, another pinned it by the nose. Hardened as he was by the annual slaughter at the killing ground, Finn winced as the wolves closed in from all sides and the stricken deer slumped to the ground with glazed eyes. The does at the edge of the herd, distracted from their grazing, sniffed the air and snorted in fright.

When, at last, it was over and the wolves were feeding and the deer had returned to their grazing, Hann lay back and looked across at Finn. Seeing the boy's face he remembered his own first sight of that same grisly spectacle, how he too had been shocked all those years ago. "Not a clean kill," he said. "Not like the killing ground." The wolves were devouring the heart, lungs, and liver, gorging themselves before crawling away to sleep or to regurgitate food for their young who lay hidden nearby. Hann pulled a piece of smoked meat from his bag and offered some to Finn. Finn shook his head, but his father insisted so he tore a strip off and chewed it sullenly. Round a mouthful of meat Hann went on, "For us the deer are hard to find and easy to kill. For wolves it's the other way round. That's why they usually kill the youngest, the weakest, or the diseased."

"It was terrible," was all Finn could say. Hann shrugged. "Bad for the fawn, good for the herd. The weak die, the strong survive, the herd prospers."

Finn did not seem to be listening. "She just left it!" he said unbelievingly. "The doe just ran off."

"They are not the best of mothers, it's true!" Hann smiled, sorry for the boy's hard lesson. "But there was nothing she could do. From the moment they're born at the end of Spring the fawns are at risk. By the time they are two days old they can run as fast as the herd—they must or get left behind."

Finn frowned. "But the herds don't move until the Autumn, when they feel the cold weather coming."

Hann shook his head. "They're always on the move. They have to keep moving to eat; they can clear an area of grazing between sunrise and sunset. Then there are the flies. In Summer, when new antlers are covered in velvet the blood in them attracts the flies. That can drive a whole herd mad, make them run for days on end, or climb up to where the air is cooler to escape."

All at once the meaning of what he had been hearing struck Finn. He turned on his father. "Have you *seen* all this?" Hann only smiled. The horrors he had just witnessed forgotten now, Finn cried out, "You have!" Hann shook his head, amused at the boy's sudden animation.

"You have!" cried Finn again, ecstatic at the very thought. "You talked of the fawning grounds, and antlers in Summer. You've seen them. You've seen the salt river!"

Still Hann shook his head. "Never!" he said. "A man might walk all his life and never reach it. That's what the old men say. They say our people came from there, that they swam across it, and it took them many generations to reach this land." Hann would have said more but Finn would have none of it.

"Then you made it up!" he said accusingly, then before Hann, laughing now, could deny it, continued, "No, I don't believe that. How then? No man has ever seen a Reindeer being born."

"I have..." said his father simply. "And one day so shall you."

"It can't be. No man could follow the deer. They travel as far in a day as would take us five or six. If we tried to follow them to the salt river we would meet them coming back!"

"You will see!" was all Hann would say for all Finn's urging, and at last to distract him he pointed across the valley to where the bucks still fought. As Finn reluctantly turned to look the younger buck began to give ground. As they disentangled yet again, it drew back and turned away. The elder stood firm, head still lowered in challenge. For a moment it seemed as if the younger wished to try conclusions one more time, but as the old buck trotted forward his adversary turned tail and made off into the distance.

Hann smiled with satisfaction. "The old fellow won . . . this time!" Then noticing how Finn's eyes strayed to where the young buck was disappearing into the trees, he prodded the boy with his foot. "The young one will have his day, never fear . . ." he laughed. "If he learns his lessons!"

That was the first of Finn's lessons, the first of many that continued as they pushed on ever deeper into the forest. He learned to recognize the tracks of the forest animals, the two rounded crescents of the deer's hooves, the paw print of the wolf, the smaller mark of the fox, and once, only once to Finn's relief, the humanoid hand-and-foot marks of the bear. He learned to foretell the weather the way the animals did, by the tightening of his hair, the way the woods smelled, and the way sound traveled farther before rain. He learned the hunters' talk of tongue-clicks, and spent whole days stalking deer, smeared with dung, and approaching them from downwind. Hann taught him to move silently, lifting his legs above the undergrowth, feeling for dry twigs or bracken with the outside of his sole before putting weight on his foot. He trained him to move slowly, keeping his eyes on the prey, holding his spear poised till his arm ached, and how to sink silently to the ground and merge with the foliage. On the march he learned how to throw his spear, Hann pointing out ever smaller and more distant marks as they jogged on through the forests. Day after day, they pressed on, Hann stopping now and then to mark the route and check his direction by the sun or the moss on the trees. Not even at night did the pace slacken, Hann teaching the boy to find among the stars the group they called "the Antler" which pointed to the "Lone Star" which guided hunters home.

At last they reached an area where the herds dwindled and the sounds of the wolves receded, and almost the only creature they saw was the occasional defeated buck, emaciated from the exertions of the rut, wandering off to die or to spend the Winter in lonely retirement before rejoining the herd in Spring. They passed on through silent forests, over hills and ridges, until Finn could have no more found his way back than found the place where the sun sets. At the end of one more day they found themselves in a valley wider and more level than the valley of the Burnt Shins. It was bounded by mountains, not so steep or craggy as the mountains of home, but rising ridge upon ridge to the clouds. Their lower slopes were thickly forested, and Finn could just see if he strained his eyes that there were grasslands high up above the tree-line. Running through the middle of the valley, in what he thought was the direction of home, was a stream a little wider and faster-flowing than the stream that flowed below the great cave.

"Does this stream join our river?" Finn asked as they descended a low ridge into the valley bottom.

Hann seemed pleased at the question, and nodded. "It joins it many days' march downriver from our killing grounds. My father first brought me here when I was no older than you are, and we returned down this river."

Finn stopped and took in the whole valley in one sweeping glance. "What people live here?" he asked.

"No men live here," answered Hann, "and few men have ever been here. My father brought me here in my last year before initiation, as I have brought you. It's good, sometimes, to get away from nagging women and the stench of people. And there is something here I wanted you to see."

By now, Finn had learned not to plague his father with questions, knowing that he preferred him to find things out for himself. No amount of entreaty on his part would get him an

111

answer before Hann was ready, so he contented himself with getting to know his new surroundings. As they descended, he ran his eyes over the lie of the land, in his mind's eye caressing it with his hands. By the time they had entered forest once more he felt he could find his way about the valley with confidence—so much had Hann's teaching already achieved. They had not traveled far when Finn began to hear familiar sounds— the clash of antlers and the bellowed defiance of rutting bucks filtered through the trees from upstream. Confused, he looked to Hann. Surely they had left the deer far behind? Hann's smile confirmed that this was what he had been brought here to see.

Nor did he have to wait long; they were following the course of the stream deeper into the valley when Finn detected a movement among the trees by the water's edge, a spear-cast away. He froze, and as he had been taught, sank slowly to one knee. The wind was blowing from behind his left shoulder—with any luck his scent would not alarm whatever beast was in the thicket ahead. It seemed perhaps that it had, for Finn caught only the most fleeting glimpse of the buck that leaped, alarmed, from the trees. What he saw, though, set his heart racing—never in all of his thirteen years had he seen so fine a creature. It was higher at the shoulder and broader-backed than any buck he had ever seen, and its antlers clattered in the branches overhead as it fled. Disappointed, Finn looked over to Hann, who seemed unperturbed and indicated that they should push on. It was not long before they saw three more deer, two does and a fawn, skirting the edge of a clearing, who also took off at their appearance. These too were fatter and stronger-looking than any he had ever seen. Finn could stay silent no longer.

"I never saw such deer as these in our killing grounds," he said.

Hann nodded. "These deer have never seen our valley, or the river, or the grasslands beyond. They are not of *our* herds."

"Whose then?" demanded Finn. "Annu created the deer for *us*."

Hann shrugged and smiled. "Another mystery for you."

"But where do they come from if not from the grasslands?"

Hann pointed with his chin to the mountain tops, shrouded now in cloud. "From up there. They Summer in the meadows up above the trees, and Winter down here."

Narrowing his eyes, Finn scanned the distant peaks. "One and a half days, perhaps two to the top . . ." he began.

"Three at the most," agreed Hann. "So?"

"So . . ." Finn reasoned even as he spoke. "So, a man could hunt these deer all year round. Could always eat fresh meat."

"That's right." Hann smiled once more. Then, as Finn looked at him excitedly, he went on, "But there are no men here, and too few deer. In this whole valley and all those mountains there are fewer than we kill in a couple of years."

"Then what use have they?" asked Finn, perplexed.

Hann shrugged again. "They are beautiful . . . perhaps that is their purpose." He laughed at Finn's face which showed clearly that the answer had not satisfied him.

▲ ▲ ▲

A fawn picked its way warily over the bracken. The best part of the day had passed since they had first entered the valley, and they had passed many small groups of deer before encountering this lone yearling. Leaning on his spear shaft as Hann had taught him, Finn sank slowly to one knee. Beside him Hann did the same; there was silence as the young Reindeer stopped and studied them for a moment, legs splayed, poised at any moment for flight. Breathing silently through his open mouth, Finn reached down and gently plucked a handful of the lichen that grew at the base of the tree beside him. His heartbeat quickened as the fawn edged nearer, so close now that he felt he could reach out and grab her. Hann, who had sunk right down to the ground, reached out and tapped his foot as a signal to him to move. Just as he was about to raise his right hand the cough of a buck echoed through the trees. The fawn looked away for an instant. Finn thought that he had lost her, but she turned back almost at once and tentatively stretched out her neck. So slowly that he scarcely seemed to move, Finn held out his open hand, sliding it under her great blunt muzzle. Her breath warmed his hand as she took the treat, and it was all he could do not to cry out loud in triumph. Hann tapped his foot once more, and Finn, taking care not to startle the beast, turned to look down at him. Hann had taken hold of Finn's spear; as their eyes met he nodded.

Knowing what came next, Finn released the spear and gently raised his left hand to stroke her muzzle. Far from frightening the fawn, as he had expected, she moved in closer and, emboldened, he ran his right hand gently down her neck. Not until he had run his hands over her whole body did he try to move off, and saw to his delight that she followed him, nuzzling at his hand until he repeated the process. Together, leaving Hann, they walked slowly across the clearing, Finn stooping occasionally to pick more lichen or break off a willow twig. At last, tiring of the game, and distracted by the sounds of other deer not far off, the fawn ran off on great furry feet. Finn watched her until she disappeared from sight, and was still staring after her like a man possessed when Hann joined him.

"I dreamed that, months ago!" he muttered half to himself, still shaking with emotion as Hann handed him his spear.

Hann smiled. "Sanu said you had good dreams."

"He told me it was true but I didn't believe him. . . . How can such a thing be?"

Hann laughed. "Young deer, like young boys, are full of questions. And like young boys they like poking their noses into things that are better left alone. And they like to be touched, and we are better at touching than their mothers are."

Finn nodded, remembering the doe that had abandoned her fawn as the wolves rushed them.

"But I never even *heard* of such a thing," he said. "Do the others know of it?"

"One or two of the Elders, who were shown it in their youth," replied Hann. "But the young ones today don't care to learn mere tricks..." He added slyly, "After all, it has no *use*."

Finn smiled, a little ashamed. "It was beautiful," he said, "that is its use."

"Now you understand!" Hann smiled too.

Just before sunset they killed a doe. It was done the way Hann favored, with the two of them crouched on all fours under his cloak, cut branches raised high for antlers with Finn imitating, as he had been taught, the cough of the deer. Twice they had enticed beasts into their chosen killing ground; twice Finn had moved too soon, and the deer—these forest deer were more wary than their grassland cousins—had bolted. But Hann had been determined that the kill should be Finn's. So it eventually was. Even though the doe was the last of three chances Hann was well pleased. The boy cast his spear well, he had mastered the timing, and now, under his watchful eye, made a passable job of butchering and skinning the beast. Later they feasted alone under the stars, on joints Finn had cut, cooked on a fire Finn had built, and reveled in the taste of fresh meat after almost two weeks of smoked rations. As was their way they gorged, consuming huge chunks of flesh, communicating only in grunts until they were both too stuffed to do anything more than lie back and stare at the sky.

After they had remained in silence for a while Finn, whose mind had not been still for days, frowned and said, "It's strange!"

"What's strange?" Hann had been on the verge of sleep.

"We love them, yet we kill them. When they are not with us we worry about them, pray that the herd may prosper. Then when they *are* with us we hunt them down and kill them till our arms ache. It's the strangest thing of all."

Hann shrugged; he had long ago reconciled himself to this mystery of men and deer.

"Most hunters think only of their stomachs..." he said. "When they pray for the herd they are praying for themselves, that it may prosper so they may prosper. Only a few love the deer for themselves."

"You do," whispered Finn.

Hann nodded, whispering too, barely audible above the crackling of logs on the fire. "If I were pure spirit and had no need to eat I would still wait by the river for the deer, still watch them in the forests, still love them."

Finn was dizzy with the food he had eaten, and the stars and the moon were a blur. "Do you know what I would like?" he said. Hann looked over to him. "To stay here with you, hunting and feasting forever."

Hann laughed. He had succumbed at last to that benign torpor that crept over a Burnt Shin who had eaten, as they said, till the meat oozed out of his toes. He had given in, too, to feelings he had tried hard to suppress. Throughout he had been trying to regard this trip as a serious business, an attempt, probably doomed, to teach the boy all he needed in time for the Spring. He had been plagued, therefore, by the uneasy feeling that he should not have been enjoying himself as much as he was.

Now, as they were about to return home, he knew that the boy would prevail; that what he had already known and what he had learned would see him through. He had longed for the day when he could pass on his knowledge — a day he had begun to think would never come. He had found in Finn a willing pupil, and more besides. He had seen in him a love for Annu's creation that matched his own, with a sense of wonder that

116

recalled his own when he had learned these things from his father. It had been a long time since he had thought of his father, first hunter of the tribe in his own day, who had lived to a venerable age and died in his forty-fifth Summer singing the praises of his God. To hunt forever with his father! Well, it would come by and by. He turned to Finn.

"It's a good dream, and a true one. We will all hunt with our fathers in time. But *I* have a hearth and a tribe to go home to. So do you."

"Even so," Finn said, "it might be good to live alone."

Hann shook his head. "We weren't meant for that."

Finn sat up. "But Annu did. When he first came down to the world..."

Hann laughed. "He was a God. Only a God and some beasts can live like that. We *need* the tribe. Our rituals, our customs, our lives together, those are the things that set us apart from everything else that is in the world."

"That's what Sanu said," muttered Finn, lying back down again.

"And since you are not a God or a beast," Hann laughed, "you had better come back to the tribe." He looked across at Finn and seeing that he was still thoughtful, added, "Besides, you would miss your friends."

"I would miss Mata, and Venn... and Gronu sometimes."

"Sometimes?"

"When he is in a good mood, warm and generous, there is no one to match him. But sometimes he frightens me, even though I am as strong as he is."

"Or stronger!" thought Hann, but he said, "Gronu is a boy, and will soon be a man of great power. Where it comes from and what he does with it, we have yet to see." After a silence he added, "I should stick with Venn."

Finn nodded, having come independently to the same conclusion. "And most of all I should miss you," he announced finally.

Hann smiled in the darkness. Then his face straightened and he said, "And Shani."

"Which is she?" Finn's attempt to sound unconcerned brought an answering roar of laughter from the other side of the fire. He felt himself reddening as his father rolled on the floor, pounding the dust with his heels. Warm, happy, and with a full stomach, Hann gave himself up to the humor of the moment. It was some time before he could find breath enough to answer. "The one who waved to you as we left the camp." Through forests that had never heard the sound of human speech there echoed the deep laughter of a full-grown man and the angry protests of a boy of thirteen Summers.

CHAPTER
SEVEN

As FINN CRAWLED DOWN into the blackness he heard a stone roll into place, sealing the mouth of the tunnel behind him, and shutting out what little light there had been. He knew that the stone had shut out more than just light; it had shut out the whole of his past life. The way back was forever closed to him. Only the way ahead, indicated by the breeze on his face, lay open. Here was a darkness unlike any he had ever experienced, so dense he felt he could reach out and hold handfuls of it. Walls of rock brushed his shoulders on either side, and he found, when once he tried to rise to all fours, that the ceiling was just above his back. As he wriggled forward on his stomach Finn remembered every tale he had ever heard round camp fires of the terrors of initiation, how some had died of shock, and others gone mad and never re-emerged into the light.

Doubtless these stories had grown with the telling, passed on by those who had been through it, to frighten those who had yet to experience it. Even so, and despite Hann's assurance that there was nothing to fear here but his own fears, he was afraid. He was afraid of the cold and the dark, afraid of the

119

unknown and the strange sounds that came to him on the breeze. Yet there was only one way he could go. His greatest fear being, as always, the fear of failure, he struggled on. It was a painful process, dragging himself along by his fingers and toes. There was no room even to bend his legs to drag himself along faster, and his legs were weak from the running.

He had been running hard since before dawn. The fastest among the young hunters had led the way. They had been followed, as they scrambled down the scree, by the wailing of the women and children—wailing for the boys who were leaving the ledge for the last time, never to return but as men. Trained by Hann all through the Winter, running every day through soft ground or knee deep in snow, Finn had been well prepared for this. He had been among the leaders from the start and by the time, toward the end of the afternoon, when they had begun to ascend the slopes of the sacred mountain, there had been only himself, Gronu, Venn, and two others close on the leader's heels. Despite the ordeal that lay ahead their spirits had been high as they had approached the mountain; light-headed from the exertion Gronu and Finn had laughed as they raced each other up the ever steeper slopes. When at last the leader had stopped on a rock shelf halfway up the mountain and indicated that they should rest, they had collapsed, laughing, side by side. Venn's arrival had stilled their laughter. Normally their keen rival, he had been content to trail a good ten paces back as they ascended. As he caught up with them they had seen how his mood had suddenly darkened and his face had become a grim, set mask. He had said nothing to either of them but sat apart, staring down the slope to where the others still toiled, arriving in twos and threes later, throwing themselves onto the bare rock where the race had suddenly, unaccountably, ended. Finn, hardly noticing them, and still perplexed at his friend's sudden change of mood, had gone over to sit by him.

Venn had looked at him, and Finn had known that the

sweat that ran down his face and neck was the cold sweat of fear.

"There is nothing to fear," Finn had said. Only he would have dared to suggest to Venn that he was afraid. Venn had not denied it, nor had he replied, so Finn had gone on, "Hann says there is nothing in there to fear but your own fears."

"I know all that," Venn had said, "and yet, somehow, suddenly, I *am* afraid."

Finn would have gone on to confess his own fear. But he sensed that it was nothing compared with that which had stolen, all of a sudden, over his friend. He had wondered what it could be—a dream, suddenly remembered, perhaps, as they reached the foot of the mountain?—or a vision? Before he could ask or ponder further, Finn had been called away and led by an unspeaking guide through twisted and overgrown paths to the tiny aperture in the rock face that led down into the bowels of the mountain.

Now, alone in the darkness, Finn had fears enough of his own. The descent seemed endless, and at least once he feared that he would pass out as exhaustion overtook him. Gradually the ground below him leveled out, and he found, on tentatively raising his back, that he could now crouch and so progressed a little faster. At last he could stand. The breeze grew stronger now, cooling and refreshing him; yet it was still dark, and he was forced to totter forward, arms outstretched like a child taking its first steps. Gradually and imperceptibly, however, he was able to make out the walls and roof of the corridor of rock along which he stumbled. He thought at first that his eyes were growing accustomed to the darkness. But as the corridor widened to a chamber he became aware that the source of light was one of three cave entrances that faced him. The light was only a faint glimmer, but there came too, wafted on the breeze, the scent of Spring flowers and the distant strains of a song. It was a song that seemed vaguely familiar yet, strangely, it was not a comforting sound. Nevertheless, heeding Hann's advice, Finn advanced to meet it. The entrance was lower than the chamber he was in, and he was forced to stoop once more. But at every step the light grew, until he found himself in a chamber where he could stand upright once more, a chamber that was lit at ground level by two small lamps.

Only then did he become aware of the row of figures that squatted around the walls, and now rose slowly and silently to greet him. Finn froze; his whole body shook as they approached. They were decked from head to foot in sleek black feathers that rustled as they stalked, ravenlike, toward him. The sounds of ravens' croaking filled the chamber and the air was hot and thick with the stench of carrion. Other figures, draped in wolfskins, joined them, and the howling of wolves joined the cacophony as they too strutted and danced about him. Wolf masks leered out of the darkness, then vanished again; Finn stood frozen to the spot in the center of their obscene, menacing dance. That small part of him that was rational told him that these were just men, men he knew, but the rest of him, most of him, was struck dumb and paralyzed with fear.

He did not resist as the figures fell on him nor when they hoisted him shoulder-high, corpselike, and bore him through another entrance into the darkness once more. Here at least the breeze blew, carrying off the smell of carrion, bringing in its place the fresh scent of flowers. Again he heard the song, again his weary mind tried to recall when he had heard it before. The mental effort tired him. As their pace slowed he felt his eyelids droop, and he became dimly aware, as his mind began to drowse, that the figures who carried him had joined in the chant. The chant! It was the chant for the dead, and he had last heard it when they had carried Hann's son to the burial place.

The horror of it engulfed him; he tried to writhe or kick himself free, but those who bore him only tightened their grip, and his tired limbs failed him. He tried to scream, but his lips were too dry to produce anything but a feeble croak which went unheard. Then he remembered Hann's words—words that he had so confidently urged on Venn such a short time ago. "There is nothing to fear in there but your own fears." He ceased to struggle and the bearers, as if in recognition, relaxed their grip. They entered another, lower, chamber—Finn could feel its roof just above his face—and slowly, gently, laid him down. By the dim lamplight he could make out their hideous shapes once more; to quell the panic that rose within him he closed his eyes. He opened them almost immediately. From below, where the ground should have been, more hands took his weight and he realized that they were lowering him not to the ground but into a grave.

He braced himself not to struggle as the two attendants who received his body and lowered it to its resting place wrapped him in fawnskin and turned him on his side to the sleeping position. He fought to restrain a scream as they laid spears, food, and flints around him. The scent of flowers grew stronger as a blossom-strewn lattice was lowered into place above him. The two shadowy figures climbed up from the grave. Then long, flat stones were heaved into place across the top of the trench, blotting out the last of what little light there had been, and the chant grew louder. Even through the thicknesses of stones he could hear voices mourning him, calling him by name, singing of the brief course of his life and lamenting his passing. Gradually that sound faded, to be replaced by the sound of a huge stone being settled into place to seal the chamber. And then there was utter silence. It was a silence more dreadful than any he had ever known. He knew that he was alone.

The temptation to fight his way free of the fawnskin, to tear at the stones with bleeding fingernails was almost too much for him. A thousand irrational fears rushed on him out of the darkness—they would forget about him and leave him here to starve or suffocate—they would lose their way and never find him again—he had been chosen as some form of sacrifice, like the hideous stories he had heard about the old times. That was why they had taken him, a stranger, into their midst; everything, all his life, had been nothing but a preparation for this awful death. He would never see the light of day or breathe fresh air again. Then again he remembered Hann's words. That fear that threatened to rob him of his sanity was indeed his greatest enemy. He told himself that whatever had been done had a purpose and a meaning: if he lay still and calm, that meaning would become clear. Even if it did not, whoever came —and his reason told him that someone, sometime, *must* come —would find him calm and composed, for his father's sake and his own.

It was warm under the fawnskin, and this, his hunger, and his aching legs continued to remind him that he was still alive. The terror of his recent experiences receded. He grew weary. He wanted to sleep but told himself that in his weakened, exhausted state sleep too was an enemy. It was a struggle to stay awake and to keep his mind from wandering. He tried to remember his past life, conjuring up every memory, however trivial, in as much detail as he could. Yet try as he might he could impose no order on the images that flooded into his brain. His whole past life seemed to merge into one confused whole, the events out of sequence, people he knew at different ages all talking to him at once and none of them making sense. Yet he felt strangely calm and detached from it all, as if he had indeed died, a very long time ago. After a while even this jumble of memories left him, and there was only the music to hold on to.

It was the sound of a single flute; a simple clear melody, but with a weird, unearthly quality. It had started faintly, worked its way insidiously into Finn's dreams, and then grown, expanding until it filled every corner of his mind and banished everything else. Finn stirred, realized that he had dozed off, but awake now, realized that the music was real. His deprived senses

124

clutched at it like a drowning man at a rescuing hand. It filtered down through the walls of rock and the piled stones above him, filling every corner of his tiny grave, seeming to flood it with light. Then, opening his eyes, he saw that the light too was real, that unseen hands had silently removed the blocks of stone that entombed him, that a solitary figure now gazed down at him. Unlike the grotesques who had laid him here, this figure was recognizably human though masked and painted from head to foot in white and red, colors of life and death. The figure beckoned and Finn rose up unsteadily on stiff legs. His mind was already working; the fact that his legs still ached suggested that much less time had elapsed than he had thought. This was the only clue he had; days and nights might have passed for all else he knew. Whatever time had elapsed, the contrast between the chamber into which he had been carried and the one which he now saw as he climbed from the tomb was startling. Where there had been gloomy half light was the brilliance of countless lamps; where there had been bare walls hung garlands of Spring blossoms whose fragrance filled the air; and in place of the croak of the raven and wolves' howling were the songs of the lark and the dove. Blossoms carpeted the floor as Finn followed his guide out into the corridor once more and down a path lighted all the way by flaming torches to a small, pebbly shore. Together they stood on the edge of an underground river whose calm surface shone black like polished stone. Finn turned questioningly to the silent figure beside him, who gestured with his arm to a point on the far side where a solitary lamp flickered. Needing no further urging, Finn undressed, bundled his clothes, and waded in; the water felt cool and clean on his body, and though its surface had seemed untroubled he could feel the current beneath. Without glancing back Finn swam on, holding his clothes above his head and reveling in the freshness of the water. Only when he had dragged himself from the water at the far side did he look back, to see the shore empty, the torches gone, and the whole scene lit only by the small lamp beside him. The water had revived him and his mind was clear again as he shook himself dry. Tired as he was, he understood. The ravens and wolves, the chant for the dead, and the women wailing as they had left the ledge that morning—they had buried his boyhood, and mourned the child who would never return. Now he had risen again, risen into manhood, awakened to a new world and crossed over to a new life—he was glad he had not looked back.

The lamp was guttering, giving off more smoke than light. As he was about to struggle into his smock once more his eyes caught sight of a well-known and comforting shape. There on a shelf in the shadows stood a Reindeer mask and beside it, neatly bundled, new clothes, cloak, smock, leggings, and a hunting spear. It was difficult, in the fitful dying light of the lamp, to guess the authorship of the spear but its feel as he held the shaft by its mid-point was familiar too. The light finally died as Finn poked his head through the opening of the smock, and he cursed for he had wanted to see his image on the face of the water. As he threw the cloak over his shoulders and groped in the dark for the mask, he became aware of a distant drumming, urgent and insistent, which he knew at once. It was the four-beat rhythm that summoned the hunters to the Reindeer dance at the end of the Summer, and it was calling to him. He knew as he struggled into the mask, stooping a little under its unaccustomed weight, and reached for his spear, that this was to be the moment that marked his passage into manhood. There was no time for delay—the beat grew faster and more urgent—and heedless of the dark he stumbled, head bowed, in its direction.

To speed his progress he felt his way along the wall with his left hand but, feeling it begin to veer away from the sound of the drum, he left the wall and stepped reluctantly forward. He had taken no more than a couple of unsteady paces when the cavern was flooded with light. Finn's spear clattered to the floor as he gazed around him, enraptured. Nothing he had ever seen,

126

nothing he had ever heard, could have prepared him for the sight that greeted him now. Never, not even in the great cave, or in his own wildest imaginings had he seen such pictures as those that adorned the walls of the chamber. Everywhere he looked he saw images of beauty, grace, movement, and color. Finn had never seen such profusion and intensity of color, and its effect was hypnotic. The sheer warmth and splendor of it all ravished his senses, and it was some time before it began to resolve itself into its component parts. As he followed it round the walls with his eyes he was able to make out the whole story of Creation.

Here was Annu, the man-bodied, antlered God, walking alone upon the face of the earth as he had done at the first dawn; the creation of his children, men and deer; the wanderings of the deer, and how they had lost the gift of speech; how Annu's daughters had stolen fire, and how the people's burnt shins had betrayed their crime; and how they and the deer, having incurred his displeasure, had been cursed to live apart with fear and bloodshed between them until they were reunited with Him and in Him in the dreamlands. Finn wandered around the chamber like a man possessed, recognizing in each group of images a story told to him by Sanu, in the many visits he had made to his cave through the Winter. They had been good stories, vigorously told, stories that posed as many questions as they answered. Finn had soon memorized them. In solitary moments he would take them out and examine them like prized possessions; but never, even in his own vivid imagination, had they come to life as they did now. Here, buried in the depths of this mountain, was the perfect, wordless expression of everything he held dear, everything he believed to be true and beautiful.

The disappearance of the light was as sudden as its arrival; the chamber was plunged into darkness once more. Although he was vaguely aware that it had never stopped, Finn noticed the drumming again. His mind still full of the wonders he had

127

seen, he groped on the floor for his spear and set off to answer the drum's insistent call. Keeping his face to the breeze, he had not gone many paces when a shaft of light spilled onto the floor in front of him. Lifting his head with difficulty he found himself entering a well-lit cavern more than a spear-cast in length and half as wide. On a flat stone to his left stood the familiar figure of Sanu, strangely comforting for all his full regalia and stern aspect, and grouped in the center of this natural arena, similarly masked and accoutered, were all the youth of the tribe who had set out with him from the ledge. Knowing at once what was required of him, Finn loped over to join their number. Before he could glance around him in the vain hope of seeing a face he recognized under any of the masks, the music had started. Though forbidden to them until this very moment, the steps of the dance were as well known as the tales they had heard at their mothers' knees. As one the youths lumbered forward, tossing heads and shaking antlers in imitation of the deer, then stamping the ground, turned and stalked back, tongues clicking, spear arms raised. How many generations of young men had performed this ancient dance here, no one, not even Sanu knew, and Finn had no time to wonder as the dance increased in pace.

Time did not pass—it ceased to be. It had no more meaning for the dancers than for the heroes who hunted and feasted on the walls of the outer chamber, caught in mid-action, made timeless in paint and ocher. Finn never knew how long they danced under Sanu's watchful eye and ceaseless stream of prayers. Gradually the words lost meaning as they mingled with the beating of the drum, and the movements of the dancers became those of men wading in deep, sluggish water that impeded their limbs. All around him Finn was dimly aware of figures falling, dancers slumping to one knee but with none to replace them, but still he danced on. All his thoughts, all memories, and all hopes ran into one another like converging streams, lost their form and flowed away from him. It seemed

128

he tried to grasp them but they slipped as if between his fingers to join with the images around him, fur and flesh, antlers and spears. All became one, and he a part of the whole, no longer knowing or caring who or what or where he was. He only knew that his limbs became suddenly strangely light, and he felt that he could dance, and *had* danced like this forever.

At last he fell, slowly it seemed, like drowning, and lay among the others like dead deer upon a killing ground. Down here on the cool stone floor all was still. Silence fell and there came among them, bathed in golden light, a figure they had seen before on the walls of the painted chamber. Its time with them was brief, but it brought with it the feel, the scent, the very essence of deer, and yet was human too, and something else, something more than both. Finn could only cry out feebly in his joy, and reach out a trembling arm to try and stay the figure before it passed once more into the darkness. When it had gone he fell back and was at peace, and all of him, even that part that might have whispered that all he had seen was a man disguised, was silent now.

By the time he had recovered full consciousness Finn was being half dragged, half carried down a dark corridor, by two men of whose identities he was content to remain ignorant. His mask and cloak had gone, and a fresh breeze, fresher by the moment, revived him until at last he felt able to use his legs once more. They left him at the low entrance to a tunnel like the one by which he had descended a lifetime ago, and van-ished wordlessly into the shadows. From ahead came the sound of running water, and the water's fresh smell was carried down to him by a breeze which he knew was from outside the moun-tain. Slowly and stiffly he began to haul himself, on his stom-ach once more, up the steep slope toward the sound and the smell of the water. The sound grew louder until it filled his ears, the slope leveled out, and the darkness gave way to shades of gray. He found himself able to stand once more and, entering a broad high cave, saw before him the light of day filtered

129

through a wall of water that cascaded down over the cave's mouth. He sat beside the waterfall, breathing the clean air that rose with the spray, and allowing himself time to recuperate before fighting his way through the torrent and out into the world again.

The steep, wooded slope on which he found himself was already littered with the bodies of some of his companions in the dance. Finn staggered among them until he found a space and threw himself down, exhausted. Their numbers grew steadily; one by one others emerged or were led round from some other exit to collapse among them. They lay about like men after feasting, Finn thought, though his own hunger told him how long it had been since any of them had eaten. Yet although their bellies were empty, their faces were those of men (for such they now were) whose hearts were full, men sated with the wonders they had seen and felt. It was strangely peaceful here after the frenzy in the cave below, and Finn lay in a daze for some time, only half aware of what went on around him. He knew that for him at least the worst was over. What lay ahead, three days and nights on the mountain, might prove testing for others, who had scarcely spent a moment alone from the day they had first opened their eyes, but he looked forward to his time in the silence of the forests. Most saw it as a chance to prove their ability to survive alone, and to return, if possible, bearing in triumph some trophy, wolf pelts, fox fur, or eagle feathers as a symbol of their skill or courage. Finn, almost alone among them, had grasped, albeit unconsciously, the purpose of this test—for him it would be a time to contemplate both the things he had seen and done and the life that lay ahead of him. Of course he was keen to show his skill and had made his plans accordingly, but he knew, as Hann had told him, that a hunter's glory lay not in wolfskins, or eagle feathers, but in full bellies at his fireside.

They did not have long to recoup their strength before one by one they were led off to begin their retreat. Finn's turn came all too soon as he sat up, flexing his tired muscles, watching friends and companions being led off in all directions. His guide was a young hunter of Hann's hearth who had often chased him down the mountain to the pool on cold Winter mornings. Although he said nothing as he handed him a small skin bag of provisions, there was something in his attitude that contrasted sharply with that of the guide who had led them here from the great cave. They were equals now, united by shared experience and a common place in the life of the tribe. The man turned and started off down a little track, Finn following as best he could.

They had not gone more than a dozen paces into the trees when they encountered another pair. The lead man was another hunter of Hann's hearth, and close on his heels was Venn. Finn wished he could have spoken with him, but to speak was forbidden, and they passed in silence. The mountain was vast and the initiates few; there was little danger that any of them would meet up again until they all returned home. He knew it was only a matter of a few days before they would be laughing and boasting round the fire together, and joining in the planning of the Spring kill. Even so, there was something in Venn's face as he passed that made Finn long to speak out, tell him that the worst was past, perhaps even mock him gently for his former fears. As they turned a bend he looked back briefly and saw that his friend was looking back too. They exchanged a smile, and went their separate ways.

Out of consideration for his aching limbs, his guide took him over the level ground at a gentle trot, though one which lasted for a good while. The sun was high in the sky by the time he halted by a small stream and declared that he would go no further. He pointed across the stream indicating with a broad sweep of his arm the region that was to be Finn's home and hunting ground for the days and nights to follow. As soon as he was alone Finn slowed his pace to a walk, and once across the stream began at once to search for a suitable camp site. The breeze that had felt so cool down below in the depths of the mountain now seemed warm and clammy, and the smell of the trees and the grass, and the prickling along his scalp told him that it would soon rain. Before he did anything he would erect a shelter, eat, and build a fire. Then he would set about finding his bearings, exploring his surroundings, and planning his hunting.

It did not take him long to select a spot, where he sat and unpacked the bag he had been given. At its mouth, where the sinew string was drawn together, was a handful of smoked deer meat, and below, packed in the way Hann had taught him, were a fire spindle and board, a bone scraper, a spare spearhead, and a length of thread. Forcing himself to stand once more on stiffening legs, he searched the undergrowth and in a short while had assembled a small pile of kindling, some flat stones, and a birch twig to cook with. Burrowing head and shoulders under his cloak to shelter his efforts from the wind, he struggled to light a fire, twirling the spindle in the wooden base with heavy clumsy fingers. Under Mata's tutelage he had become an accomplished fire maker, but he had never worked before in this exhausted state. An age seemed to pass during which he was several times tempted to devour the meat cold, before at last the spindle end began to glow. Within a few moments by hastily juggling tinder, kindling and stones he had built a passable fire. After placing the skewered meat over the flames, he stuck his spear point first in the ground, and improvised a wind break with his cloak. He knew Hann would not approve. He could almost hear him reminding him always to keep his spear within easy reach and ready for use, but he was too tired to care, and he flopped down behind it gratefully. Later, his mood greatly improved by the hot, smoky-tasting meat, he laughed at the thought, but resolved to follow Hann's advice in future. Once having eaten he sank back against the grassy bank behind him and closed his eyes, soaking up the warmth of the fire. He thought that he had been under the mountain for two days and nights, and had probably emerged on the morning of the third day. During that time he had been dragged from the very depths of terror and despair to heights of ecstasy hitherto unimaginable. He tried to think of the hunt, but his mind was still grappling with the enormity of what he had undergone. He was too tired even to feel the joy that he knew he should have felt at this moment—that would come later.

As his head dropped to his chest for the third time he knew that he had been right to stop and rest; to go on in this condition would have been foolish. There was time enough later for hunting. He could hear the sound of distant thunder, like the drumming at the dance. Thunder and rain could help him, much as he disliked them. The noise could set the deer running in panic, make them less cautious, as well as masking his approach. He needed a good kill early on, to feed himself and lure the wolves; he had set his heart on a cloak of wolfskin, or at least a hood, and the wolves had had a bad Winter. He had never known them to come for carrion, though the old men said it had happened before. There were too many of them, they were saying back at the camp, for too few deer. So be it, it would make his task easier. But first he must rest. His head slumped to his chest and he jerked it up sharply and looked around him from under heavy eyelids. This place was far from ideal, he must move on . . . would move in just a few moments more.

· When he awoke the rain had extinguished the fire, and was running in a torrent down the slope at his back, wetting the edge of his cloak. He was alert at once. Heavy thunder clouds raced through the sky, blocking out what little sun there had been. It was impossible to know how far the day had advanced, but he reckoned it to be late afternoon. Stuffing his few possessions into the bag, he raced with his spear and cloak to the shelter of a nearby pine, and dressed hurriedly. The site he had chosen had been a bad one; he should have seen, tired as he was, that the rain would run down into it, and he had been lucky to escape so lightly. Although he felt a little better for the sleep, he knew he had not recovered sufficiently to hunt, and resolved that as soon as the rain showed signs of slackening, he would set off in search of a fallen tree under which to shelter for the night. The rain did not slacken, but increased in ferocity until it bounced off the earth and the rocks around him. The sky roared out its anger, hurling great spears of fire across the sky. Finn, afraid now, knew that he had no option but to brave the rain and seek better shelter. No fallen pine or deerskin cloak would keep out this rain. He would have to climb the hillside, to where he could see bare rock, and try and find a small cave. It was risky, he knew, such places being favored by all manner of dangerous beasts, especially bears, but he knew also that in his present state the weather posed the greatest threat. Hauling his hood over his already wet hair, he stepped out and, bent against the wind, began his ascent. The way up to the rocks was exposed and the wind buffeted him as he climbed, but he could see, close by the cliff face, a clump of pines that would afford him temporary shelter while he caught his breath. The whole sky was slate gray now, darkening the earth, and Finn thought as he battled through the stinging rain that this was not how he had imagined his time alone on the mountain. He had imagined a peaceful, joyous Spring morning, not this, the whole of Creation seemingly in a rage, the sky boiling, the earth rumbling under his feet, and even the pines above tossing their heads in disapproval. Like all of his tribe, Finn feared storms, seeing them as things of ill omen. He wondered how his friends, and one friend in particular, were faring now.

There was a movement among the pines. Not trunks or branches shaken by the wind, but a deliberate animal movement. Frightened as he was, and eager to take what little shelter the trees could offer, Finn raised his spear. Normally most animals, even bears, avoided men, but in storms they were unpredictable and it was best to be prepared. If, as he suspected, it was deer, then this inauspicious day might turn out well after all. Breathing heavily from the climb, he entered the trees. Even through the spray and the driving rain he could see the tangled foliage ahead of him shaking, as something tried to creep away toward the other side of the copse. Finn stopped, dropped his bag, wiped the rain from the shaft of his spear, and began to stalk. The foliage shook again, whatever it was made a break for the far side of the wood, and as it ran Finn caught a glimpse of doeskin. He judged it to be out of his range. While he knew a doe could easily outrun him, there was a chance that she might get caught in the undergrowth or stumble before she reached open ground. Ignoring the branches that tore at his face and legs he plunged in after her, crashing through a tight clump of trees at the wood's very heart. It was he who stumbled, though, almost losing his spear, but he sprang to his feet to find himself standing, in a small clearing, spear raised with Shani crouched at his feet staring up at him.

She was clad from head to foot in doeskin, and Finn had just time to bless the instinct that had restrained his arm from casting when the full horror of what he saw struck him. It was no wonder the heavens were raging or that the earth shook. It was no wonder that the very stones and trees of the mountain rebelled. If Finn had expected to encounter any human on these slopes, it would have been one of his companions who had strayed there in search of shelter. Shani's presence here, or that of any woman, was taboo. And as he stood above her, spear arm frozen, they both knew that his duty was clear. He must kill her. Not to do so would be to invite disaster on himself, on her, on the whole tribe. Enough had been profaned already—this fearful storm was sign enough of Annu's anger. He must slay her now, swiftly and mercifully, before it was too late. Yet his arm did not move. Finn had never seen a human face in terror before, and to see that look on a face he knew and loved, tore at his vitals. Her face was pale, her dark hair plastered over her forehead, as she crouched beast-like below him, clutching handfuls of wet earth. Finn could see in her face that she expected the thrust of the spear, was anticipating the physical pain of it in her heart. It was well known what the penalty was for her being here. Any man, even her own father or brother, must carry it out or face death himself at the hands of the others. Everything he had been told by Hann and Sanu, everything he had ever believed, everything he had felt more strongly than ever in the cave that very morning, now screamed at him that he must strike.

Yet Finn knew, even as she looked fearfully up at him, that he could not, *would* not do it. That this spear head, worked by his father with such patience and love, should bite into human flesh, and hers at that, was unthinkable. He was astonished that she could not see this. Did she really think that he would kill her? Did she not know that he could not conceive of a world that did not have her in it? No, she had no reason to know it; he had not known the strength of his own feelings himself until this very moment. There was nothing to be said, even if he could have made himself heard in the din around him. They remained rooted, the rain seethed around them, hissing off the tree trunks, thrashing the earth, and the sky growled overhead. At last, broken, he lowered his spear and turned away, rainwater and salt tears mingling down his cheeks as he stumbled blindly away to where he had left his bag.

Darkness had fallen and Shani had been swallowed up in it before Finn trudged wearily back through the wood toward the cliff face. The storm had redoubled its ferocity now, but Finn paid it no regard and wandered, hood down, cloak hanging loose, spear trailing in the mud along the side of the rock face. At a crack in the rocks, more out of instinct than any desire to escape the rain, he crawled into it until his head struck rock, and lay down wrapped in his sodden cloak. He knew what Shani had been doing there, he had known from the first instant he had seen her. Now he, she, and the whole tribe were cursed, victims of her curiosity. People had always said it would be the death of her and, but for his own weakness, it would have been. He had passed his first day as a hunter, and nearly killed a girl he loved; he had faced his first test as a man, and failed it miserably. Outside, the whole world continued to bellow its fury at him, and at the end of this day that should have been his happiest, he sobbed himself into a tormented sleep.

▲   ▲   ▲

Directly below Finn the wolves slavered and bickered and snapped at the meat and offal. Like most animals they rarely looked up. Even if they had they would not have seen him crouched in the branches above. Before dawn he had crawled from his miserable niche in the rocks and made his kill a short while after. It had been an easy kill; he had caught a doe, heavily pregnant, making her way down to join the herds massing at the edge of the forests for the migration to the fawning grounds. Even at this urgent time they could be waylaid by a salt-splash of urine against a tree, and lured within spear range. Butchering the creature on the spot, he had eaten a portion raw, without enthusiasm. Enthusiasm was dead now, dead with his boyhood and his stillborn manhood. Then, mechanically, to relieve himself of the torment of thinking, he had gone through the motions of his plan.

Now these wolves feasting eagerly below him offered him more than the prospect of a wolfskin cloak or the honor it would bring. They offered him release. He watched their jaws tugging at the meat in all the frenzy of hunger, saw them worrying it, rending muscle from fat, flesh from sinew, and thought what a hard death it would be.

"For them the deer are easy to find, hard to kill"—Hann's words echoed in his mind. Not even easy to find, this winter, or why would they fight like this over the remains of a dead beast that he had laid out for them? It would be the simplest thing in the world to slip down from his perch into their midst. They would scatter at once, but once having tasted meat and seeing that he

137

did not stir, they would close once more. It would be a hard death, but no harder than he deserved. Perhaps by his own death and suffering he could wipe out the offense that he and Shani had jointly committed. Perhaps his life, offered in place of hers, would avert disaster. Yet he was no more capable of doing it than he had been at dawn when he had pressed the point of his spear against his side and considered falling on it; no more capable of killing himself then he had been of killing her. You did not wipe out one blasphemy by committing another.

Almost too late, as most of the wolves were gorged and starting to wander off, Finn struck from his hiding place. All his frustration and anger was behind the spear throw that pinned its target, a full-grown dog, to the earth as the rest of the pack scattered into the surrounding forest. He dropped from the tree, removed the spear, and began to skin the carcass. Tears welled in his eyes as he thought of the way he had anticipated this moment, and the joy it should have brought him. Now it meant nothing to him; nothing he did seemed to have any point. He felt like a dead man, still able by some strange mischance to walk upon the earth. It would be better, he knew, if he could have summoned the courage to let this beast gut and skin *him* instead; yet here, again, he had failed. Having rolled the pelt, he slumped back to his cleft in the rocks. It was a dismal place but it suited his mood, and he sat at its mouth for the rest of the day and well into the night, staring gloomily ahead, pondering his future.

He wondered first of all what had happened to Shani. It was possible that someone else had found her, and slain her on the spot as he should have done. Who might it have been?... Venn? Gronu? Could either of them do such a thing? Could anyone? He told himself that they could, that he should have done it. Then he was struck with a new fear: if someone had killed her, had she told them before she died of meeting Finn? Then he cursed himself for the unworthy thought. Yet it had to be said—he wished deep down that someone other than himself had met her, had done what had to be done, so that all would be well once more, not for his sake but for the tribe's. Even so, he also knew that if she were to walk up to him now, beg him for the tribe's sake to do it, he could not.

He tried to imagine his homecoming, and found he could not. It had been easy enough to picture it before: Hann's welcoming smile, Mata's pride at seeing him a man at last, the comradeship of the older hunters, and Venn and Gronu once more. When, finally, he could summon up an image it was quite different— hostile faces ringing him, spitting curses, spears, perhaps even Hann's, brandished at him. He considered fleeing, going to the valley where Hann had taken him, where he had dreamed by the fireside of living alone, but which he had left because he had a home to return to. Perhaps he could draw the curse after him, free the tribe from the results of his blasphemy. Yet he remembered Hann's telling him that only a God and some beasts can live alone; he had never felt less God-like, and knew himself now to be lower than any beast. In any case there was no escaping what had been done or that it affected everyone.

On the morning of the third day he crawled reluctantly from his gravelike bed, packed his belongings and started for home. Whatever had happened, the ledge was where he belonged, and if ever he could undo the harm that had been done it would be there. If it had been found out they would be waiting for him; perhaps Sanu would know what was to be done. If his death was decreed he would accept, even welcome it. Whatever the outcome, he felt instinctively that he belonged among these people. It was late in the day before he crossed the stream below the great cave and looked up toward the ledge, afraid of what he might see.

At first sight all appeared unchanged. As he crossed the stream Finn indulged himself in the fancy that all that he had seen upon the mountain was an illusion, brought on by the delirium of the dance and his own tired state. It was almost possible to believe it. There above him was the camp, seemingly at peace, the usual wisps of smoke creeping up the cliff face at its back, a few figures, almost recognizable at this distance, moving about it, and a small cluster of people at one end. Only when he entered the trees on the home bank, and his legs began to strain at the slope leading up to the scree did he hear the cries of anguish.

The crowd at the edge of the camp was larger than he had first thought, and by the time Finn had completed the climb, he could see that it comprised the whole tribe. Even without the awful burden of what he already knew, Finn would have known at once that something was wrong. Strong men blundered from the crowd, covering their faces to hide their grief. The women, less constrained, were keening already, their disordered hair hanging about their shoulders. Even the Elders, who had seen the beginning and the end of life time and again over years beyond number, stood dazed and mute, shaking their heads in disbelief at what they saw.

As Finn fought his way to the heart of the crowd he saw, over the heads of those in front, the leading hunters of all the ten hearths grouped around a shapeless bundle of skins. Gronu was foremost among them, grim-faced and bloody. He was answering in short, sharp bursts of speech the questions addressed to him from all sides, but he never once took his eyes from the bundle at his feet. From it, Finn now saw, protruded a human hand. It was all Finn could do to keep from throwing himself to the earth and tearing at it with his fingers. Gronu had found her; Gronu, who loved her too, had killed her. If the curse was lifted, and the tribe might live, even so what price now his own life?

Faces turned toward Finn as he shouldered his way forward and, recognizing him, the crowd parted. Hann was by the body too, and looked up from it to him as he approached. Instead of the accusing glare he had nerved himself to expect, however, there was pity in his eyes and in the eyes of the hunters who surrounded him. Had all the tribe known, all along, of his feelings for Shani? This thought, which would have horrified him once, seemed trivial now as he joined his father and forced

140

himself to look down at the corpse. Gently Hann stooped to uncover the face, but Finn could not draw his eyes away from the hand. It was hard to believe that this cold, pale hand was the same that had so recently rested upon his shoulder, shared meat with him and been held out to him in a friendship that had meant more to him than life itself. Yet it was not the hand he had looked for; this was broad and callused, and it *had* been strong, and the face when he turned to it was Venn's.

Finn had the story that night from Hann as they sat under the night sky digesting the feast that Mata had prepared against his homecoming. It was a gloomy meal, eaten in silence. Mata had eaten nothing and, seeing them settled, had gone to the tents to lament with Laela and Venn's cousins. They were keening now as Hann told how Gronu had arrived below the camp in the late afternoon, dragging the body of Venn on a sled like a slaughtered deer.

"He had dragged him like that all the way from the mountain. He almost fainted at the foot of the scree, but he wouldn't let us help him."

Finn noticed the respectful tone of Hann's voice and recalled how he had once spoken of Gronu.

"It was during the storm . . ." Hann continued. "We were all thinking of you on that night. It seems Gronu headed for the cliffs looking for a cave. I suppose you all did . . ." Finn nodded grimly, remembering his own miserable night . . . "Well, Venn had done the same, headed for the same cliffs. He must have disturbed a bear in the darkness. Gronu heard the noise even over the storm; by the time he got there Venn was on the ground, with the bear coming in to attack him once more. Gronu got himself between them—you should see his shoulder —speared it with his own spear, and finished it off with Venn's. He tried to revive Venn, but his head was crushed. There was nothing he could do but bring him home."

They sat in silence, Finn remembering Venn's foreboding and what he himself had seen and done in that same storm.

Hann was still marveling at Gronu's courage. "All the way back from the mountain with his friend dead on his back, that's a hard thing for a young man." He shook his head and looked at Finn. "He turned out all right, that one!"

Finn could not find it in himself to answer. He longed to tell Hann of his own dark secret, tell him that the tragedy he had just recounted, Venn's death and Gronu's wounding, were *his* doing, his and Shani's, but he knew he could never do so. Without a word he left his father and walked out onto the scree. Venn was gone. Venn who had saved him from the river, who had been his friend when all the world disowned him, who had sworn to be his brother, was no more. There would be no hunting together, stalking deer through the knee-deep snow, spearing salmon in the stream in Autumn, no feasting, no laughter at the fireside. Never again would he hear him tease his sister at the morning meal, see his broad face crease into a broken-toothed smile. The beast that had crushed Venn's head had torn Finn's heart out too. (Would that that were true!—even the pain of death could not be worse than this of parting!) Venn who had saved Finn's life had in that same moment forfeited his own, saving the boy who would one day bring about his own death.

"Forgive me, Venn, I beg you!" he whispered to the night sky, tears scalding his cheeks. He tried to say more, to wish for death that he might fulfill his promise and hunt with his friend. But somewhere between his heart and his mouth the words became a wail of anguish and despair. The sound of the women keening seemed to answer him, to taunt him with how soon his blasphemy had borne its bitter fruit.

CHAPTER
EIGHT

▲ ▲ ▲
▲ ▲

V ENN'S DEATH ON THE MOUNTAIN was recognized by all to be an extraordinary event, outside the experience of anyone then living. Some among the old muttered that it was a bad omen, a warning of worse misfortunes to come. Most, however, felt that a young boy's death on the brink of manhood was surely misfortune enough for one generation. The herds were massing in the forests for the Spring migration, marking the beginning of the yearly cycle and reminding them all that life must continue. So, after Venn had been buried and suitably mourned, life on the ledge returned to normal. As the immediate shock of Venn's death wore off, it became just one outstanding event, an aid to memory in a life where any one year was little different from the one that had passed or those that lay ahead. Mothers would tell their children, "You were born three years before Venn died"; hunters' tales would begin, "In the year Venn was killed on the mountain, . . ." but beyond that it ceased to mean anything except to those most intimately affected.

Of these, Shani was the most obviously changed. It was widely expected that after a decent interval she would marry

143

Gronu. Nobody expected this more than Gronu himself, but to his and everyone else's surprise she showed little inclination toward him or any other. In the three years that followed the events on the mountain she became gradually more and more withdrawn, avoiding the company of both Gronu and Finn, and spending the greater part of her time alone. People agreed that Venn's death had affected her more than anyone could have foreseen but that in time she would become her old self again. After all, even Laela had overcome her grief and had married a hunter of Hann's hearth. To this end, and in increasing desperation, Shani's family continued to press suitors on her only to see each one rejected more vehemently than the last. It seemed that in her grief she had resolved never to marry. Since she usually got her own way, that at least had not changed, she remained unmarried and childless, an unusual condition for a woman in her sixteenth Summer.

Gronu made little secret of his dismay at Shani's strange conduct; it was the only setback in what was for him a time of growing power and influence. After the shock of Venn's death had worn off, his own part in the events of that time came to be remembered. Songs were composed about Venn's tragedy and few failed to mention the conduct of his friend, his attempt at rescue, and his own climactic battle with the bear. It was not long before the bear's skin re-appeared in the form of a cloak which, its great paws resting on his shoulders, Gronu wore proudly at all the great councils and tribal rituals. These and the scars he gained in the combat were taken as further evidence of a prowess which many claimed to have been the first to observe in the boy, and which all now rushed to recognize in the man. With his strength and skill at the hunt, the respect with which his words were heard at the great Councils, and the way even older hunters would seek his advice and opinion, it was little surprise that his band of followers should have swelled over the years. More surprising was the fact that this group crossed over the usual bonds of hearth and family and attracted the best of the young men from throughout the tribe. These, under Gronu's guidance, soon developed their own code of conduct, their own bonds of loyalty, even their own hunting language, impenetrable by outsiders. They would take off for days on end, sometimes for as long as a month at a time, into the forests or onto the grasslands; what they did there or what they talked about round their campfires remained a mystery. Not all of the older men welcomed this development, and some of the young, notably Finn, stood aloof, yet it was agreed by all that Gronu was a young man of whom great things could be expected.

Finn, too, had grown strong and wise in the knowledge that his father passed on to him. He was well liked both by those of his own age who admired his strength and skill, and by the Elders for his quiet wisdom and respectful bearing. His voice was not heard in the Councils as Gronu's was; but it was widely agreed that his judgment, when sought, was shrewd. It was well known that Venn had been his first and best friend and that since his death he chose, when not with his father, to be alone. Such a thing was understandable, a throwback, no doubt, to the bitter experience of his early life. None except Shani, who generally avoided him, guessed the true cause of his self-imposed isolation from the body of the tribe. From the moment he had gazed down on Venn's dead face, he had been haunted by the knowledge of his part in it. Even then, believing Venn's death to be a visitation on the tribe, his torment had been almost more than he could bear. Three lean years and three hard Winters later, when men began to remember the old ones' forebodings and to date their troubles from the moment Gronu had appeared dragging Venn's body behind him, his anguish had increased. It was clear to him that the tribe's misfortunes were his fault, his and Shani's, and that the loss of his friend had been a mere portent of worse things to come.

If the sun had suddenly gone out, if the river had dried up or turned to blood, if the earth itself had rolled over and shaken

145

the people off like fleas, their destruction could not have seemed more certain than in the years that followed Venn's passing. Yet calamity did not fall upon the tribe and devour them at once but crept up on them like a wasting sickness. Its first symptoms arrived unseen by any Burnt Shin, beside a distant seashore, where vast lands lay strewn with carcasses. Buzzards and ravens, too glutted to fly, preened and bickered in a petrified forest, whose branches of bone and antler shed leaves of tattered skin. The most hardened hunter of the Burnt Shins would have wept to see such killing grounds as these, that stretched as far as a man could have seen in every direction. As though struck down by unseen hands dead deer smothered the moss of the Summer grazing grounds and, as the herd moved off, stirred by the Autumn winds, it left a trail of dead and dying in its wake. Many weakened, foundered and fell easy prey to wolves and scavengers; many reached the river scarcely strong enough to swim across; and many more, most damaging of all, had never lived to leave the fawning grounds.

Thus, the lifeblood of the people, which had flowed ceaselessly as long as men could remember or their stories could recall, grew sluggish and began to fail. It was imperceptible at first; in his first Autumn as a hunter Finn had not noticed anything wrong, carried away as he was by the exhilaration of the kill and the joy of feasting. Nor was he alone in this. The few old men who grumbled were ignored as ever. He did notice though, that Hann's mood continued to darken as time passed, and that despite his best efforts, and the growing closeness between them, Hann never again recovered that easy good humor that had been his during their expedition to the forests. By the second Autumn, the state of the herd had become the subject of anxious talk among the hunters, and it was a leaner tribe that descended to the river for the Spring kill. A year later, when the whole herd came and passed through the killing grounds well within the space of one day, it seemed that even the children could remember a day when the deer had covered the earth from one horizon to the other.

What had so angered Annu as to bring His wrath upon them in this way, only two of the Burnt Shins knew, or thought they knew. As to more immediate causes of the herd's dwindling, whether pestilence or over-grazing, wolves or other humans at the far end of the earth, each hunter had his own ideas. Even so at the Autumn kill, herded together, racing down corridors to the killing grounds, they still seemed sufficient to all but the keenest eye; but in the Winter, dispersed in the forests, that same number seemed pitifully few. When the smoked meat ran out and the men took to the forests once more, those who had not seen the problem felt it in their empty stomachs. Anxious groups of women would wait on the edge of the scree day after day, quieting crying children and staring down into the trees for some sign of the returning hunters; as often as not these returned home empty-handed. The arrival of a fresh carcass was a cause for rejoicing all along the ledge. The subsequent sharing became an ordeal for the successful hearth and a strain on the already fragile relations within the camp.

It was after one such meal that Hann first admitted his fears to Finn. The two of them had hunted the forest for two days, floundering knee-deep in snow, straying ever farther from home, seeing few deer and finding many corpses. At length and with great good luck they had killed a young buck, and together had dragged the undersized carcass back to the ledge. By the time they reached the tents around Hann's hearth a crowd had gathered, men, women and children from many hearths. They had sat around Hann's fire while the two of them skinned and butchered the beast, making room for them when at last they, too, had sat at the fireside. The talk had been casual, of matters unconnected with deer or hunting. But both men had seen how their eyes strayed to where the beast hung, and the way the nonchalant crowd about the fire had slowly swelled as more

147

visitors ambled up—as though out of idle curiosity—and joined the gathering. Only the children, not understanding the etiquette of these matters, crowded around the beast, dipping their fingers in the blood and looking back at Hann with appealing eyes. Unable to resist this for long, he had offered the expected invitation to all present to eat with him, an offer that was received with an affectation of mild surprise, pondered at length and finally, casually, accepted. There had been little casualness, though, in the way they had devoured the small portions allowed by the division of such a beast among so many. As Finn had eaten his share, he had looked at the faces of the men around him, respected Elders, renowned hunters, feeling pain for them, seeing how it shamed them to eat at another's hearth.

Now, as they sat gazing out at the distant mountain tops, Hann looked back now and then at the dispersing crowd. Sensing his frustration, Finn tried to make satisfied noises, shifting his position and wrapping his cloak tighter round him. There was no denying, though, that the deer had not gone far.

"Not much," said Hann, "among so many." Finn remained silent, hoping he would leave it at this, but he went on, "The deer are smaller this year, the herd thinner."

This was obvious, a commonplace observation around the campfires, but Finn had always managed to avoid discussing it with his father. He laughed dismissively. "They say that when a man thinks the deer are getting smaller, it is because his beard is getting longer."

Hann did not laugh, as he usually did at Finn's jokes. "Even the children notice it," he said sourly. "Don't pretend that you don't."

Of course Finn had noticed it, and he *had* been pretending, trying not to admit it even to himself. That second Autumn, when the thinning of the herds had first become noticeable, he had tried to convince himself that it was a passing thing, that the following year all would be well. It had taken that third

Autumn, when the gray and brown tidal wave that had used to descend upon them from the grasslands had become a succession of rivulets, to convince him of the truth. And the why of it only he and one other knew! There could be no doubt now that this evil that had beset the herds and therefore the tribe was his doing. Even so he sought reassurance from his father.

"What do you think has caused it?" he asked.

Hann shrugged morosely. "There is no way that we can know. It could be many things . . . wolves, disease, poor grazing at the fawning grounds, as well as whatever we have done . . ."

"We?" Finn reddened as he spoke.

Hann nodded. "The herds depend on Annu. It must be that this is a sign of his disfavor."

Now—and not for the first time—Finn longed to break his three years' silence, longed to pour out his heart and his troubles to the one person who, if he did not understand, might at least have pity. Yet he knew even as he fought with this urge that he would never do so. Such knowledge would kill his father as surely as his spear would have killed Shani had he only had the courage to wield it.

Hann, wrapped up in his own grim thoughts, had not noticed the change in his son. When he spoke once more it was almost to himself. "Whatever it is, we must pray that His anger passes soon for if the herd suffers we suffer too. As its numbers fall so will ours. If the hunting goes, everything else goes with it."

They sat for a while in gloomy silence, the crowd behind them now scattered to their tents to sleep or lounge listlessly about their fires. It was not long, though, before a sound from below roused them both from their thoughts, and brought others running to the edge of the scree. It was a sound unfamiliar enough this close to the ledge at any time, but it was especially so at the end of a bitter Winter. It was the cough of a deer. As all eyes strained down into the gloom of the forest, they saw a buck limping through the snow, a trail of blood from

149

a wound in its hind quarters marking the path it had taken. Some men ran at once to their tents to grab spears; they set off down the side of the scree in hope of working their way round behind the struggling beast. Others remained at the camp's edge with the women and children, stupefied by this sudden apparition. Finn looked to Hann; he was shaking his head as though in disbelief. Then suddenly Hann lowered it into his hands, and looked no more. Amazed, Finn turned again to where the deer labored reluctantly up the slope and away from the cover of the trees. Every now and then it turned, trying to find a way back down the slope, but now Finn could hear the cries from among the trees that were driving it upward. Within a few moments a thin line of hunters emerged from the cover of the trees, with Gronu at their head. At once the men on the ledge and those who had begun to descend stopped, remaining rooted to the spot as Gronu's men drove the wounded and now frantic deer up the hillside to the edge of the scree.

For a few moments Finn did not grasp what Hann had guessed at once; that they had wounded the deer a long way off and driven it home to save themselves the effort of dragging its carcass up the hill. The faces of the men and women around him registered their shock at this act of cruelty, but as the beast reached the bottom of the scree and began to drag itself painfully up toward them, their hunger got the better of their nobler instincts. They began to cry out in praise of Gronu and shout encouragement to the young men below. Only Finn, it seemed, was spurred to action. Without a word to his father, whose face remained buried in his hands, he leaped to his feet, and grabbing a spear from a startled hunter at the edge of the camp, raced down the scree toward the deer.

Seeing him come, the beast turned once more to face its pursuers, searching with wild eyes for a path down to the safety of the trees. When it tried to move it fell and slumped to its wounded side, but rose again just as Finn cast his spear. These days he seldom missed. The spear, thrown from above, struck the beast squarely in the back of the neck, killing it instantly. Before it had stopped kicking Finn was astride it, wrenching the spear free. With the spear point he ear-marked the beast, oblivious to the angry cries and threatening gestures of the young men running toward him up the slope. They gathered round him still shouting, but he turned to face them, one by one. Silence fell. Angry as they were at his intervention none was willing, such was his strength, to push the matter further. Finn now turned to the one man who had not run up the slope, and who now passed through his fellows to stand facing him. The years that had passed had taken with them any fear Finn might have felt of Gronu. When he spoke he spoke boldly.

"Don't worry. It has your mark," he said, nodding down to the dead buck at his feet.

Gronu seemed more amused than angry.

"I never doubted it." Then reaching into his legging for a blade, he held it out to Finn, adding, "No doubt you'll want to carry it up for us."

Finn took the blade without a word and strode off down to the trees to cut saplings. He did not look back as he heard the angry mutterings of Gronu's companions, nor even when he heard Gronu bid them climb to the ledge and light a fire. By the time he had cut two saplings and some smaller branches for supports, Gronu, still smiling, had joined him once more.

"They think you are mad . . ." he said, offering Finn a handful of twine to bind the sled, ". . . making work for yourself."

Not taking his eyes from his work Finn shrugged. Then, turning to Gronu who leaned against a tree beside him, he asked, "How far did you drive it?"

"We wounded it across the stream, in a glade in the foothills halfway to the Sacred Mountain. We were lucky."

As he bound the framework together, Finn thought how ill the word "luck" sat with the image Gronu had conjured. He thought of the pain and fear the deer had suffered—surrounded by enemies, thrashing through the deep snow, leaving a bloody trail as its life drained away. Reading all this in his face, Gronu pointed with his chin to the ledge, where a mixed crowd of men, women and children were peering down at them.

"I save my pity for them," he said, but Finn remained unimpressed.

"There was no need for this," he answered. "They can be fed without this."

Gronu smiled once more. "Do you think *they* care so long as we fill their bellies? Look at them beckoning to us. When we divide the carcass who will even stop to think how it died."

Finn continued working in silence, heaving the carcass onto the frame, binding it in place, and finally hoisting the end of the sled onto his shoulders. Taking Finn's spear as well as his own, Gronu walked alongside him as he started up the hill.

"Of course some still care. You care, and I admire you for it," he was saying as Finn bent his back to the task of hauling the dead weight up the scree. "But for the rest of them . . ."—and he spat.

The gesture of contempt shocked Finn almost as much as the deer's cruel death. As though the thought had just occurred to him, Gronu suddenly said, "You should join with us," in a tone that just failed to hide the urgency he obviously attached to it. "You could learn a lot," he said.

Finn shook his head. "I learn all I need from my father."

Gronu shrugged. "So pass it on!" he said. Then, leaning closer, he all but whispered in his ear despite the fact that they were a long way out of earshot of the camp. "Hard times are coming, and the answers lie with us. Great things are in the wind. You can choose to be a part of them or remain burdened by the old ways." That said, he sprang a few paces up the slope and placed himself in Finn's path, staring down at him, his expression eager and hopeful.

There was nothing in Finn's face to justify his hopes, nor in his voice when he spoke. "This much I have seen of your 'great things,' " he said, jerking his head back to indicate the dead deer on his back, "and I think I have seen enough. It doesn't seem to me that much luck lies for us that way."

For an instant Gronu opened his mouth as though to speak again. But studying Finn's face he changed his mind, turned and started off up the hill at his own speed.

"Bring it up to my hearth!" was all he said over his shoulder. By the time Finn had reached the edge of the camp, a great fire was burning. Those at the edge of the crowd that had gathered round Gronu broke off to relieve Finn of his burden. In an instant men and deer were gone, swallowed up in the rejoicing crowd; Finn turned, flexing his aching shoulders, to rejoin his father at the other end of the camp. He reached the space that they had scraped in the snow to find it empty, and Hann gone, retired to his tent.

▲   ▲   ▲

The Summer that followed was among the best that anyone could remember. The state of the herds at the Spring kill was a cause of much disquiet but there were still many more than the hunters could kill, and to those not inclined to speculate on the future this was enough. The sun came early; the drying went well, and long lazy days followed—bathing in the stream, lying around on the warm rocks, singing and telling stories. The woods teemed with small game, and as if to compensate the people for past sufferings the salmon filled the stream in greater numbers than ever. It was possible, in that time, to feel that the worst was past and that the hard times of the past few years were simply an aberration, a timely reminder sent by Annu to teach them the value of things. Even so, when the dried meat ran low, and the Autumn winds began to blow, men once more cast anxious eyes toward the horizon.

In midsummer Gronu and his friends had departed, as was their habit, to roam the grasslands. They returned with the first

153

blowing of the chill winds, running through the camp shouting the news that Gronu wished to address the Council that very night on a matter of great importance. It was every hunter's right to be heard in Council if the Elders agreed, and such was the esteem in which Gronu was held that the cave was at once prepared and a messenger sent to summon Sanu. Finn had been fishing in the stream all day and had missed the excitement of this hastily summoned meeting. On reaching the camp—fishing spear on his shoulder, with four salmon dangling from its points—he was surprised to find it silent and deserted. Hearing the murmur from the cave he threw down his spear and made his way through the lines of tents.

The tribe had assembled within, the Elders and older hunters seated to the fore, the young men, women, and children standing in the rear. As Finn approached he could see the backs of the crowd filling the cave mouth, but guessed from the presence outside of Gronu and two of his friends that the Council had yet to start. The friends were arraying Gronu's bear cloak, laying the great paws upon his shoulders, while Gronu himself was engaged in rubbing vigorously at the scars those same claws had made, so as to render them vivid and prominent. As Finn approached he looked up, saw that he had been caught out, smiled and shrugged. There was self-mockery in the smile. But in his eyes was that eager, predatory look that so disfigured men's faces at the killing grounds. Finn nodded a greeting, restraining a shudder, and pressed through the crowds into the cave.

At the front of the cave, on the open space where the speakers would stand, men were milling around examining the red hand prints left there by generations of hunters, identifying them by name and hearth and explaining to each other and anyone who would listen their own relationship to these long-departed heroes. The cave was humming with gossip and speculation as to what this meeting could mean. What message could Gronu have to impart that was so urgent?

154

Sensing their impatience, perhaps a prey to it himself, Sanu rose and walked onto the floor. At once the hunters took their places, and silence settled on the crowd.

"After many days away. . ." he began, "Gronu has returned to us. There are things he wishes to say, things he wishes to offer for our judgment. Gronu is a young man, but his deeds and his wisdom are well known to us. I, Sanu, say he should be heard!"

As one the Elders signified their assent though it was a mere formality once Sanu had spoken, and the holy man took his place once more in their ranks. Nothing more happened—the crowd began to stir; even the Elders, Sanu excepted, began to glance over their shoulders toward the cave mouth. Not until the cave was filled once more with the hum of conversation, and several hunters had risen to their feet to try to restore order, did Gronu appear. Flanked by his colleagues cleaving a path through the crowds, they moved as a body down through the ranks of the tribe. The body gradually diminished as his supporters dropped out in ones and twos, threading their way into the crowd until Gronu arrived alone at the floor.

He turned and faced them, arms folded, legs splayed, cloak thrown back to reveal his scarred shoulder. Not until complete silence had fallen once more did he begin to speak.

"The herds are dwindling," he announced simply. "For two years we have watched their numbers fall. For two Winters we have barely survived. How much longer can this go on? How many more such Winters can we survive?"

Gronu paused for effect as the question, one that had been asked by many, passed among the crowd. At last, satisfied with the result, he drew himself up to his full height. "The time has come for great changes."

At the word a ripple ran through the ranks of the Elders and some older hunters. They looked to one another, concerned, and then at Gronu, who stood regarding this with evident satisfaction. To their surprise, though, he merely folded his arms

155

and said nothing further. A murmur arose from the crowd packed behind, and many voices urged him on, but still he stood, allowing his words to take their full effect.

"What is it you propose, Gronu?" asked Sanu at length.

Gronu affected surprise. "Is it for me to propose? A hunter in his third year? No. I ask what do *you* propose? I, Gronu, ask it!"

With that he held out his arms in a gesture that seemed to embrace the whole tribe but was aimed specifically at the men who sat before him. These looked baffled, and for the first time unsure of themselves. Gronu had departed from the usual way of such meetings and by so doing had taken them by surprise. One or two at the back began to shout suggestions. But before Gronu could respond, Sanu had risen to his feet and quelled them with a glance. Turning to Gronu he spoke, his voice shaking now with suppressed anger.

"It is not for you to question us! We came here because we were told you had something to say and we were willing to listen. We did not come here to talk about the herds or the future of the tribe. *We* will decide when such things are to be discussed."

Before the approving growl from the older men had died down Gronu was shouting. "And when will that be? When another Winter has been and gone? When our teeth have fallen out, and our ribs stand out so you can count them? I say now is the time!" This time there was a louder response from the crowd, with voices raised in agreement. Gronu had timed his attack well. With Winter now no more than a dim memory, the good humor of early Summer had evaporated. Now he had the support not only of his own companions but of a growing number at the back of the meeting.

"The Winter is almost upon us once more," he cried. "Even as we sit here the herds are massing. Again I ask, what do you propose?"

The clamor in the cave increased, and from all sides the

question was repeated. Gronu strode forward to tower over the rows of men seated before him. With well-planned words and the organized support of his friends scattered among the crowd, he had taken control of the gathering. At one stroke he had managed not only to discredit the Elders for their inactivity, but to dictate the course the talk would take. Taken by surprise by this challenge, the Elders seemed nonplussed; compared with this powerful sardonic presence that now cast his shadow over them, they suddenly looked pitiful and confused.

During these words Finn had worked his way forward until he was behind Hann, and now leaned forward to whisper in his ear.

"Why don't you speak? He'll soon back down."

Hann shook his head. "Not yet. So far it all goes his way. Let him put his own plan forward, and we shall see how it stands up."

Almost as if to echo his words Sanu spoke out. "Tell us what it is that you propose, Gronu . . ."—his voice betrayed the distaste he felt for the young man's manner—"tell us now or quit the floor."

Gronu stepped back, swept his cloak behind him and stood regarding them, hands upon his hips.

"It is in the Winter that our troubles come," he began. "In the Autumn at the killing grounds there are still more deer than we can kill. But when the snows come and the smoked meat is eaten up that's when we go hungry, that's when the women and children sit starving on the scree and the men come home empty-handed. Am I right?" The hunters nodded in agreement. He turned to the crowd. "Am I right?"

He held out his arms, appealing over the heads of the Elders and hunters to the crowds at their back, and with their shouted assent receiving the confidence to go on.

The Elders stirred uneasily at this clamor from behind. Gronu was breaking all the traditions of the Council—using the floor to tell them things they already knew, and appealing to the crowd whose presence at these meetings was normally only just tolerated. Opinions were being openly voiced behind them by those who had no business speaking at such a gathering. Worse, there was no doubt that the bulk of those angry voices that shouted from the darkness agreed with Gronu.

"Wolves..." an elderly and much respected hunter of Finn's hearth was on his feet now.

"It is the wolves," he said. "They follow the herd throughout the year. They are whittling away at the herds. After the Autumn kill we must go out in strength and hunt wolves." There was a chorus of agreement for this from the front two rows, but Gronu, emboldened now, sneered as he replied.

"And how will you hunt them? How will you kill them in any numbers? Will you drive them like deer? And while you hunt wolves who will feed our families? When they cry for food will you give them wolf meat?" From the back of the cave Gronu's supporters laughed aloud. The old hunter, used to respect from his youngers and confused by Gronu's quick tongue, sat down in confusion.

Gronu was suddenly conciliatory, sensing that he had perhaps overreached himself, gone too far in his mockery of a respected member of the tribe.

"You have spoken wisely," he said to the elderly man. "It may be that in your wisdom you have struck to the heart of the problem." Finn was wondering whether he was alone in resenting Gronu's patronizing tone, when a voice from the darkness cried out, "Who are you to judge?" Some muttered in agreement. Gronu chose to ignore them. Still addressing the old man, he continued, "But we can never kill wolves in such numbers as would make any difference. And every day out after wolves is a day without meat. The answer lies elsewhere."

"Where then?" snapped Sanu, by no means mollified by Gronu's change of tone.

This was the moment for which Gronu had been waiting.

Every man, woman and child in the great cave hung on his words as he spoke.

"We must kill more deer at the Autumn kill."

It was the turn of the Elders and hunters to laugh. As the mirth spread from them to all corners of the cave and even to the small children in their mothers' arms, Gronu stood serene and aloof, as though what he had suggested was the most obvious in the world.

"More carcasses, more smoke-houses, more meat," he intoned his simple formula, "... enough to see us through the Winter."

As one of those who was supposedly to perform this miracle, Finn laughed as loudly as any. Had Gronu left his wits out on the grasslands somewhere, to summon a Council for this? Yet among those who understood the least, the images Gronu had invoked spoke more powerfully than reason could. To people dreading the onset of the snows, his vision of bulging smoke-houses stacked with meat, and a Winter of ease and comfort free from the fear of starvation, was a potent one.

"What is this?" Sanu's voice, coldly scornful, scattered the images like a stone cast into a pool. "How can we kill more? Our hunters slay deer till their arms ache. What would you have us do, arm the children?"

The scattered laughter that greeted this affected Gronu no more than that of a few moments earlier.

"We abandon our killing grounds," he announced calmly. Then, raising his voice against the cries of outrage, "We meet the deer farther out, far beyond the river, we plant the staves in one long line, split off a portion of the herd and..."—he was shouting now to be heard above the outcry—"and we drive them over the flats."

For the briefest of moments there was silence. It seemed to Finn as if the whole world had suddenly stopped in its tracks. If he had heard that the river below had stood still, or the trees

159

no longer tossed their heads in the wind, it would not have surprised him. A man had spoken words, given utterance to thoughts like none that had gone before; as when a falling tree or a rock toppling from a cliff seemed to hang in the air for an instant, there was a moment of stillness before the cave erupted.

Then all was chaos. The whole tribe seemed to be shouting at once. A dozen hunters, including Hann, were on their feet mouthing their protests, unheard in the din. A few Elders tried feebly to rise, and fell, toppled by the press from behind. Sanu alone was still staring ahead of him as one in a dream.

The flats—beyond the river, a long level shelf of rock culminating in a sheer cliff. A place where the grasslands fell away to the low ground at the mouth of another valley, a valley most of them had never seen, the valley where Hann and his father had emerged after their expedition into the forests many years before.

Oblivious to the tumult all around him, Finn tried to envisage the flats. He had been there once as a child. He had amused himself rolling stones over the cliffs, counting on his fingers, sometimes as many as four, until he heard them thump on the hard earth below. Then, bored with that game, he had lain on the sun-warmed rocks and slept until it grew cold, then returned to the camp long after dark. It was across those same rocks and over that same precipice that Gronu now proposed they drive the deer. Bucks, does and fawns all tumbling through the air in a terrified thrashing mass to lie shattered at the foot of the cliffs—this was what Gronu and his friends had been planning all Summer. This was what they had talked of round their fires and dreamed of as they lay under the stars.

The silence that had fallen once more dragged Finn away from these dreadful visions, and he saw to his joy that Hann had taken the floor. He was facing Gronu. All were silent as Hann denounced Gronu's scheme.

"No man can know what has blighted the herds," he was

saying. "Some unnatural act perhaps"—here Gronu paled for the first time under Hann's accusing glare. "Or something amiss in this world or the other. Perhaps it is wolves..." Hann turned to the old hunter and they nodded to each other in mutual respect, "or poor grazing by the sea, or another people in another part of the earth. It has not been given us to know. But whatever it is, *this*"—he gestured at Gronu—"will solve nothing. If the herds are dwindling, the answer does not lie in killing more. That may fill our bellies till the Spring, but what then? Fewer deer still. And what *then?* Another massacre?"

Hann's reasonable, measured tone seemed to have restored sanity once more. Even Gronu shrugged.

"If you have a better answer," he said softly, "I would gladly hear it and just as gladly submit to your wisdom."

All eyes turned to Hann once more. His voice had stilled their frenzy, brought them to their senses and now, as always in the past, they looked to him for answers. Yet, as Finn looked at the rows of faces turned trustingly to his father, he knew that Hann had no answer that would satisfy them.

"Let us consider the matter calmly," Hann said, "and take the counsel of wise men. Let us do what we can—hunt down wolves, range farther when we go out after deer. But nothing will be solved by a deed so frightful as this that Gronu proposes. Annu tells us to love the deer. We must hunt them, yes, that is our lot, but with reverence and respect. Whatever has been done by us or by others to cause this blight cannot be undone by greater evils. Let us pray and dance. In time the herd may recover..."

He got no further. Defying the conventions of the Councils, Gronu stepped forward and interrupted. "The herds *may* recover!" he cried, seizing on the one word that had sounded lame even to Finn. "And in the meantime we *will* starve!"

An answering shout filled the cave. Hann stood dumbfounded. Suddenly he seemed old beside the imposing figure of Gronu. However wise, however true his words had been, they had fallen on deaf ears. Just for a moment Finn saw a look of shame pass across his father's face. It was the look of a man who felt that he had failed, that his wisdom had deserted him. Finn felt that, if had been standing next to Gronu, he would have felled him there and then; he had the strength and, now, the confidence. Hann had never been known to lay violent hands on any man, though, and he stepped aside as Gronu spoke again.

"There was a time, Hann, when I respected your wisdom above all others. But that time has passed. What have your dancing and your prayers brought us?" There were angry growls from the front of the meeting at this, but they were all but drowned out by the swelling chorus of agreement behind.

"They have brought us to the brink of starvation!" cried Gronu in answer to his own question. Before Hann could say a word he turned on him. "You used to say that a hunter's glory was full bellies round his fire. Where's your glory now?" As the shouting filled the cave once more, Hann could only stand, struck dumb by Gronu's vehemence and the violence of his language. Worst of all, the words rang true, as Finn looked around him; the exposed ribs and drawn faces he saw proclaimed them to be so.

Nothing could stop Gronu now. "Let the old men pray and dance if they can, and tell their tales around the fire," he raged. "The fault does not lie there..."—he gestured vaguely to the heavens—"it lies here!" With this last word he stabbed his own chest with his fingers, crying, "It is time for *us* to take control of *our* world!"

"Blasphemy!" Sanu was on his feet once more, his whole body shaking.

"Blasphemy?" shouted Gronu before the dread word could begin to echo. "I'll show you blasphemy." He turned to shout to the people massed at the cave mouth. "Hana, of Rann's hearth, where is the baby you had last Autumn? Bela, where is your first-born? Konn, your father died in his fortieth Winter too weak to rise to greet you when you returned empty-handed from the hunt." As the sobbing and lamentations that answered him from the dark died down, he turned once more to Sanu. "There is blasphemy!" he snarled. "Tell me when it was that Annu said we should starve to death?"

Sanu, who had never been spoken to in this way, stood amazed. So did Hann beside him. It seemed from their silence, from the reluctance of any other to stand up and be heard, and from the clamor that now greeted Gronu's every utterance, that he had carried the day.

Finn had never before spoken at a Council, but before he even realized what he was doing he had stepped forward. "Gronu claims to speak for the young men," he cried, unsure himself of what he was going to say next, "but there are still those among us who respect our Elders...." This drew quiet approval from the men seated before him. "And are not so fast to reject the wisdom of our ancestors."

"And whose ancestors are these?" inquired Gronu. As he spoke he slipped his own cloak down over his left arm in the same way Finn wore his to hide his tattoo. The gesture and his comment caused the cave to fill with laughter.

In an instant all Finn's righteous anger drained away, all the old anxieties returned. It pained him to know how easily it could be done. How quickly he could become again the timid outsider he had once been. The few voices raised in his defense were lost amid the laughter and he felt suddenly isolated. At that same moment there came upon him the renewed realization that all of this—the blighted herds, Gronu's terrible plan, and the bitter divisions that had arisen that night—all were his fault, his and Shani's. Confused, he began to withdraw into the shadows. As he did so his eyes met Gronu's. The look that passed between them left neither in any doubt that from that day forth they were enemies: Gronu's offer of friendship on the day he had driven home the stricken deer had been his last. Even though he knew Gronu could not help himself, that he was the unknowing instrument of Annu's anger, Finn would

163

never forgive the injury that had just been done him. Or the insults that had been heaped upon his father's head.

Before the shadows had swallowed Finn or the laughter had subsided, Gronu brushed past him, appealing directly to the tribe.

"My way is clear!" he declared. "My path is chosen. At dawn I go to the flats with my companions, your sons and brothers. Their choice is made. It is you, now, who must make yours!"

A great roar, a torrent of sound, engulfed Gronu and the Elders as the crowd, led by his own supporters, swept forward to acknowledge him. The old men and hearth leaders, those who had not themselves surged forward, barely had time to dash for the walls. It was as though the cave had been flooded. Finn, pressed against the rock wall, saw among the legs of the crowd some of the Elders attempting to rise, others sprawling, as the tribe thronged about Gronu chanting his name. Resisting attempts to hoist him to their shoulders, he forced his way triumphantly through them, acknowledging the plaudits of his well-wishers, and marched out into the gathering dusk. One or two of the hearth leaders, Hann among them, still tried to make themselves heard on the fringes of the crowd. Finn joined them, tugging at any man or woman who would listen, crying the folly of what was proposed, but it was futile. A collective madness had seized them all—bewitched by Gronu's words and Gronu's vision they had eyes and ears for no other.

The camp was ringing to the sounds of celebration, as though the deer were already slaughtered and the feasting fires already lit when, later that night, Finn passed again by the mouth of the cave. Hann alone had managed to sway the men and women of his hearth, as well as a few stragglers from the others, convincing them to keep to the old ways. Over at his tents they were preparing for the dance that Hann had declared immediately in the hope that once begun the sight of the old familiar rituals would bring the tribe to its senses. Finn knew better though. He knew, as his father could not, that this was the visitation of their God's anger on the people. He knew that all was lost, and as he wandered by the mouth of the cave he saw that others knew it too. The cave was filled with the smoke of a dozen dying lamps, by whose dim light he could just make out the huddled figures of Sanu and the Elders, still and silent, gazing with doleful, tear-filled eyes at the images of the deer and the hand-prints of their ancestors.

CHAPTER
NINE

▲ ▲ ▲
▲ ▲

SQUATTING IN THE GROVE among the Reindeer dancers, Finn
heard Sanu's voice drifting across from the center of the dancing ring.

"Touch the earth, Lord, as you did in our fathers' time..."
The prayer sounded joyless and forlorn now, a worn-out formula
stumbled through by a half-crazed old man, in an all but deserted arena. Only a handful of women and children, mostly of
Hann's hearth, stood about as he repeated the familiar words;
only eighteen dancers, ten to start with and eight reliefs, waited
in the shade.

"Lead the deer under the spears of Your children..." cried
the holy man, but the spears of the Burnt Shins would lie idle if
Gronu had his way. Even as Sanu spoke and the pitiful rump of
the tribe led by Hann were preparing for the dance, Gronu's
plans were coming to fruition. Across the grasslands, toward
the flats, men of every hearth were laying out staves in two
long, converging lines, a vast funnel whose mouth lay at one
end of a low shallow valley, and whose ending was the cliffs
themselves. There was no dancing there, no ritual, but there

was joy, that wild exultation men feel when they cast off all restraint and launch themselves heedless into the unknown. There was singing there as they hammered the staves home, and the women and children sang as they paced the ground over which Gronu assured them the deer would come.

The sound of their singing did not filter down to the dancing ring where Sanu was finishing the traditional prayer to the muffled beat of the drum. With arms still raised, but with chin sunk to his chest he uttered a final appeal of his own, so low that only those nearest could hear.

"Have mercy on us, Lord, have pity on Your children!" With these words he left the ring. Still mumbling to himself he made his way to the foot of the track that led up to the ledge and his cave beyond. As Finn loped into the ring, leading the dancers at his father's side, he could see the figure of the holy man wrapped in his cloak, making his way up the hillside, his eyes cast down as though searching for something he had lost.

As the drumming increased in pace the spirits of the dancers soared. Finn felt it all around him as, spear arms raised, they began the first pass. Amidst the turmoil of recent times, the bitter words in the cave, the divisions of the tribe and all their fears for the future, here at least was comfort. It was a relief to have done with words, to take refuge in vigorous action, stamping out the old familiar steps, stalking forward, tongues clicking, or lumbering back, deerlike, as their forefathers had done since the first day. It was possible to believe in those first few moments that all would be well, in spite of everything. It was possible to believe that, if they only persisted with the dance, things could be as they had been, and that the dance would bring not only the deer, but the tribe too, their friends and brothers, coming shamefaced and laughing shyly to watch the dance and prepare the killing grounds, leaving Gronu to rave alone at the flats.

Yet even as he strained and sweated under his great deer mask Finn knew that this dance was a poor thing, at best a pale imitation of how it should be. Where there should have been twenty, ten men danced, one for each hearth, and most of them were of Hann's. Of the ten hearths of the Burnt Shins, seven were not represented save for the old men who huddled at the ring's edge. Beyond them the crowd was already thinning: in ones and twos, with feeble excuses, weak jests or vague promises to return they were melting away into the woods, streaming down to the river and the grasslands beyond.

It was always the way with the dance that one lost track of time, but it seemed to Finn that they had hardly crossed the ground a dozen times before the first dancer dropped to one knee and dipped his antlers toward the grove where the replacements waited. In time-hallowed fashion the dancers passed on, while a fresh man emerged, symbolically "slew" the weary man, and joined them as they returned. Time passed, but not enough, Finn thought, before another dropped out and was replaced, and then another, shortly after. The fourth man was not replaced. The dancers had passed on, turned and were coming back, spears held low, grunting and coughing like deer when they saw him still kneeling, still waiting. Finn glanced across at Hann; even beneath the mask he could see the concern on his father's face. Both men guessed the truth at once; the waiting dancers in the grove had gone too. It took a while to dawn on the slumped figure, who continued to look in that direction as the dancers stumbled around him. At length he staggered to his feet and tried to rejoin the dance. But his weary legs did not carry him far before he fell once more, this time to lie face down in the dust. By the time they had turned again he had crawled to the edge of the ring where an old man removed his mask and tried to revive him. As the dance progressed and the sun moved across the sky more fell, each to lie until he could crawl off, and the old man drew their cloaks over their faces as the onlookers drifted away.

By the time a fire showed on the hilltop there were only four dancers in the ring—Finn, Hann, and two more of his own

169

hearth, watched by a few old men and a scattering of women and children. As one, they turned to the other horizon to scan the distant peaks for the answering fire. Finn felt himself weakening but sustained himself with the hope that in a matter of moments fire would blossom on the other peak, proclaiming the coming of the herds. They passed across the ring again and again, each time, Finn thought, surely the last, yet still no answering beacon came. He could hear voices shouting questions or mocking the men on the heights. But still there came no signal, still they danced on. At last Hann simply stopped so abruptly that the dancers behind, taken by surprise, almost careered into him. For a moment he looked at the single column of smoke, and then walked unsteadily to the edge of the ring. Finn and the others followed, knowing the dance to be over. Here was no brandishing of spears, no jokes, no boasting; just relief that a wearisome task was done. Hann's shoulders were slumped as Finn staggered over to him. Lowering his mask to the ground, Hann strained through sweat-stung eyes to the bare hilltop.

"They've gone," was all he said. Then, "They've seen the deer and gone to join Gronu. It's time for us to move."

As they moved down to cross the river Finn saw for the first time how defections during the dance had thinned their numbers. There were old folk enough of all hearths to set up camp at the riverside, but many women, even of Hann's hearth, had gone to the flats, taking their children with them. There were only four boys to guard the funnel mouth, and many hunters, too, had taken to the woods. While Hann and Finn had led the dance a fight had broken out, and a hunter loyal to Hann had been wounded in the arm. Among the men who lined Hann's butts would be eager boys and old men who had never thought to wield a spear again.

By dawn the wind was up, and banks of cloud rolled over the horizon toward them. The wind brought the cries of gull and raven and the sound of distant hooves, and Finn and others felt the old thrill again. Sitting on the butts, Hann was glum. His sharp ears had picked out other sounds—the cries and whoops of women and children, not his, who as yet still crouched in the long grass before his killing ground, but those who followed Gronu. Finn climbed up beside him, reading his father's fears in his face, seeing how the hunters, boys and old men all around saw them too, and grew restive.

"We are enough here to kill in the old way," he said. "However many deer Gronu's people divert . . ."

"Gronu's people?" Hann interrupted. "We used to be one people."

Finn ignored this. "However many they divert the rest will still come through us . . . down to the river. When the people see what Gronu's way means, see it with their own eyes, not only in their minds, they will be sickened. Then they will see what we have done in the old way, and we will prevail."

"At what cost?" said Hann. "What's done can never be undone. Such a blasphemy once committed, what will it matter if the whole tribe comes back? What they will do will destroy us and our children for generations to come."

"But not those who are faithful," pleaded Finn, as much to his God as to his father. Hann looked at the faces down the line of butts, and across the killing ground, men looking to him for reassurance, men occupied with their spears and with their nagging thoughts—there had been other defections overnight.

"And how many are they?" he asked. "And how many will they be by the time the deer come?"

His question remained unanswered, which was answer enough. Finally he turned to his son.

"You must lead here. I have other things to attend to."

What Hann had to do that was more important than the hunt, Finn could only guess at, but there was no time for guessing. His father had dropped to the ground and gathered up his

171

spears before Finn could stop him. He jumped down after him and hissed in his ear, "If you go now, for whatever purpose, they will all leave. Look at them!"

Hann looked at the faces once more; some could not meet his eyes, others looked uncertain. "If they would have stayed with me, they will stay with you," he said.

Finn had only the vaguest inkling of what his father intended, feeling only that it must surely be futile, but there was little time for argument. "We need you!" he cried, so loud that even those across the killing ground heard him and turned from their tasks to watch.

Hann pointed with his chin to the horizon from where the sounds of the deer and the people floated on the wind. "They need me!" he said and, turning, trotted off up the rise toward the grasslands. As Finn watched him go he wondered whether Hann had meant the people or the deer.

The herds were scattering. Startled by figures who sprang up in the grass before them long before they had begun to descend to the river, the deer were now divided into two distinct groups. One, the largest, had veered away to the left and now, scattered across the tundra, spilled over the brows of low hills and down narrow valleys toward the river. They could smell the water and the forests beyond the empty killing grounds, and timeless urges—to feed, to rut, and to shelter from the Winter—drove them on. The others, driven by fear away from where their instincts urged them, had turned to the right. There, packed ever tighter by the moment, their leaders entered the mouth of the funnel that led to the flats. Hundreds followed, long columns of gray, white, and brown maddened by fear, driven onward by the wild shrieking figures that threatened on either side.

Behind the rows of stakes that formed the funnel, men, women and boys of all hearths, even some of Hann's, yelled and cheered as the deer raced past toward its narrow neck. Waving cloaks and rattling the shafts of redundant spears they urged the prey on to their destruction, calling Gronu's praises to the sky and shouting across the backs of the frantic deer to friends on the other side. In all the dust, noise and confusion of the herd's headlong flight no one noticed the solitary figure who, having come up from the river, now followed the line of stakes down to the cliff's edge.

Down at Hann's killing ground, Finn sat on the butts where his father had squatted before, his cloak wrapped closer round him now because of the wind. Now and again he would look up at the faces of the few who remained. Since Hann had gone there had been a steady trickle of defectors. The first had been a group of women who had hailed Hann as he passed and, receiving no answer, had come down to the butts to collect their menfolk. The first few hunters had offered Finn their excuses, even urged him to come with them. He had ignored them, staring through them, knowing all was lost. As he looked now at the few that remained he could read their minds. He knew the question each man was asking himself, "Can a whole *people* be wrong?" He knew that when the deer came to Hann's killing ground there would be no women and children to drive them, no spears to meet them at the river; those who avoided Gronu's trap would have safe passage to the forests.

Gronu's trap was long; it had taken the stakes of all the old killing grounds, and new, improvised ones, to lay the route to the flat rocky ledge before the cliffs. Before they could plunge to their deaths the deer had to crowd and jostle down a winding lane of staves that followed the line of a fold in the ground, cheered on and pelted all the way by the whole tribe. At the funnel's neck the ground was too hard for stakes. It was here that the bulk of the hunters waited. Here was the point of maximum danger; if the plan could go wrong it would go wrong here. Seeing the drop ahead, the leading deer could veer suddenly left or right, break out from the trap along the cliff's edge and then race down to the river where the rest of the herd would be crossing. Gronu had seen the danger and placed lines

173

of hunters from the end of the funnel to the very cliff's edge, leaving the deer no way to go but forward, no choice but death on the rocks below. As they heard the deer approaching there was a stir among the hunters; they crouched and braced their spears, pointing them inward on both sides of the trap, an impassable fence. Necks craned, eyes strained in toward the grasslands, up toward the bend round which the deer would appear at any moment.

Finn was sitting alone now. One old man had stayed with him to the last, saying nothing, leaning on a spear he was too weak to throw. Neither had been able to offer the other any comfort, and when Finn had slumped forward with his head on his arms the old man had shrugged, let fall his spear, and climbed wearily up toward the flats. Young men can please themselves, feed themselves, the old must go where the food is.

The head of the column had reached the flats. Eyes staring, backs steaming, they tumbled forward, driven on by terror and the ceaseless press from behind. Their feet clattered on the stone, they saw the way ahead, saw the drop, turned this way and that in their frenzy, but spears hedged them in and the herd behind drove them on. The men at either side laughed and howled at the spectacle, drunk at the prospect of such easy meat. In no longer time than it took to skin three deer there would be enough meat to feed the tribe now and through the Winter. Yet even as the hunters on the river side of the trap dreamed of the feasting to come, something unforeseen shook their ranks. Men were bowled over from behind, others were sent sprawling by a clubbed hand or swinging spear shaft. The line was broken and out onto the rock ledge, in the path of the oncoming herd, ran a familiar figure, broad-chested, dark-locked and with a beard as wide as a hand's span. Only Hann could have broken through a double line of the strongest hunters in the tribe, only Hann could have reached the cliff's edge before the panic-stricken deer. As he stood directly in

174

their way, waving his cloak and mouthing unheard words, the scattered men tried to restore their line, some shaking their fists at him, others lying dazed or cursing him through bloody teeth. The deer, confronted by this new threat to their front, veered away to their left where a straggling line had been reformed. Spears were leveled once more, a few were thrown, and as one the deer turned again. Hann still waved and shouted, noiseless above the din, striving hopelessly to drive them from the precipice. He stood there for what seemed an age, ignoring or not hearing the warning cries of those still well disposed to him, with certain death at his back and irresistible force ahead. A few bucks crashed past him, eyes glazed and nostrils flaring as they trod empty air and began the plunge. Then two immediately to his front tried to turn, collided with others, skidded and fell. They slid kicking and struggling toward him, trying to rise, with others already attempting to climb or leap over them driven on by the pressure from behind. Distracted by the horror to either side Hann hardly seemed to notice the danger to his front. When at last he saw the welter of hooves and antlers rolling in on him, it was too late. There was no way out, no time to move—he was still shouting as they bore him over the brink.

Down past the killing grounds, the leaders of the main herd were already nosing their way out into midstream. Behind them in long columns the deer streamed down to the river's edge past the piles of turf that had for generations meant death for their kind. No spears flashed, no hunters laughed and cheered as they made their way toward the river and the forests, oblivious to the fate of their fellows at the flats. Before the killing ground that had been Hann's. A few women and children started up from the grass, causing momentary panic, but those deer who turned between the lines of stakes had an untroubled passage down to the water. A solitary hunter was there, sitting on the butts, his head in his arms, his spear thrust point-down in the turf, not even watching as they raced past. After they had gone the women and children who had run down to cheer on the men stopped short, saw the bare earth of the empty killing ground and the silent unresponding figure on the butt, and turned sadly for the flats.

At the foot of the cliffs below the flats the whole tribe danced and capered among the bodies of more dead deer than any man had ever seen. The stones were blood-spattered and the deer lay in heaps, piled so high in places that it seemed a man might climb the cliffs on their corpses. Does, bucks, fawns, all lay mingled, some crushed beyond recognition, some still kicking. Many were useless, so mangled as to be fit only for broth; many more would have been spared at the killing grounds, the does and the yearlings. Yet amid the carnage there was only rejoicing at the prospect of the coming feast so cheaply won. Gronu, his bear cloak flung back to reveal his scarred shoulder and strong arms, stood on a boulder directing the butchery. Everywhere men and women were dragging the best carcasses from the heaps of slain, frantically ear-marking all they could, racing against time and their neighbors to lay claim to their portion. Arguments broke out; where each man's claim was as good as another's, Gronu's judgment was in constant demand, and his companions raced to and fro making decisions and allotting portions on his behalf. The unity of the drive had given way to discord, and they bickered like ravens over their carrion. Only one corner of the field remained untouched. There the ravens themselves held sway, strutting and preening on the mounds of carcasses. There, some hunters of Hann's hearth, late arrivals at the slaughter, had stood for some time watching a single human arm that protruded from the tangle of furred limbs, heads and antlers. They had waited, uncertain what to do, distracted by the cries of their comrades urging them to lose no time in cutting up the kill. At last the lure of fresh meat and the ancient fear of hunger proved too strong;

one by one they drifted away though with many a guilty backward glance.

If, as they skinned and butchered, any of them noticed Finn's arrival, few showed any sign of it. Finn himself was too appalled at the sight that greeted him to notice the way their eyes avoided his, or how they hurried away at his approach. He wandered as though in a dream, trailing his spear behind him. "We must become like beasts so we can continue to live like men"; so he had told himself at every hunt. But what beasts could have made this random slaughter? So many of the carcasses were useless—killed at the wrong season, and in such a manner! Annu had given them the hunting to make men live together, work together; from the hunting came their rituals, their customs, everything that placed them apart. But this had been murder, not hunting, and far from bringing men together had caused the discord and the fighting that now raged all around him. Finn thought of the Winter to come, of the arguments that would not be resolved and the resentments that would continue to simmer. What kind of a life lay ahead for them all, what would their rituals mean now, and having become beasts this time, not beasts of prey but scavengers, would they ever be men again?

Finn seemed not to recognize the faces that surrounded him, changed as they were by fear and greed and something else. He searched the crowd for some sign of his father, fearing to find a man driven mad by what his people had become, but in need nonetheless of his comforting presence. Here and there in the crowd he came upon faces he seemed to know—Gronu's face clouding for an instant before turning sharply away; Shani's face pale and shocked, about to speak before being tugged away by her mother—but of Hann there was no sign, no word. He was already making for the place all others were avoiding when Laela found him. She and her second husband had been skinning a beast close by and as Finn passed she broke off and stopped him. Their eyes met for an instant then hers flickered over to the pile of carcasses topped with ravens, and Finn knew at once what had happened.

"He tried to stop them," she said. Finn nodded, seeing for the first time the human flesh among the fur and bone.

"Where's Mata?" he asked.

Laela shook her head. "She was with us at the drive, and when we went down to the killing ground. We called to you but you didn't answer..." Her words trailed off—there was nothing more to be said.

Saying simply "Help me" and crossing over to where his father's body lay, Finn began to haul aside the dead deer. He did not look back to see whether Laela followed, but within moments she and her family were beside him. The horror of it all was more than Finn could bear; he performed the task as though in a trance, straightening the shattered limbs and covering with his own cloak the bloody mask of a face. Still numb, he rose when his work was done and saying to Laela, "Keep the ravens from him," he strode off through the crowds, out of that awful place and down to a copse by the river to cut saplings.

As Finn built a frame to carry his father's body to the burial place, the people dragged the best carcasses down to the camp they had made in the shadow of the cliffs. He cut the saplings and bound them with sinew, hearing in the distance the strains of the familiar feasting songs and seeing the glow of the high-banked fires light the darkening horizon. At the place of slaughter only the children of Laela remained, crouching uneasily among the bones and bloody corpses and casting stones at ravens that threatened the body of their dead leader. Only they saw the lone figure who stood on the clifftop above, wrapped in the flawed white cloak her son had given her on a day such as this years before. Only they saw her lift her face to the sky, saw the tears course down her scarred cheeks as she mourned the man who lay below among the deer he had loved. They heard odd words of her chant carried down to them on the wind, an eerie sound that made them almost forget their mother's words and flee down to the warmth and safety of the camp. At last, her song finished, they saw her spread her arms as though she would embrace the sky, then step forward from the cliff. She fell among the bones a stone's throw from her husband. The younger child cried, but his brother crept forward. Afraid to touch her he arranged her bloody cloak as best he could, flung a piece of bone at a hovering raven, and prayed for Finn to return.

▲   ▲   ▲

Nervously Finn twitched the curtain that covered the mouth of Sanu's cave. He glanced over his shoulder to where Laela and her family waited in the dark with the sled bearing Hann's and Mata's bodies; they had come across the river to bury them with their ancestors. For some time now they had called to the old man, knowing from the sound of his chanting that he was in there and alive. Finn twitched the curtain once more; getting no response he crouched to enter the cave. It was an awesome step. Few men had ever been allowed within the cave though Hann had, and as his heir Finn supposed he had the right. The cave inside was dimly lit by a small oil lamp in front of which sat Sanu. He seemed not to see Finn but stared ahead of him singing softly to himself. As he drew nearer and his eyes grew accustomed to the gloom, Finn could see that the cave was littered with ritual objects, some familiar to him, others whose significance he could only guess. The old man was unkempt and grimy, and Finn felt sure he had been sitting there since he had returned from the dancing ring two days earlier.

For a while he sat patiently, waiting for Sanu to speak or at least indicate that he had seen him. But he waited in vain. At last Finn moved closer until he faced the old man across the light, and spoke. Softly, so as not to startle him he whispered,

179

"Sanu, my father and mother are dead. They need your prayers to assist them to the dreamworld."

There was no reply. The holy man's eyes remained fixed on a point on the wall behind Finn's head. Neither by sign nor gesture did he hint that he had heard.

Finn went on more urgently, "There is no hearth to mourn them, no tribe to assist at their rites. There are only we few outside. We need you now as never before." Still there was no response; Sanu was no longer in this world and, watching him, Finn wondered if he would ever return. A phrase the old man had used of Hann's child, years before, came now into his mind. "He liked it there, so he stayed." Finn looked about him, wondering if there was anything he could do to help the old man. Seeing that there was not, and feeling too that Sanu was more to be envied than pitied at such a time as this, he crawled from the cave.

They buried Hann and Mata by torchlight beside their son, with food, clothes and weapons according to custom. Laela sang the chant for the dead, while her husband helped Finn lay the stones in place. Her children looked longingly over their shoulders toward the river, where even now hunters were dragging fresh meat up to the ledge. The rituals done, Finn stood a long time before the cave mouth, remembering the last time he had been there on a day that had held so much promise for him. He had sworn then to bring them comfort, to grow to be worthy of them and to do them honor. Instead he had brought death upon them and destruction on their people, and now, with this sad inglorious burial, even in death he had failed them. He was shedding bitter tears when Laela laid her hand upon his shoulder. Finn turned to her, nodded to where her husband already waited on the track that led down to the ledge.

"You must go," he said. "You have done enough, lost enough already being here while they. . ."—he spat this last word to the wind—"divide the spoils."

Laela took him by the arm and tried to tug him away from

the cave mouth. "You must come too. There is nothing further to do here."

Finn shook her arm off, and turned once more to face the cave. "I can never go back."

"But you must! To lead your father's hearth..." Before Laela could say another word Finn had turned back. Casting his eyes around the space before the cave where once the whole tribe would have gathered he muttered, "What hearth?"

When Laela and her family had descended the slope and he was alone at last, he sat at the mouth of the cave, composed his lament for Hann and Mata and, that done, sang it to the stars. He sang of the deeds of Hann, who had been a father and a teacher to his hearth, who had walked all his life in the ways of his ancestors, who had loved the Reindeer more than life itself; and of Mata, who had led her people at the drive and at the feasting, who had not turned away, in her grief, for the orphan and the outcast, whose whole life had been lived in praise of Annu. He sang in grief at the passing of Hann and Mata, who had been all the world to each other and to him, who in life and death had been as one, and whose children had brought only sorrow into their lives. At last, weakened by hunger and fatigue, he laid himself on the cold stones of their grave, and prayed that the dawn might never come.

CHAPTER

TEN

▴ ▴ ▴
▴ ▴

STANDING WHERE HE HAD STOOD that day when he had returned from his first talk with Sanu, Finn watched the activity on the ledge below. On that day, so distant now, the old man had described to him the workings of an ordered world, whose foundations were respect for tradition and love of their God's creation. Now that world had come apart—respect had died, their God was forgotten, and the old man had fled this world despairing. Yet to look at the scene below he would never have guessed that such things had come about. Below was rejoicing as parties of hunters arrived dragging bloody carcasses up from across the river, or new parties set off to the slaughter ground. Smoke-houses were being erected on every available open space and were starting to sprout along even the edges of the scree where the women and girls squatted scraping skins. Beside each group was a mountain of pelts. Some, piled too high, had already toppled and slid down the scree where they lay unregarded. Already there were more skins than the tribe could use in a year. Even as they worked, men at the place of slaughter were skinning more. Armfuls of meat were being loaded into

183

bulging smoke-houses or, as these filled up, stacked in rows among the tents until someone could think of what to do with them. At every moment or so it seemed, more carcasses arrived from the river, each carrying party being greeted with shouts of acclamation and another outburst of singing in praise of Gronu.

At length a flurry of activity at the far end of the ledge and a tremor of excitement running down the lines of tents, proclaimed that Gronu himself was coming up from the river. Work was abandoned, skins cast aside, meat dropped to lie where it fell, and the people flocked to greet him as he emerged at the head of the track, carried shoulder-high by his comrades. Finn strode to the edge of the trees the better to see this triumphal entry, and those immediately below him saw him for the first time. As they called to him, urging him to come down and join them, Finn looked at their faces. There were some there from Hann's hearth, though most were flocking to the far end to greet Gronu. Laela was there, beckoning, and Shani too, though she stood apart regarding him solemnly.

Still they called to him, still he did not reply—he was looking on their faces for the last time. Seeing him unmoved, they shrugged and left to swell the much bigger crowd that thronged around Gronu and his companions. When Gronu had gained the center of the camp, Finn turned away, shouldered his bedroll and his father's spears, and began his descent into the forest.

Where he intended to go and what he meant to do he had no idea. He did not know whether he meant to die or simply live alone. He only knew that he could no longer bear human company, or live with either his memories of how things had been or the reality of how they were. At the valley bottom he turned to his right, upstream, deeper into the forests, the way Hann had led him years before. The forests were full of deer, fewer though than in former years; the herds had not recovered, and the slaughter at the flats had thinned them still further. They too were on the move deeper into the forests, but Finn

184

hardly noticed them. Soon the exhaustion of the past few days caught up with him; his accustomed lope trailed off into a stumbling walk. He became aware of the dark shape of the Sacred Mountain across the stream to his left, and reflected on how bitterly it had fulfilled its promise to him. On first leaving the camp he had thought of going there to die. But now he knew his only wish was to remove his accursed presence from the tribe and everything that belonged to it. If he could take at least part of Annu's wrath upon himself, he might yet do something to help the people his father had loved. For himself he found it hard to love them, remembering how they had deserted Hann, but for Hann's sake he would do it. That night he sheltered in the trees from the wolves who now ranged the woods, and at dawn he continued his course upstream. The next day he killed a doe, and cooked the meat over a small fire under the branches of a fallen pine. He ate sparingly, slept fitfully, and in the morning moved on, leaving the carcass half-consumed.

On the fourth day he thought he smelled snow in the wind blowing up the valley from the grasslands. It was early for snow —even the seasons were in turmoil now that the tribe had turned the world on its head. By nightfall he was stumbling forward in a blizzard, snow coating his hood and cloak and dragging at his legs. He sat down with his back to a tree to brush the snow from his shoulders and tighten his leggings. Where he was he no longer knew—it was impossible to see any farther than he could spit—he knew only that he had wandered away from the stream and into the foothills. He grew weary and his mind began to wander, but he knew that to sleep here would be fatal so he dragged himself to his feet and stumbled on. The wind blew stronger, so strong at times as almost to send him sprawling, yet he felt warm, and threw back the folds of his cloak. He tripped, and finding himself on his knees in the snow, clutched handfuls of it to his chest to cool himself. As he rose and floundered on it seemed he heard voices calling to him on the wind. He knew the voices, and knew in the same moment that he was dying. Here was Annu's will at last revealed, here the relief he had longed for. It grew unbearably hot and he let fall his spears and bedroll, and tugged at the neck of his cloak. His numb fingers wrenched at the cord until he was free of it at last. It was quiet now, ahead was light. It was the light of a Spring morning, and he knew that in that light or beyond it waited Hann and Mata, Venn and the sick boy who had been his first friend. He tried to step forward, tottered childlike, swayed, recovered then sat down sharply in the snow. Laughing, he called to them to come to him, help him to his feet. Then he opened his arms and gave himself up to death.

▲　　▲　　▲

The darkness receded reluctantly and only a moment before the warm, soft light. It battled with the shadows, creating fantastic shapes and bringing to his mind a small boy, he had forgotten who or when, who had stared at a sky and made pictures from the clouds. He tried to cling to the boy, but his image faded, the light faltered, and the darkness held sway once more.

The second time the light was stronger. It had cleared itself a place in the center of the world, banishing the darkness to the fringes from where it constantly threatened. He remembered another such light, summoning a man from his boyhood's tomb. He doubted if he could rise now. If he had a body he could not feel it. All there was was the light and the darkness, which was starting to encroach once more. Just before it swallowed him again, he heard a curse, a little, muffled curse.

With the third awakening came remembrance; childhood, manhood, hunting and feasting, family and friends. Yet all of it seemed somehow remote as though it had been finished with long ago, and none of it mattered. This, then, was the dream-world where nothing mattered. Then why the curse? He re-

186

membered the curse just as a hand slipped behind his head and drew him into the light, hurting his eyes. A face he knew looked down at him, though not a face he had expected. He wanted to laugh and ask her how *she* came to be here. But as his cracked lips tried to form the words a raven croaked feebly. Shani shook her head and lifted him higher, holding to his lips a steaming bowl. Its contents seared his lips and he gasped— that raven's croak again! Another curse; she dropped his head and he heard her blowing furiously into the bowl. Then she lifted him once more and fed him, bitter broth made with bark. Warmth flooded his body, pain racked his limbs—now he knew he had a body. The bowl drained, he tried once more to speak, but she held a finger to his lips, and after wiping broth from his beard and lips, laid him back more gently this time. His eyelids drooped and closed as she crawled back to the fire she had been struggling with all day. He slept while she banked it with small sticks, tending it with as much care as if the flames contained his very soul and she were feeding life into him.

"It kept going out . . ." She was chattering now, and he was wrapped in her cloak and propped against the cave wall. "There was no dry wood or not much, and I didn't have time to grab kindling, you left the camp in such a hurry. My mother . . ." she paused for a moment, swallowed, then continued, "My mother always scolded me for not listening when she told us how to build fires in the wet, but I used to say 'What use is that, the way we live now?' And anyway there are always people to light fires. Well, there always *were!*"

For the first time in a long time Finn felt the urge to laugh, but she did not seem to notice, and prattled on.

". . . And anyway I was exhausted from dragging you here, and following you for days on end, and sleeping up in trees, and not eating except for that doe you left. And then you had to go and decide to die in the snow. Like that old man—do you remember him?—the year all the smoke-houses blew over in

187

the wind, and he decided it was his time and threw off his cloak and went up to the mountain, and everyone said what a beautiful thing it was. I could never see any sense in it myself."

Now he did laugh, weakly, to himself, and straightaway felt guilty, as though laughter should have died with Hann and Mata. Shani seemed brighter and happier now than he had seen her since before Venn died. She scarcely looked at him as she turned the stones in the fire and talked on, as much for her own benefit as his. It was her old self talking, as though she had been silenced for years and was now miraculously restored to speech. As he watched her and listened, Finn wondered what had brought this about. Did she feel that by saving his life she had somehow undone what had happened all those years ago on the mountain? Could she really believe that by this she could appease their God? It was not yet his time to die, that much was clear. Since it was true that nothing happened that was not Annu's will, then she must surely have been His instrument. Yet what purpose He could have in preserving Finn's worthless life he could not fathom, unless it was to torment him further.

At least, it seemed, he had drawn her away from the tribe, and it might be that they could take God's anger on themselves. Even so, he thought, that was little enough to justify her mood. Even if much of her chatter seemed forced, like a child's singing in the dark, there was no mistaking a feeling on her part that she had been relieved of some great burden. There would come a time soon, he knew, when he would have to explain all this to her. But for the moment he was too weak and content to lie back on the skins and doze, lulled by the sound of her voice.

By the fifth day he was strong enough to tend the fire, propped on one elbow, while she went out to check her traps. She was away for most of the day and he began to grow concerned, was even considering crawling to the cave mouth when she returned, a hare swinging at her belt. She smiled seeing him upright and so far from the skin where she had laid him, and flung the hare nonchalantly down beside him.

"You men think you can do *everything!*" she said warming herself by the fire.

Finn smiled as he began skinning. "How many traps?" he asked.

"Five." Rubbing her arms and legs, she looked over at him and saw that, engrossed in his work, he was still smiling.

"Ten really!" she added.

She ate only sparingly, leaving the greater part of the meat for him, and filling herself up with the remains of the broth. Draining the dregs, she pulled a face. "You must get strong quickly and go out after deer, I cannot face much more of this. Your spears are by the cave mouth. I brought them back yesterday from where you fell."

Finn could remember nothing of where he had lain down to die, nor did he care where his spears might be. If Annu had ordained that he live on then so be it. He would make no further attempts on his own life. But neither, when he looked within himself, could he find any great desire to sustain it. Shani seemed to assume as a matter of course that he would soon go out to hunt for them both. Yet, for Finn, to take up his spears once more would be an act of faith, a recognition on his part that their lives were worth sustaining. Shani had already made such a profession, dragging him through the snow to a place of shelter, chafing life into his frozen limbs, dragging him slowly back from the death he had been seeking. To nurture life at all costs, knowing its value, that was her women's wisdom; his was to question its worth. Shani had acted according to her nature and he could see the sense of it, though doubt still nagged at him.

Later, revived by the fire and the hot food, Shani was telling him more of how she had trailed him from the camp. "I didn't sleep much either. I had to be sure of waking before you so as to follow you. Of course it got easier when the snows came, I could follow your tracks. . . ."

"Why did you do it?" he interrupted suddenly. "Why did you follow me?"

"It was in your face when you left, what you meant to do. So I followed you to prevent it." She raised the bowl to her lips.

"But why? What could it matter?"

She lowered the bowl, grimaced, and said, "Once on the mountain you gave me life. I simply returned the gift."

"And bitter gifts they both were..." he muttered staring into the fire, avoiding her eyes. "It were better that neither of us had been born than that we should have lived to bring this calamity on the tribe."

Shani shrugged. "Even so the debt is paid. If you seek death no doubt you will find it."

He quoted the old prayer, "I fear it not, I have faith in the life to come."

She snorted. "So do I, but *I'm* content to wait. If you want to die, give me the hare. *I* don't."

Suddenly, with a piece of meat halfway to his mouth, Finn felt foolish. He lowered his head, regretting his lofty tone. Taking pity on him she crept nearer, and whispered in his ear, "There were other reasons. Reasons why I *had* to leave."

Finn looked up and she went on. "Gronu is leader now of all the hearths. The people's hearts are full of him, their tongues all sing of his wisdom, in their eyes he can do no wrong. Even on the day you left I saw how he looked at me, and how my family looked at *him*. The people will refuse him nothing now, and my family will want to bind themselves closer to him. And so I followed you."

Finn was intrigued now. "Would it have been so bad? You felt something for him once."

"Once maybe..." —she spat—"now I hate him!"

Even remembering her aversion to the various suitors who had been pressed upon her, Finn was taken back by her vehemence.

"You don't understand," he said softly, "he is our victim too,

190

as much as any of the tribe. If what has happened is the result of what took place on the mountain, then he cannot be blamed. He is merely the instrument of Annu's wrath."

To his surprise she laughed. It was a weary, sad laugh. When she spoke she could scarcely conceal the contempt in her voice. "I don't understand? You, who know nothing and understand nothing, can tell *me* that!"

Finn was about to explain further when she closed her eyes, leaned back against the cave wall and began to speak once more.

Her brow furrowed as though she were reciting by memory an oft-repeated tale, but what she told him that night had never been heard by another living soul, and never would. The telling of it pained her, Finn could see that, but it brought her comfort too, to be unburdened of it at last. She spoke quietly and fast, as though she were talking in her sleep, but Finn knew, as her story unfolded, that it was no dream. No one could have dreamed such a story as this—the mere telling of which changed his world more completely than anything had done since the night Mata had welcomed him into her arms. At times as she talked he cried out, struck the ground feebly with his fists, even tried to reach out to silence her, but she seemed not to notice. When her story was at last finished she slumped back against the wall and seemed to sleep, and the fire burned low as Finn lay back and grappled with what he had heard.

In the brief time she had spoken Shani had upset his vision of the world. Even in all the agony of what had happened, Finn had felt that he at least understood it and what lay behind it; now even that had proved illusory. The truths she had revealed had brought Finn little comfort, merely replacing old fears with new and worse, but they had transformed him. He was no longer the man who had sat raving in the blizzard, arms spread to welcome death. That man *had* died, not in the snow but here in the cave while Shani talked; with him had died the guilt that had been his torment. Thus, as the fire fell away to ashes, a man who had begun the day uncaring whether he lived or died, now fought with the ghastly images that crowded his brain, anxious to sleep and to conserve his strength.

Shani awoke to the sight of a cold hearth beside an empty bed space. She stretched and shivered, and saw in the gray dawn's light Finn sitting at the cave mouth, tightening the binding on one of his spears. He was still pale, his limbs still bore the scars of the frost, and his hands shook as he worked. Yet as he turned to face her she saw in his eyes that which she had feared never to see again. She smiled and crept over to him.

"You are going to hunt?" She hardly dared ask the question.

"First to hunt..." He nodded, and she beamed as much at the prospect of fresh deer meat as at his change of mood. His next words removed her smile. "And then I am going back."

"Then you go alone," she whispered.

Finn looked at her astonished until she explained, "I will not go back. My family will marry me to Gronu, whatever I say. He will have me, by force if necessary. As it was done in ancient times. But either way with my parents' consent. And so I say, if you go back you go alone."

"You need not fear him," insisted Finn, "I'll be with you!"

"And what will you do?"

"What Laela would have had me do. Lead my father's hearth. Show the people the error of their ways."

She turned on him angrily. "Will they listen? What will have changed them from what they were ten days ago? Tell me!"

Finn could find no answer. In his tired, weakened state, she could see he had not thought things through. More patiently now she explained, "If you go back and if you speak out—and knowing what I have told you could you stay silent?—they would turn on you as they did before. They would pelt you, mock you, call you outsider."

Finn blushed for shame at the memory. It hurt her to say these things to him, but she knew that she must at all costs dissuade him from going back.

"They might even kill you, in their present madness, as they would have done the day Venn died. The things you know can never be told."

Finn was still defiant. "But I can tell them what my father would have told them. I can try again where I failed before—in the Council."

Shani shook her head. "Their bellies are full and their hearts are full of Gronu. They would say you spoke through jealousy or bitterness at your father's death. Besides, Gronu would see to it that you never spoke . . . he fears you."

Finn was shocked at this last remark. Shani struggled to hide the irritation in her voice as she explained, "He fears you because he knows that only you can match his strength, and he envies the knowledge passed on to you by Hann. That alone would make you his enemy. You now are his only rival." That they both understood the full meaning of this showed in the look that passed between them.

"He does well to fear me," grunted Finn, cutting himself a length of twine.

Shani nodded. "But now is not the time to challenge him. You are not strong enough, not even armed with what I have told you. This is *his* time. One day perhaps yours will come."

Glancing across at her as he worked on his spear, Finn marveled at the change that had come over her in the years since that day on the mountain. In that time, during which hardly a word had passed between them, that spoiled, willful child who had been at once the delight and despair of them all had become a woman, with a wisdom beyond her years. The feckless, carefree girl who had haunted his dreams and his solitary moments had grown watchful, learned to read men's faces and see into their hearts. The old Shani was still there, prattling by the fire as she stirred the broth, lying cheerfully about her prowess with the traps, but tempered now by bitter experience and both their cruel fates. He could see that what she said was true.

When he looked at her again there were tears in her eyes. "For now," she said, "the people have made their choice, and I fear it will bring them much sorrow. Not yet, not this year, perhaps not for many years to come. Great wrongs have been done, but not by us alone. We have suffered..." She looked around her. "We suffer now, and so in time must they. That, I fear, is the will of Annu."

His spear finished, Finn laid it down. Using the wall for support he hauled himself to his feet and stood at the mouth of the cave, staring out at the snow-covered valley. The voice behind him sounded less certain now.

"What will become of us?" she was saying. "And how will we live? You can hunt the deer now, but in the Spring when they go down past the camp and over the river... where will we go then?"

Finn was only half listening as he peered between the trunks of the pines to where the stream wandered, following it as far as his eye could see up to its source. He was thinking of a far-off valley, silent now, but which had once echoed to the sound of his father's laughter.

"I know where," he said.

CHAPTER
ELEVEN

▲ ▲ ▲
▲ ▲

Kɴᴇᴇ ᴅᴇᴇᴘ ɪɴ sɴᴏᴡ, Finn leaned on his spear, gazing down on a land he had not seen for many years. The snowfall had re-shaped it, creating new hills and valleys that would melt away in the Spring, but there was no mistaking the line of the stream buried now under snow and ice or the shape of the mountains beyond. Here it was that he had first stood with his father, discovering a new land and a new life, apprehensive, but full of hope for the future. Now he was back; the future was as bleak as the Winter landscape that stretched before him, and the new life had proved an illusion. For what was this valley, he asked himself, as he scanned the silent forests, but another bolt-hole? Now, in his eighteenth Winter, almost at the mid-point of his life, he was again running and hiding. Even so, the sight of this familiar ground, like the face of an old friend, lifted his sagging spirits, while a sound from behind dispelled his bitter thoughts.

Loaded down with sleeping mats, bowls and kindling Shani was struggling up the slope to join him. In the five days' journey from the cave she had never yet managed to find a way of carrying them comfortably, and her complaints and curses had been a constant background noise to their laborious trek through the snow. She arrived out of breath, threw down the mats and sat on them. One of the bowls began to slip from the skin bag around her neck, and she struggled to stuff it away. Finn tried to stop himself from smiling, and seeing this she resumed her complaint.

"I don't see why you can't carry some of this!"

"I have told you. I need to keep my spear arm free," he repeated patiently. "If we come across deer..."

"Deer! Ha!" She threw the bag away from her with a curse. "We left the last deer behind days ago!"

Finn smiled. "You will see. You have been so patient, don't spoil it now!"

Shani ignored this gibe, and continued to complain under her breath. He slipped down the bank a little to examine some tracks a stone's throw away.

"Come and see this!" he called, and reluctantly she hauled herself to her feet, and slid down the bank toward him. Finn indicated the tracks. "Fox!" he said. He had been teaching her to recognize the tracks of the forest animals.

Shani seemed unimpressed. "Can we eat it?" Finn shook his head. "Then don't bother me with it," she replied and flounced back up to the mats.

Finn laughed. It was not the first time he had laughed during this journey; she was teaching him, too. He climbed back up the hill to join her.

Finn's joy on seeing this valley once again was not shared by Shani, who viewed it for the first time. "This is a wilderness," she said as he threw himself down beside her. "How many days must we starve here before you admit you were wrong and turn back?"

"We shan't be turning back. These forests are full of deer, finer, fatter deer than you have ever seen." She looked at him doubtfully. "Why even now you might hear them..." he laughed, "if you could stay silent long enough!"

196

Later, as they descended into the valley, even Finn began to have his doubts. The forest seemed ominously silent. He struggled to remember exactly where he had first seen deer all those years before. It suddenly seemed possible that whatever had blighted the grassland herds could have struck this smaller one too, that Shani in her ignorance had spoken the truth and they would have to struggle back the way they had come, to face starvation. Sensing his fears, noticing that he became more irritable by the moment, she ceased her teasing and trudged along behind him in silence. They had put the stream well behind them and were climbing the gentle slope on the far side of the valley when Finn first heard an unmistakable sound. Still struggling and shifting her burden, Shani had missed it; but seeing his raised hand she stopped and listened. Now she too heard it—the cough of a deer followed by a series of grunts and the sound of heavy, furry footfalls in the snow. Finn turned, beckoned her to shed her load and follow in his footsteps. It was hard to move silently in the snow, but the wind in the trees and the noise from up ahead masked their approach. Crawling up to where Finn lay at the crest of a fold in the ground, Shani saw a sight that caused her heart to leap. Across a patch of open ground just out of spear range was a group of five deer. Just as she snuggled into the snow beside Finn, a large buck broke away. Even now, thinned by the exertion of the rut, its antlers shed, it was the finest buck she had ever seen. No beast like this had ever run through the killing grounds by the river, not even in the memories of old men. Beyond, a fawn tugged at a patch of lichen from which its mother had just driven the buck; like the grassland deer, these does retained their antlers after the males had shed, giving them the dominance they needed to secure the best feeding for their young. Shani watched them in silence for a while, enjoying the beauty of the scene, the gray and brown of their sleek coats against the snow, and the way their breath blew up in clouds as they browsed at the patch of green they had cleared.

"Is it here where the strongest come?" she whispered, unconsciously echoing Finn's first question of years ago.

"These deer never saw the river, or the grasslands," he answered in his father's words, then adding for himself, "these are *our* deer!"

By the time Finn killed the buck it was dusk and, as the pelt steamed in the snow, the sun stained the whole valley blood red. It was the first time he had seen the sun in many days, and it seemed to him, as he dragged the carcass back to where he had left Shani, to be a good omen. Shani had not been idle in his absence. On their long march she had become adept at improvising shelter. A lively fire guided him in to where she had set up camp in the angle between the hillside and a fallen pine. She had cleared the snow where they would lie, packing it on either side, and stretched her cloak and bedroll overhead for a roof. Inside the two of them would be dry and warm, with the fire at the door to ward off wolves.

They ate ravenously, even licking the spits and the bowls where the fat had dripped. The cold meat they had brought with them from Finn's last kill had run out days before, and the hot fresh meat in their stomachs brought that euphoria that seized people at the feasts. His own fears forgotten now, Finn teased Shani about her doubts and she replied in kind, praising the wisdom of the deer whose women ruled till the Spring. In the heat from the fire, reflected off the polished snow on either side, they grew drowsy and at last ate lazily from the same spit. Shani had fallen silent now. The only sounds were the crackling of the fire and the sighing of the wind outside. Finn leaned forward to stoke the fire, and when he turned he saw that she had been watching him. What he saw in her eyes pleased him; he had read many things there before, affection, sometimes laughter, most often pity. But now, at last, he felt he had earned her respect. Not that he would have guessed it from the way she talked. Looking round the shelter she began to complain once

more about the things she had to carry, and chided him, laughingly, for his bad temper as they had descended into the valley.

He did not attempt to reply but sat smiling as she chattered.
Her hair was tousled from her fight with the branches of the
tree, and without thinking he reached out to smooth it. At
once she fell silent, not resisting when his hand strayed down to
the softness of her neck. Gently she took his hand and laid it
on her shoulder beneath her smock. As children of the camp,
life held few secrets for them, and they had both known that
this moment would come. The time for shyness between them
was long past and they came together untroubled by guilt or
fear. Outside, the wolves grew bolder, drawn by the kill despite
the fire and the unaccustomed scent of Man. Poised for flight,
they tugged at the carcass that hung from a branch, and lapped
the bloody snow beneath, casting nervous eyes at the small
shelter nearby whose occupants no longer thought of them or
cared.

The cave was halfway up a small snow-filled valley down
which in Spring a small rivulet would run to feed the stream
below. From there Finn could scour the valley floor in search of
prey or explore the grasslands high in the mountains, and still
return before dark. The cave was not lofty like the great cave at
home—they still talked of "home"—but it was high enough for
Finn to stand upright and small enough to be warmed by a
single large fire. Below the snow and ice was fresh water, and
the surrounding forests were filled with deer, so they thrived
despite the bitter cold. Killing enough for their meager needs
took up but little of Finn's time, yet even so the Winter passed
quickly. They would spent whole days sitting at the cave
mouth; he making tools from bone or antler or refining the flint
heads he had roughed out the previous year, she preparing the
kill or making cups and bowls from the odd-shaped lumps of
wood she found when out gathering. At night, by firelight,
Finn would tell her of the things he had learned from the deer

or the places he had discovered while out hunting, while she worked on the skins for the tent they would need when the snows receded and the deer began to wander.

Spring caught them unaware, heralded one morning by the sound of rushing water outside the cave. Ice blocks were breaking up and the rivulet became a torrent as the mountain snows melted. Gradually the valley bottom melted under the sun into the landscape Finn remembered. Now they could go abroad together and explore the farthest limits of their new world. Soon the herds were on the move, wandering in small groups up to the high ground, to the better grazing and the fawning grounds. Day by day, bucks, fawns, and swaying pregnant does passed by the mouth of the cave, and Finn had to wander farther and climb higher in search of meat. At last, reluctantly, they left the cave, securing their more immovable goods against their return in the Autumn, and set off up the mountain themselves.

They set up camp beside a mountain lake that fed the stream, pitching the tent where the grass had been trampled by the feet of many deer. The tent proved misshapen—Finn taunted her with it but she merely laughed, blaming it on the skins he had selected—but it served its purpose. The hills and trees sheltered them from winds, and the deer were always with them, browsing in the forests, and coming to the water's edge to drink at dusk. It was like that lazy time, Autumn on the ledge, when the kill was done and the woods below teemed with deer, except that now the days grew longer and warmer, and they had no need to fear the future. For them there would be no more hungry Winters or endless Summers gazing anxiously out to the horizon; they would eat fresh meat throughout the year, following the herd in its leisurely progress up and down this same mountain.

The last of the snows melted, the sun warmed the meadow, and the glade and the forest floor were filled with flowers. Freed from the fear of hunger, Finn and Shani had time to explore their new world. It was possible to imagine—as they climbed up through the pines whose pollen drifted through the air like golden smoke—that they were the first man and woman on earth. Hand in hand like children, they climbed to the mountaintop and gazed down on their world: the small tent at the forest's edge, and the lake whose waters tumbled into the valley past their Winter home, down to the river and away. Shani showed the same delight in it that Finn had years before, and gave each place a name. They gathered flowers by the armful to deck the tent or scatter inside, filling it with fragrance. On these too, she bestowed names, new names of her own devising. Starting as a device to hide her ignorance in the face of Finn's questions, it became in time a point of faith with them that every flower and herb should have a new name.

When the sun was past its height they would bathe in the waters of the lake and crawl out onto the rocks to enjoy the last of the sun's warmth. There, gazing at the sky one evening, Finn found himself telling Shani of the things he saw in the clouds. He had not indulged himself in this way since before Venn's death, yet he found, slightly to his surprise, that he had not lost his ability to conjure images from the random patterns in the sky. He found in Shani a willing audience.

When the last of the clouds had passed overhead she said, "Now I know what you were doing all those times!"

Finn felt his face reddening. Even now the very thought of those times could re-open old wounds. "What times?" he demanded angrily.

If his tone affected Shani at all she gave no sign of it. "All those times you thought you were alone. I used to look up at the sky where you were looking but I could see only clouds. Now I see them through your eyes."

Her voice soothed him but the awkwardness remained. "It's just foolishness," he grunted.

Shani shook her head. "It's what makes you different, more

201

than anything else. You see things that have never been, that no one has ever seen. That's why I used to follow you, and why I followed you here."

"I thought you came because of..." Finn faltered, but she cut him short. Her words came out in a flood. "My heart was always with you. Not Venn or Gronu or any of them. Without them, without all that's happened, I would still have followed you. I would have followed to the end of the earth, and if you had died in the snow, I would have lain down and died beside you."

There were tears in her eyes now. Finn held her in his arms, breathing into her ear. "All those years, I never knew. You said nothing."

"It was for *you* to speak," she whispered, "but you never did."

Finn spoke softly. "As a boy, I learned to keep silence. By the time I found my voice, there were things between us that could not be said."

Shani looked down. The sun was sinking into the trees but it was not from cold that she shivered. For a few moments they re-lived the past, as they had both done so many times before. Neither spoke, holding each other close until the bitter memories passed. At last Shani sat up, seeming with an almost physical effort to shrug them off.

"Yet this life, our life here, would never have been, without..." She hesitated, reluctant still to speak of it. "Without what happened. So good things can come out of bad, and our prayers don't go unheeded!"

Finn took her hands in his and drew her to him, touching with his lips first her forehead, then her mouth. She had put into words what both of them, without knowing it, had come to believe once more. As together they watched the sun go down, Finn blessed the memory of his father who had first brought him to this land that had so healed them and restored their faith.

202

Deprived though they were of human company, Finn and Shani had the deer always at hand, and they ranged far and wide, learning the nature of this new herd. They were larger than the grassland deer, traveled less far and in smaller groups, yet their lives were much the same. Wolves were an ever present danger, always circling, waiting for an unwary yearling, a tired old buck, or a heavily pregnant doe to stray from the main group. With the advent of Summer the bucks resumed their dominant role, as the herds sprouted velvet-covered antlers. Flies, drawn by these blood-filled new growths, plagued the herd, driving them up to the cooler air of the mountaintops where Finn and Shani followed, glad too to be free of them. The velvet shed, falling in bloody tatters, or rubbed off on the trunks of trees and the deer descended once more, when the does took themselves apart to fawn in peace and solitude. Finn and Shani knew as they watched this miracle from a distance that they were seeing what no human eye, not even Hann's, had seen before. But it was a harrowing lesson. Hardened as they were by the annual slaughter at the killing grounds, it shocked them to see the number of newborn deer who fell to the wolves before they could even leave the fawning grounds.

Although he had never before seen such things as they witnessed that Summer Finn had at least heard of them from his father or from the stories of the Elders; to Shani they were a constant source of wonder. The hunters of the Burnt Shins guarded their secrets well even from one as determined and curious as she. Now thanks to Finn she had learned more deer lore than any Burnt Shin woman and most men. Yet she was still unprepared for what he showed her one morning in late Summer shortly after the fawning.

They had been crouching in the bushes for what seemed to her like a lifetime. The flies were driving her to distraction, and her legs ached, but Finn had hissed at her so violently the last time she had stirred that she suffered now in silence and longed to be away. With the patience of a hunter Finn continued to stare stonily ahead. Shani's thoughts began to wander. She was staring longingly back in the direction of the tent and the cool waters of the lake and considering creeping away when she felt his hand tighten on her arm, and turned to him once more. What she saw disappointed her—a fawn still unsteady on its legs but fast enough to leave its mother if its curiosity was aroused—had entered the glade to their front, and was nosing among the lichen only a spear's length away. This was, it was true, the closest she had ever been to a living deer but, she felt, she had surely seen fawns enough in the last few days. There was nothing remarkable that she could see about this one although its fur looked particularly soft. Still, since she could feel the warmth of its breath, she was hoping Finn would not kill it. To her surprise he laid down his spear and slowly stretched out his left hand.

As he watched, transfixed, the unbelievable happened: he gently touched the fawn's neck. It started, leaped back, then seeing that it was not hurt, came forward cautiously to be touched again. Slowly Finn stroked its neck and muzzle; as it gained confidence he drew himself to his full height and ran his hands over its whole body. Oblivious of her cramped legs and a fly that crawled across her cheek Shani watched, scarcely daring to breathe, longing to touch the fawn as he had done. At last he beckoned her to join him. She knew enough already to make no sudden moves but stole forward silently. Seeing her the fawn darted back and she felt a pang of disappointment. But to her delight it came forward again to her outstretched hand. A moment later she felt the unutterable thrill of the beast's warm body beneath her hand and its breath upon her upturned palm. Enraptured, she turned to Finn but he had stepped quietly back into the shade, leaving the two of them alone. How long she spent stroking and petting the creature she never knew, only that she wished at the time that it would never end. As each grew more confident she walked a little way across the glade, followed by the fawn; she ran and it ran with her; it darted off to one side and she chased it. Tiring of the game it stopped to browse and she stroked it once more. Feeling its heart beat under the soft fur Shani understood at last that love that had caused a man who had killed deer all his life to throw himself in their path at the flats—a love that man had passed on to his son. She felt also, for the first time, the sorrow of Man's condition; that to live he must kill that which he most loved.

In time the fawn, hearing its mother close at hand, or merely distracted, wandered off into the trees. Shani watched it until it was out of sight and then ran back to the edge of the glade where Finn waited.

"I never believed such a thing could be true!" she cried, her eyes brimming with tears of joy.

"I told you..." Finn smiled, remembering his own joy at this same discovery. "Did I ever deceive you?"

"Many times." She shoved him and sent him sprawling. "But not this time." She looked in the direction the fawn had gone. "I called him Fleetfoot."

Lying on his back in the long grass, Finn howled with laughter and she threw herself upon him pounding him with her fists. "It's a good name..." she protested, blushing, slightly ashamed now at such foolishness.

Rolling away from her, Finn at last regained control of himself and sat up, looking after the departed fawn. "Well, now *I* have seen something new," he declared finally, "something no man ever saw before. A deer with a name!" She sprang at him again but he avoided her and ran, still laughing, down to the tent, with Shani still protesting on his heels.

The naming of the fawn was the object of much banter and laughter between them for the rest of that Summer, but it was not until they were about to follow the herds back down to the valley bottom that its full significance dawned on them. Finn had gone off to hunt, to provide a carcass to last them until they set up camp at the cave again. As the day wore on, Shani waiting by the tent grew impatient, wanting to bathe in the

205

lake and lie out on a warm rock as they usually did on those sunny afternoons. It was not until dusk that Finn returned, tired and empty handed. He threw down his spear and replied to her questions with noncommittal grunts. Finally, embarrassed, he told his story. "Your Fleetfoot got into trouble..." he said, and seeing the alarm in her eyes quickly added, "he's all right now. I found him in the pines up by the white rock, he'd wandered off again. He had stumbled and hurt his leg, not badly, but enough to slow him down, and the wolves were all around him. I had to hold them off until I could get him in among some bucks. He was all right then."

Finn looked at the ground; he, who had watched a hundred fawns killed by wolves, had wasted a whole day saving one. As he recounted his story Shani had listened first with horror, then relief and gratitude and now, worst of all, with amusement.

"I did it for you..." he said as gruffly as he could manage. Then, "I just couldn't let a thing with a name be torn apart by wolves."

That night as Shani slept beside him Finn remembered his words and considered what Shani had done, unknowingly, that day she had played with the fawn. By naming it they had established a claim on it, and given it a claim on them. Now its fate was a matter of concern to them—he had intervened not just for Shani's sake but for his own too, and by so doing had changed forever his relationship with the deer. Here was a oneness with the herd no man had known since Annu walked the earth, and the thought of it thrilled and frightened him.

The Autumn migration began, and they followed the herd down the mountainside and moved back into the cave. Killing only as and when they needed, they had time to fish for salmon in the stream, make new tools and repair the old, and improve the tent sufficiently to make it habitable throughout the Winter, setting it up at the cave mouth. Finn was happier now than he had ever thought possible. There were days, it was true, when he felt his parents' death as keenly as he had on that first day, and nights when the horror of the flats came back to haunt him. But his life here was too active, too full of joy and discovery for him to brood. He rarely thought of the tribe—his only links with them were dead and buried, and the only one of them for whom he still felt anything was here at his side. He was still, at heart, the boy who longed for solitude, who had once dreamed of just such a life as that which he now led. But it was not the same for Shani. With all her love for Finn, and her joy in their life together, there was no escaping thoughts of home, family and friends, especially at the times of the tribal rituals. And, while Finn was quite happy to not have the extra burden of a child, Shani was disappointed that she still had not become pregnant.

One night late in the Autumn, Finn awoke, missing Shani's head on his arm and the soft sound of her breathing beside him. The space where she had lain was empty and cold; hearing no sound from outside the tent he crawled out into the night. Still half asleep and blinded by the light of a full moon, he spent some time before he found her. Where the stream rushed between the rocks she sat, bathed in moonlight, gazing at the sky. Only when he crept closer, reluctant to disturb her, did he notice the tears that glistened on her cheeks. He knelt beside her, wrapping her doeskin cloak across her shoulders while she wiped away a tear with the heel of her hand, still looking up into the sky to where the "Antler" pointed to the "Lone Star."

"I was weeping for the Lone Star!" she whispered. "He knows how sad it is to live alone. That's why he points the way home. For men, like stars, belong together."

There was nothing he could say, he who in former times had thought that star his own, and Finn kept silent.

"I was thinking of home," she admitted at last. Still he did not reply and after a long silence she said more quietly, "This is no way to live!"

Finn looked around him at the forest he had grown to love; it seemed more beautiful than ever in this cold light. "I like it well enough," he said.

Shani shook her head. "You were always the lone one, always the 'Little Wolf...'" In spite of all his efforts the memory of Mata's name for him touched his heart. "But I miss my mother and my sisters. You have the forests and the deer, but when you are gone there is silence here. I am not a hunter; I hate the sound of silence. I was used to the noise of the camp and the jokes and the laughter at the gathering. I long for the sound of a human voice other than yours..." She touched his bloody arm and added placatingly, "... much as yours pleases me."

Finn could understand her longing, nor was he immune himself from such feelings. But he could find no words to comfort her.

After a silence she said wistfully, "They will be feasting now."

"We will feast too. Tomorrow!" Finn offered, but she rounded on him.

"You see? Even our words make mock of us!" she cried. "We speak the tongue of a tribe, we talk of a 'feast' when the two of us sit at the fire, we call this lone tent a 'camp.' When you pray to Annu you use the old prayers, calling upon Him to protect His children... what children? You? Me? We don't belong, Finn, we don't mean anything... there is not even a word to describe us, not 'hearth,' not 'family,' nothing!"

There was no consoling her that night nor in the days that followed, and Finn, knowing that she had spoken from the heart, did not try. Not until days later, when he came back to the cave to tell her that he had seen her fawn among a group of does and yearlings wandering up to the upland pastures, did she smile again. As the days lengthened and the deer began to stream up from the valley floor, their own move in the wake of the herds left little time for thoughts of home. Encamped once

208

more by the lake, with the sun warming the meadow, it was difficult to mourn the life that was gone, the more so after Finn emerged from the forests one Spring morning with Fleetfoot following at his back. The fawn, it seemed, had not forgotten his first contact with men, and Finn had had little difficulty in re-establishing the bond and luring him back. Soon, encouraged by Shani's attentions and the tidbits of lichen and moss that were usually to be had, he took to hanging round the camp, and throughout that long Summer was never far away. So Shani's spirits revived, and if thoughts of home were never completely banished—not even Finn could do that—they were pushed into the back of her mind.

The seasons came and went, and for four Summers Finn and Shani followed the herds and prospered. Their new world became as comfortable and familiar to them as had been the valley of the Burnt Shins. The valley floor, the lake, the Summer pastures, and the small cave where they wintered, each now held memories for them that dimmed, if they did not replace their memories of home. Fleetfoot, grown to full maturity now, continued to appear at odd intervals. Whether flourishing an imposing rack of antlers and with his own following of does, or tired, worn, and thin from the rut, his appearances were always a joy to them both, and something else besides. They served also as a reminder of the bond that had grown up between themselves and the forest herd, an affinity with the deer that Hann would have envied. Not only did the rhythms of their lives accord with those of the herd, but realizing its growth must benefit them too, they had become its guardians. They spent whole days in Winter clearing areas of snow where the best mosses and lichens could be found, or in Summer protecting does and fawns, as best they could, from the ever present threat of wolves. It was not a role they had looked for, it sat uneasily with Finn's life as a hunter, and the irony of it was not lost on him. Years before at the killing grounds he had been struck by the paradox that men both hunted and revered the

Reindeer; now in his new role, both predator and protector, he had found it again.

Pleasant as their lives were, neither of them was ever entirely free from thoughts that most of the time they managed to suppress. Shani, though her bouts of depression grew less frequent, was still tormented at times by memories of home and family, while Finn found refuge in his continuous quest for knowledge. Even this, though, had its dangers and sometimes led him where he would not go. One day in their fifth Summer by the lakeside he was jointing a freshly slain carcass, quartering the trunk and breaking the limbs, and threading the joints with sinew to hang them in a tree. Nearby, Shani pegged out the skin by an anthill whose occupants would pick it clean, ready for drying. Finn worked silently, lost in thought. When he had finished, and the last joint swung from the branches, dripping blood onto the ground below, he suddenly turned to Shani, and said, "What have I done?"

Used as she was to his strange fancies, Shani looked at his handiwork and could see nothing unusual. "You've hung the meat. Well done!" She returned to her own work.

"But why?"

"To make it tender, and to keep the wolves off it!" She was curious now.

"Right! . . ." Finn seemed unusually excited now. "To keep the wolves off."

It was possible, Shani thought, that Finn had lost his wits, nor did his next question reassure her. "What is the difference between a living deer and a dead deer?"

She laughed a little nervously, and nodded to the tree. "Try getting a living deer up there and you will see!" To her relief Finn laughed, too, and took her head in his hands.

"But what is the difference to *us*? What is the difference between a deer I have just killed, and a deer I am about to kill, above which I am standing with my spear raised?"

210

Shani shrugged. "I thought only women and holy men talked in riddles."

Ignoring this, Finn answered his own question. "There is no difference. Both are meat to us. Yet I keep the wolves away from the dead deer, and not from the living."

"So?" Shani was interested now.

"So, when I saved Fleetfoot from the wolves, I cursed myself for a fool, but I was right. We protect the deer we *have* killed. Why not those we mean to kill?"

Shani tossed her head dismissively. "You fought all day to keep the wolves off one deer. How would you protect a herd?" It was always this way with them, Finn dreaming, reasoning as he spoke, Shani practical, preferring the evidence of her senses.

Finn smiled, trying to imagine places he had seen in the mountains. "In the right place . . ." he began.

"With enough men?" Shani's words brought him to earth once more. Far from following his train of thought she had left him far behind, seen where it was leading. There she now waited, smiling. "One man alone could never do it," she said, "not even you."

There was little more talk that day. In the evening, having eaten, Finn rose from the fireside and strode off into the forest to be alone. He was angry at the way Shani had turned away their talk, angrier still that it was in a direction that his own thoughts increasingly seemed to take. In this land he had found a happiness he had thought impossible, had banished from his mind all thoughts of the past; yet now everything, his dreams, his new discoveries, even Shani herself, seemed to be in league against him, reminding him of that which he had put behind him.

From that day Finn was haunted by the vision that had come upon him almost by accident—of men driving off wolves with spears and fire so that the herd might flourish. Despite what Shani had said he had kept back the wolves with ease;

they would not attack a man unless crazed with hunger. How easily a larger group of men could keep wolves from the fawning grounds. How then the herd might grow! The thought would not leave him; it colored his dreams that night and many another. However many times he thrust it angrily out of his mind, however many times he told himself that it was all futile dreaming, he was never again free of it.

Shani, seeing him thus troubled, knowing where it must lead and how it must resolve itself, bided her time. She had not long to wait. Some days passed in which she ignored his moody silences and left him to his gloomy reflections. One afternoon, as she was sitting in the sun repairing the stitching on the tent, he spoke.

"Do you remember the Autumn kill by the river, the year we all sat together at Gronu's fires...?" She nodded. "I killed my first buck, the biggest that came through Hann's ground that year."

"Yes..." she said feigning boredom. "We should all have seen then what a great hunter you would be." He either failed to notice or chose to ignore her teasing.

"That buck, if it had lived, would have fathered many more, and strong ones like himself."

Shani shrugged. "We had to eat!"

Finn nodded. "True, but a smaller, weaker buck would have fed us just as well. I killed it, and it was lost to the herd forever."

He had lost Shani; she turned to him frowning. "So?"

Though Finn spoke calmly she could see in his eyes the excitement he was suppressing. "I have been watching the wolves...how they kill. We used to blame them for the thinning of the herd, but if there were twice as many wolves it wouldn't make any difference."

Shani shuddered. "There are wolves enough for me."

Finn would not be distracted. "My father once told me that

for the wolves, the deer are easy to find and hard to kill. For us it was the other way round..." Still Shani looked blank. "Wolves cannot kill a full-grown buck, so they kill the weak and the lame or the very young. So the strong survive and breed and the herd prospers. Whatever else was killing the herd, *we* made it worse. Yet we blamed the wolves."

"So what would you have us do?" asked Shani. "Become wolves?"

"Yes!" cried Finn. "Hunt like the wolves, follow the herd, pick out the weak, and leave the strong. Not like them because they must, but like men because we choose to! It was there all the time, my father saw part of it..."

"Why not all? He was a wise man!"

Finn threw his arms wide. "He might have had he lived. The Burnt Shins never thought of it before because for them it was impossible. The grasslands deer could outrun them in a day, they couldn't follow the herd. When the herds did come in Spring and Autumn there was no time to select, they had to kill all they could. It could only work *here*, and most of them had never been here."

Shani smiled at him. "And what would the poor wolves eat?"

Finn was not smiling. "Let the wolves eat each other. If we could keep them off too, we could take their places then!"

"The two of us?"

Finn had seen all along how Shani was steering the talk in the old familiar direction. She knew as well as he did that such a life as he proposed would need the whole tribe to make it work. From the start of that day he had known where his train of thought was taking him, and he had not liked it. Now he hung his head. "The people have made their choice," he said sullenly, arguing as much with himself as her. "You said that."

"And if what you say is true, as bad a choice as they could have made," her voice whispered, urgent, insistent in his ear.

"Killing the deer randomly, in greater numbers than ever. Young, old, weak, strong, they all go over the cliffs. They're killing the herd, and killing themselves, if what you say is true."

"It is true," he said. "I am sure of it."

"Then they need you now as never before," she pleaded.

Finn glared up at her. "Hann needed *them*. In life and in death he needed them, and where were they? Crowing over the carcasses of the deer they had murdered!"

Shani sat down beside him and stared into his face. "You and I both know what caused all that. Once you wanted to put it right. When I first told you in the cave you were all for going back. I had to stop you, remember?" Finn could not look her in the face as she continued, "I said then that it was not our time, but that one day your time would come. I think, I *know* that time is now. And so, I think, do you."

Without waiting for a reply she rose and went to the lake to swim, leaving him alone to battle with his conflicting emotions. He knew that she had steered their talk that way on purpose—to force that issue that had often before come between them. Finn had grown to love this life of theirs; they had been the whole world to each other and had walked the earth alone like the first children of Annu. With the passage of time his desire to return to the Burnt Shins and to right old wrongs had diminished. But his angry outburst proved that, if old loyalties still remained, then so did the memory of past injuries. The Burnt Shins were the people who had persecuted him as a child, deserted his adopted father, and abandoned their own traditions to rush headlong to destruction. Yet there was another side of them—and even as he brooded on old resentments he remembered the old women who had sewn his ragged clothes, the families who had shared their meat with him, and the laughing hunters who had carried him home long ago from the fight by the river—a child abandoned in the first few days of his life. Then he thought of Hann and Mata who had taken him into their lives, Venn who had befriended him when no other would, Laela, his sister, who had begged him to stay, and Shani. She who had shared his life here and who meant more to him than any living soul—she too was Burnt Shin, and so was he. Most poignant of all came the memory of Hann telling him, down in the valley the Winter before he was initiated, that men were not meant to live alone.

"We need the tribe . . ." he heard him say, and as he closed his eyes he saw him lying beside him, smiling over at him, as he had that night beside the fire. "Our rituals, our customs, our lives together, those are the things that set us apart from everything else that is in the world."

By the time Shani returned and sat beside him, smelling fresh from the water, the battle was lost and won, as she knew it would be.

"If we find them prosperous," he said, "we stay a day, no more, and then return."

Her eyes told of her joy at his decision, but her voice betrayed her forebodings. "They have not prospered," she said, "if what you say is true."

215

CHAPTER
TWELVE

▲ ▲ ▲
▲ ▲

As LAELA APPROACHED Sanu's cave the evening shadows were already falling across the valley. That and the fact that she was bowed under the burden of the child on her back—he was too weak to make the climb unaided—meant that she was almost at the head of the track before she saw the two strangers seated at the cave mouth. At once she dropped to one knee and, burdened as she was, crawled over into the bushes to watch from a place of hiding. Exactly when and how suspicion had come into her life she could not say; if she had stopped to think she might have remembered a time when such behavior would have been alien to her, but now she acted out of instinct. Among the things she might expect to find on these journeys to visit the holy man, this was not one. They were few enough who bothered to climb up here with food for him, fewer still who would tolerate him in his distracted moods or listen patiently in his few lucid moments. Those who did, like herself, did so in strict rotation, and avoided the place at other times. So, struggling to quiet the wriggling infant on her back and also keep hold of the small parcel of food that she clutched, she

217

peered out of the bushes through narrowed eyes. Then—with a cry of delight that startled the child—she burst from the bushes and lumbered heavily forward across the clearing into the arms of Shani.

Sanu was seated just inside the cave, already eating food that Finn and Shani had brought him. He said nothing but smiled at them, seemingly aware of what was being said as they greeted each other and sat down on the grass at the cave mouth.

"I knew you would come back," Laela said. "I and others have prayed for it. We needed you then"—there was a slight note of reproach in her voice—"we need you even more now."

Finn nodded. "There were reasons at the time why I thought I could not stay. I learned later that I was wrong..." He looked for a moment as though he would say more, but Shani caught his eye and shook her head slightly. Laela had not noticed what passed between them; he shrugged and added, "There was little then that I could do or say, and none who would have listened."

"But all that is changed now," interrupted Shani. "We have much to tell you. But first tell *us*..."—she spoke fearfully—"how my family... and the tribe fare."

Laela looked them both over: Finn strong limbed and broad chested, half a head taller than when he had left, and Shani with her clear skin and sleek dark hair. Then she looked down at herself and at the child who peered timidly from behind her cloak. The contrast between them told its own story.

"Your family are all alive," she said finally. Even the words she chose next had an ominous ring, "Which is what we call thriving."

Shani buried her face in her hands for a moment. But Finn leaned forward and almost whispered his question. "And Gronu still leads?"

"Gronu rules," she used a word unfamiliar among the Burnt Shins, "and he thrives. But he has changed from the man you

218

knew, has become more like a beast. It started when you left . . ." She turned to Shani. "Some people blamed it on that and set off to find you. But most agree it would have happened anyway."

"And the hearths?" persisted Finn.

"Exist in name only. Rann led his hearth away across the grasslands in the second Summer, knowing how the coming Winter would be. Some few straggled back in time under his brother; what became of the rest no one knows. Sanu . . ." She nodded at the old man who in turn nodded at Finn and smiled. "He has hardly spoken at all, and never in Council. Rann's brother who came back spoke out once, urged that we return to the old ways. But Gronu's men shouted him down. The next day he was gone. They said he just wandered off, but no one saw him go."

At this a look passed between Finn and Shani, before Shani asked, "Yet they would defy him if they could?"

Laela nodded vigorously. "He is killing the herds. It has been as Hann said it would. Each year it gets worse. The ground below the flats is a forest of bones now, a dirty, diseased place fit only for ravens. You can smell it from here when the Autumn winds blow. The first Winter was bad enough. True, there was plenty of meat. But it was far more than we could smoke or dry—much of it rotted, many skins were spoiled. Then half the smoke-houses blew down—they had been thrown up in such a hurry. There were fights over the meat, the skins, and the smoke-houses. When the smoked meat ran out—much later, it is true, but it ran out just the same—the men took to the forests but the deer were scarcer than ever. So there was more fighting whenever anyone brought home a kill. Gronu had to divide the spoils; his friends and supporters got the best, the rest of us got by as best we could. And the next winter was worse still, and so it continues. . . ."

Laela could say no more; her head drooped and tears ran down her hollow cheeks. Finn and Shani sat in horrified si-

219

lence, unbroken save for the sound of Sanu singing to himself in the shadows and the infant whispering in his mother's ear. At length Laela looked up at them once more.

"If you think you have heard the worst, you are wrong," she said. "I could tell you of hunters who devour their prey raw in the forests rather than bring it home, of meals cooked in secret in the burial caves or the woods below the scree, of people who die in agony from eating rotten meat . . . or worse . . ."—she began to sob—"of children who disappear, who one morning just aren't there, and everyone looks guilty and pretends not to remember them, and their mothers cast off their cloaks and walk off into the forest to die."

Shani laid her hand upon Laela's arm and spoke softly. "All that is over now, and soon to be a thing forgotten." She looked at Finn for support, but he was watching Laela's child. He was remembering the Burnt Shin children who had raced about the ledge like fawns, or wandered from hearth to hearth at the feasts without fear, fighting and sprawling, even clambering over the hunters as they talked. Was this pale creature, bright-eyed but not with health, belly swollen but not with food, quiet and watchful, what those children had become?

He turned to Laela and placed his hand upon her shoulder. "When the time came to bury my father and mother," he said, "you alone did not fail me. Yet when you begged me to stay I failed you. You owe me nothing, yet again I ask your help . . ."

Laela looked him in the eyes now, her tears gone. "Only lead your father's hearth, and you shall have it . . . anything."

"Go to the camp and tell them I am come home, and that I wish to address the Council tonight."

"Come yourself, now!" she cried eagerly.

Finn shook his head. "Soon. But first," he looked at Shani, "there are things we must prepare!"

▲ ▲ ▲

"Why has he come here?..." It was Gronu's booming voice that echoed round the great cave. "Whom our fathers took into our midst, and who at our time of need chose to flee the camp and dwell alone among the beasts? Why has he come here now?"

Waiting to one side at the back of the cave, Finn looked at what had become of the Council. The center of the floor was now taken up with a large stone seat covered with skins, from which Gronu held court flanked by his friends and advisors. Before him, cross-legged on the floor, sat the Elders and hunters and behind them stood the people, row upon row of old faces —even the children had old faces.

Between Gronu and the assembled tribe stood Laela's husband. He was sweating profusely despite the chill, and he cowered under Gronu's glare. He swallowed hard and began his answer. "He says he has something to say, something that affects the whole tribe..." He got no further.

"The tribe he neither belongs to nor cares for," stormed Gronu, and his supporters growled their assent. "The time when he could speak in Council is long gone!"

From the back of the crowd a female voice that Finn recognized as Laela's cried out, "Let him be heard!" and was joined almost at once by a chorus of voices from all sides crying, "Let us hear him, let him speak!"

For a few moments the cave was in an uproar as Gronu's supporters, recovering from their initial surprise, tried in vain to shout down the protesters, whose numbers seemed to be swelling.

"Enough!" At Gronu's bellowed command silence fell. He had sprung to his feet and stood towering above them in the lamplight, his eyes blazing, his lips quivering with barely suppressed rage. "*I* say he shall not be heard!"

The crowd shifted uneasily, and many eyes darted over to where Finn stood waiting in the shadows. Finn could read what was in those eyes—"We have spoken out, put ourselves at risk, it is for you now to act!" He was about to step forward into the light to the long-awaited confrontation, when a frail voice from the back of the cave broke the silence.

"I say he *shall* be heard!" Even after years of silence, and feeble as it was, it was a voice known to all. Stupefied by this most unexpected intervention, Gronu fell back into his seat as the crowd parted to reveal Sanu in his ritual finery, making his way unsteadily to his place of honor among the Elders. His progress was slow, yet he shrugged off the many hands that reached out to assist him as he made his way through the hushed assembly. Acknowledging the Elders who rose to greet him, he walked out onto the open space before Gronu's seat; scarcely giving its occupant a glance, he turned to address the people.

"It is he, Finn, who would speak, the son of Hann of whose deer-luck you all remember, and whose voice, wise in Council, is sadly missed." Many among the old men and the hunters nodded, and more in the crowd murmured their agreement. Such was the shock of Sanu's sudden re-appearance that few noticed the effort that these few words cost him. None dared to interrupt as he continued, "He has come to us from far away to tell us of things that he has learned. I have heard what he has to say and know that it comes from Annu. It *shall* be heard, I, Sanu, say it!" With that he took his place among the Elders, and leaning on the arms of companions he had not seen in years, sat cross-legged on the floor staring straight ahead of him as though oblivious to what might follow.

Finn knew that now was his moment. Laela and Sanu at great cost and great risk had done all that could be dared. If he failed now many would fall with him. Banishing all such thoughts, he strode forward into the light, eyes fixed on Gronu, who rose to face him. It was the first time they had confronted each other since the night in that same cave when Gronu had insulted his father, creating an enmity between them that had lost none of its edge in the intervening years. As he stared into Gronu's eyes Finn saw there the fear that Shani had spoken of, and something else that he had never seen before—something terrible. Turning away to be free of that baleful glare, he stepped forward and threw back the folds of his cloak to reveal his body. For hours before coming to the cave he had gorged on all the food they had brought with them, and his belly was swollen tight as a drumskin; Shani had rubbed his body with deer fat so it glistened in the lamplight. He waited, allowing the crowd to see his condition and compare it with their own emaciated state. At last he spoke.

"As I look around me I wonder what has become of the Burnt Shins who used to live here—what became of the ten hearths. Time was when the Council cave rang to the sound of many voices, now I seem to hear but one!" There was a threatening growl at this from Gronu's friends but also some muffled laughter from the crowd.

"The hunters of the Burnt Shins were proud and powerful and lived joyful lives, hunting and feasting. Here, the men lie around the ledge counting their ribs. Flies walk across their faces." He saw with satisfaction and with sorrow how his words hit home, and how many of the hunters hung their heads.

"The women of the Burnt Shins were comely and clean-limbed, with eyes like does. Now the woman are tired and care-worn, old before their time. The sound of their children's laughter used to fill the valley, now the camp is quiet as the grave. Again I ask, what became of my father's people?"

Gronu leaped to his feet, thrust himself forward. "We have had hard times," he shouted. "*That* everybody knows. Hard times you chose not to share with us, but we have come through."

Finn looked Gronu up and down, slowly and silently. He

223

was as strong as ever, though Finn now was the taller. Gronu's body too glistened in the torchlight.

"I see that some, at least, have prospered!" said Finn. Again there was laughter. He turned once more to the crowd. "Five years ago Gronu stood here in Council and said that the time had come for great changes. Now I stand here, and in my father's name declare that the time has come again!"

Finn allowed his words to take their full effect and for the murmuring that greeted them to die down before continuing, "What has befallen the tribe is the result of great blasphemies, great crimes..." He turned to Gronu, seated now, who shifted uneasily.

"Gronu urged the slaughter at the flats in defiance of tradition and the wisdom of the Elders, and what has it brought? It has brought the tribe to the verge of starvation. The herds waste away and the people with them. In the time I have been away, children have been born and died..."

A chorus of sobs and the shouted names of children greeted this but was cut short by Gronu, who was on his feet once more.

"If you have come, as I hear, many days' walk to tell us of things we already know, then I fear your journey has been wasted!"

"I have come to tell you things you do *not* know, but which those of wisdom among you may have wondered about. I come to tell you of things I have seen and done in a land I first saw with my father, Hann."

"Your father!" Gronu scoffed, but Finn saw the effect the name had on the hunters and, ignoring Gronu, leaned forward to address them.

"In the year I was initiated he showed me a herd, deep in the forests, whose deer are strong and hardy, who live their lives in one valley and the mountains above. A man may follow them in two days from Winter grazing to Summer fawning grounds. When he had fled this life, I went in search of them, and with Shani, I have followed this herd for five years!"

Most of the people assembled in the cave knew nothing of the forest herd. Finn's words brought confusion as claim and counter-claim flew back and forth.

"But Finn"—the stir he had caused was stilled by the voice of one of the Elders—"I too have seen this herd . . ." The Elder turned to the people massed behind him. "In my youth *my* father took me to the valley Finn speaks of. But the deer there are too few to feed us all."

The groan of disappointment that greeted this remark was almost drowned out by the victorious baying of Gronu's supporters. In truth, they were as ignorant as the youngest child present of the matter in question.

Amid all this noise Finn held up his arm for silence which slowly settled once more. He told the old man, "Since your day that herd has grown and continues to grow. It has grown even in the time we have been there. Yet what you say is true—*if* we hunt in the old ways."

"What other way is there?" cried a voice from the crowd. "Gronu's way?" cried another.

Finn was unruffled. "From my father I learned to watch the wolves," he began, "and from them I have learned their secret. They never starve, Winter or Summer. And why? Because they follow the herds, killing and eating as they need."

Gronu scoffed. "What of it? They follow the herds! Is *that* what you would have us do? Sprout wings and fly across the grasslands?"

Finn rounded on him. "The grassland herds are dying. You, with your murders, have seen to that!" Many gasped at the harsh words, expecting Gronu to fly at him in rage; to their surprise he recoiled as though struck and, suddenly drained of color, slumped into his seat again.

Finn shook his head. "I have watched the wolves, seen

them hunt the forest herd, Winter and Summer. They cannot kill the strong or fast deer, only those that wander or fall behind—the old, the unwary, the weak, the lame. The strong survive to breed more like themselves, while the weak strains perish and the herd prospers! Already there are more deer in the valley than ever Hann saw."

"If what you say is true, why don't the grasslands deer thrive?" cried a voice from the darkness.

"Because of us!" cried Finn. "What is killing them across the grasslands no one knows. But here it was we, not wolves, that did the damage. The killing grounds were bad enough. But then, as their numbers began to fall, we took to killing them in ever greater numbers. Young and old, weak and strong, all herded over the cliffs together. That was Gronu's way—a cure worse than the sickness."

Gronu, seemingly recovered, stormed forward. "Silence!" he bellowed and continued shouting until nothing could be heard but the hissing of the fat in the lamps. He turned to Finn, sneering, "You'd have us live like wolves?"

Finn ignored him, addressing the people. "I'd have you hunt like wolves, so that you might live again like men!"

In an extravagant show of disdain Gronu turned away, but among the hunters and the Elders, Finn's words hit home.

Llin spoke. Once a hearth leader and friend of Hann, he thought aloud. "We could never follow the grassland herd. To do as you would wish, Finn, we should have to follow you into the forests, leave the valley, our home and our holy places."

"The caves where we have lain our ancestors," added someone in the crowd.

"And where we now bury our children!..." said Finn. It hurt him to use such words, hearing in the sobs from the back of the gathering the pain they caused. "I know what it is I ask of you. But what will our holy places or the graves of our fathers mean, if we are no more?"

Many, even among the Elders, nodded at this. Yet others

among Gronu's supporters cried out, accusing Finn of blasphemy. He turned on his accusers.

"It was not I who abandoned our customs, or forsook the wisdom of our ancestors. It was the wisdom of my father that went unheeded here, that took me to that land where I have thrived. I might have stayed there and prospered alone, but I was drawn back by a vision. It was a vision sent by Annu, of a time that was when He walked the earth, and a time that will come again; when the Burnt Shins will live among the deer as His sons did. I saw a tribe of men following the forest herd Winter and Summer—killing only what they needed, *when* they needed, choosing their prey with care, keeping the wolves at bay, nurturing the herd, making it grow that *they* might grow. Once the deer ensured our survival —now we must ensure theirs!"

"Enough!" Gronu pushed past him into the torchlight. He had seen the effect of Finn's words, and how many, even among his own supporters, had been swayed by the image he had conjured. "I have heard enough!" he shouted. "Even if we were fool enough to follow you to the end of the world, even if we could find this herd you talk of, this life you describe is the stuff of dreams!"

By way of answer, Finn stepped toward him and threw back his cloak once more; even beside Gronu he was an imposing figure. "I have lived this life for five Winters and five Summers," he declared. ". . . Do I seem to you a figure from a dream?"

In the roar of acclamation that followed Finn had his answer. Beckoning for silence once more, he concluded, "Soon I go back to the valley I have spoken of. Those who would follow me I will welcome. Of those who would stay I will take my leave without bitterness."

From the babble at his back Finn knew that his words had impressed many, though many others, possibly the majority, recoiled from such a bold step as he had proposed: abandoning the home of generations and trekking, with Winter at their heels, into an unknown land. For now, in challenging Gronu and reminding the people of their fallen state, he had done

227

enough. Pointedly turning his back on Gronu, he addressed the tribe once more.

"It is for the hearth leaders and hunters now to consider what I have said. In the morning I will return and, if you wish it, say more of the forest herd."

"Tell your tales to the trees!" shouted Gronu. Without a backward glance in his direction Finn made his way through the crowd toward the cave mouth. Gronu's taunts were almost drowned out in the tumult; some cried out for Finn, his own supporters raged and spat, and many others shouted questions or jostled and fought among themselves. Oblivious alike of friend and foe, seemingly unaware even of the hunters of his own hearth who now formed themselves in a body around him, Finn wrapped himself in his cloak and strode out into the moonlight. Dismissing his escort at the edge of the scree, he was soon swallowed up in the night, leaving the camp in turmoil behind him.

▲　　▲　　▲

Before dawn the next day, Shani had risen leaving Finn sleeping in the shelter they had erected beside Sanu's cave, and made her way down to the camp to see her family. The sun was overhead in the treetops—though the holy man still slept exhausted—before she returned to tell Finn of the effect of his appearance at Council.

"The whole camp was astir even before I arrived. Laela says there has been nothing like it since Hann's time. The Elders and hearth leaders have been talking all night, the hunters are going from hearth to hearth, the women are gathering in groups at the edge of the scree. Some of them are packing already!"

Finn nodded grimly; he knew the battle was as yet but half-won, and could still be lost. "And Gronu?"

Shani was dismissive. "Oh, he's stumping round the camp

with his friends, pouring cold water on everything. But he knows it's over with him."

Finn was less sure. "How many do you think are with us?"

Shani counted on her fingers. "My family and all their hearth, Hann's of course, two others for sure . . . most of the women."

"What about the hearth *leaders?*" Finn persisted.

Shani shrugged. "They don't tell me their plans! I think if they stay, they'll have only each other for company."

Finn shook his head. "They are the most important of all. If they stay we will be leading a rabble into the forest and Gronu will have won, have destroyed the tribe. They must decide . . . and be seen to decide for things to be as they were!"

Shani laid a hand on his arm. "Things will never be as they were," she said gently, "not for us, not for them. Nothing can bring back the old life. Even our life in the valley is gone now."

Suddenly fearful, Finn looked at her. "This will be our last time alone together . . . is this what you wanted?"

In an instant the resolute hearth leader and the visionary vanished before her eyes, to be replaced by a figure from the past—the friendless child hovering uncertainly at the edge of the firelight. She came to him, took his head in her hands. "Nothing can spoil what has been between us, what *is* between us. But if, in our love, we turn away from those who gave us life, what then would that love be worth? What would our lives be worth, lived knowing of their suffering, and choosing to ignore it?"

"I know it!" Finn hung his head. Knowing what ailed him, Shani stroked his hair.

"Put aside your fears," she whispered. "There will be time for us again. I left this place once before, broke all ties of home, hearth, kinship, not for fear of Gronu, but for love of you. It is that same love, grown stronger with the years, that now bids you go and do your duty as a man, a hunter, and your father's son."

He did not go at once but held her close, savoring this last moment, knowing that change was in the nature of things but longing already for that life that they had both lost. At last he rose and dressed, preparing himself for his second appearance before the ten hearths.

"When the moon is clear of the trees!" he reminded Shani as they parted.

"I'll be there!" was all she said, and as he descended to the camp she set off alone, leaving Sanu's cave and their small tent behind her, and disappearing into the forest.

The camp was as Shani had described it; Finn was met at the edge of the scree by a body of hunters of Hann's hearth. Though he felt uneasy going about the camp with an armed retinue, he was glad of them when he saw the look Gronu gave him. They avoided each other for the rest of the day, but both ranged the camp ceaselessly, arguing with leaders and Elders or addressing mixed groups from all hearths and of all ages. Among these last, Finn found, lay his greatest body of support. Many of the hearth leaders still wavered.

"What if the forest herd dies out?" asked one as Finn talked with them late in the evening, shortly before the whole tribe was due to assemble once more in the great cave. "We have heard they are fewer than our grassland deer."

"They will not die out," repeated Finn patiently, "if we hunt them as I have said. And, whatever happens, there are enough to see us through the Winter. In the Spring, if you're not satisfied, there is nothing to stop your coming back. At the very worst the grassland deer will have had one Autumn and Winter free of us, to recoup their strength."

Finn noticed many of them nod at this.

"And what of the holy places?" This was an Elder, voicing the fears of many of his fellows.

"From the top of the mountain where the forest deer graze in Summer, you can see our Sacred Mountain," declared Finn. "Our boys will have farther to run"—there was some laughter —"but they will be stronger, I promise you! As for the burial places, the dead have their world, and we must do what we can

230

to live in ours. How can it serve our dead to linger here and pile our bones on theirs?"

To Finn's relief there was no outcry at this last. Reading the thoughtful faces before him he felt at last, and for the first time, that victory was in his grasp. Yet even as he felt this the sight of Gronu and his companions reminded him that the greatest challenge lay ahead. Even after all his efforts, even with the bulk of the tribe, Elders and hunters behind him, there remained Gronu to deal with. Those who had listened to Finn—agreed with him, even spoken in his favor—had sat silent through five years of Gronu's misrule and would do so again until Gronu was overthrown. Finn knew better than any what Gronu would do, *had* done, to achieve his preeminence in the tribe. He knew better even than the spearmen who formed a protective huddle around him, as they made their way in darkness to the great cave, what this man was capable of. That knowledge would destroy one or the other of them before the sun had risen.

As the tribe filed into the great cave Gronu took his seat in the center of the floor, flanked by his henchmen, watching carefully which people greeted Finn as he made his way to the front of the crowd. Already Finn noticed a change of atmosphere; some who had promised great things during the day now looked away or at the ground as he passed, intimidated by the menace of the dark, bear-cloaked figure who glowered at them from the depths of the cave. Pausing only to bow to the Elders, a custom fallen into disuse under Gronu, Finn walked out into the center of the floor, and took his stance as one who would address the tribe. It was Gronu who spoke first, however. Standing on his seat so that his words would carry even to those at the back who were crammed into the cave mouth, he began at once to pour scorn on Finn.

"Last night Finn told us a pretty tale . . ." he began. "His people, whoever they were, must have been great tellers of tales!" Gronu's adherents roared their approval at this, but among the crowd it had less effect. The gibe was a tired one;

doubts about Finn's status had been laid to rest many years before.

"You would not have said that in Hann's time!" someone shouted from the crowd, as if to confirm the fact. The crowd murmured their assent.

Gronu wavered only for a moment, then went on. "How he came upon this tale we'll never know—gazing at the sky perhaps. If so I fear he let his wits go with the clouds. There is no forest herd, and if there were why should we leave our homes to find them? The deer will come to us, as they always have. He talks of the wisdom of our ancestors, then bids us leave them and all that binds us to them, to follow him and chase a fable!"

The cries "I have seen them!" and "Finn speaks truth!" coming from the darkness whipped Gronu into a frenzy. "Finn speaks from bitterness," he raged, "blaming you for Hann's death, and he would lead you into the forest to die!"

There was uproar in the cave now as Gronu's supporters backed this claim and others in the crowd shouted their dissent.

"I say he will lead you to destruction!" bellowed Gronu, his voice carrying over the din. The crowd surged, and blows were struck. Judging the time right Finn stepped forward, placing himself between Gronu and the crowd and raising his arms to indicate that he would speak. As if by magic, silence fell at once, each man and woman—even Gronu, scowling behind him—wondering how Finn would refute this charge.

"I will lead you nowhere!" he announced simply, and stepped back.

Gronu's eyes narrowed, suspicious that he had won so easily. "What new nonsense is this?" he demanded, his voice echoing now in the startled hush that had settled.

Finn moved forward once more. "When my father, the wisest man alive, walked the earth, who led the Burnt Shins then? Did he? Or did you . . . or you . . ." He appealed to two of the most eminent Elders seated at the front. Seeing his meaning, they smiled and shook their heads.

"In my youth, the Burnt Shins came and went as they pleased—obeying even their hearth leaders only as the mood took them. . . ." There were wistful smiles at the memories he evoked. "So who am I, born among strangers, to claim leadership? No man has that right, no man ever had!"

Again there was pandemonium. With a snarl Gronu leaped forward, grappling for Finn's throat. In an instant Finn found himself surrounded once more by the hunters of his own hearth. To his joy, he saw many others with them. In the confusion, Gronu had been swept from his seat. Climbing up in his place, Finn cried above the noise, "I have not come to lead, but to tell you what I know, and what I mean to do. It is for you and your leaders to decide what you will do. I have asked to be heard. I have been heard. I ask no more!" With that he strode through the crowd toward the cave mouth. The bulk of the crowd was close on his heels, spilling out from the confines of the cave into the fresh air and the moonlight. As the people surged out, chanting Finn's name as they had once chanted his own, Gronu stood aghast. He turned to his friends; and saw to his dismay that some had already joined the crowd that heaved and jostled at the cave mouth. Those who still clustered about his seat looked at one another in their uncertainty.

"He deserted you once . . ." he tried to shout at the departing press of people, seeing from the corner of his eye all but two of his supporters rush past.

Outside Finn found himself pressed on all sides by well-wishers but, aside from acknowledging the promises of the hearth leaders, he did not linger. The moon was above the trees; he knew that Shani was close and that she was not alone. Shaking himself free of his escort—gesturing to them not to follow—he strode off toward the scree, and without looking back descended at speed toward the tree-line below. He could hear the shouting and cheering above him. But as the ground leveled out, and he slowed his pace, he was more concerned with the shadowy figures who lurked in the trees ahead. Glanc-

233

ing over his shoulder he saw that the multitude who had surged out of the cave had halted at the edge of the scree, and now stared down into the gloom after him. The moment was perfect; waiting in the trees Shani knew it too.

The crowd at the camp's edge had seen many wonders. They had seen a man they had thought dead return in triumph, they had seen an old man they thought mad break a five years' silence to assert his authority in Council. Yet these were as nothing compared to the sight that now greeted their eyes. From the cover of the trees emerged a Reindeer buck, taller and stronger than any of them had ever seen, which trotted across the grass toward him at Finn's beckoning. As Fleetfoot approached, Finn reached out and stroked the soft fur at his cheek, calming his fears as he shied at the noise and smell of the crowd above. Then, with his hand on the beast's shoulder, Finn turned to face them.

Emerging from the cave, Gronu had found to his surprise that the crowd had fallen silent. He stalked to the edge of the scree, shouldering his way forward through the press until he saw what had stopped them in their tracks.

"It's a trick!" he cried. "I've seen it before...done it myself!"

Many of the hunters in the crowd nodded. But trick or not there was no denying that it was a fine beast, a silent witness to the state of the herd Finn had spoken of. To those less versed in deer lore, the sight of a Reindeer buck at all in late Summer was a miracle that confirmed Finn's claim that his vision came from Annu Himself. But Gronu, implacable, breaking free of the crowd, scrambled down the slope to where man and deer stood. Fleetfoot, unnerved already by the unfamiliar sounds and smells of this place, and calmed so far only by Finn's soothing hand, started at Gronu's approach; before Finn could hold him, he raced off into the darkness, his heels clicking as he went. Unaware that many in the crowd nodded to one another, seeing in this an omen, Gronu was triumphant. "You'd best be off too"—he indicated to Finn where the deer had disappeared into the trees—"you may have won the women and the children with your trickery and your talk of Annu..."

"Annu has revealed to me many things," Finn cut him short. "Some are fit for their ears, some not."

Gronu frowned and eyed him warily. Glancing up to the ledge to be sure the people were out of earshot, Finn leaned forward and said, almost in a whisper, "He told me of a young man, strong, brave, and generous, a young man of whom great things were promised, who went out on a mountain one day to hunt. This young man's heart was high because this was the first day of his manhood, and he looked for some trophy to take back to his people. He wandered all day and found nothing, but late in the day he came by chance upon his friend. Luck had been with his friend and he had killed a bear. Seeing the young man he hailed him, called upon him to help him skin his prize. And the young man's heart was dark, because the friend was also his rival in the hunt and in love, and he knew that when they went home it would be *his* praises they would be singing, and to *him* that those eyes they both held dear would be turned..."

Gronu's jaw fell. He trembled from head to foot, and sweat poured from him as Finn continued, "And as the friend stooped to continue the skinning, the young man laid down his spear as though he would help and, unseen, he took up a rock and..."

"No!" It was like the bellow of a wounded buck, not the cry of a man. Having uttered it Gronu lurched forward to try to stanch Finn's flow of words. He tripped, and Finn sidestepped as he fell, and leaned over him as he lay, hissing in his ear with vehement emphasis, "He took up a rock and struck his friend. The first blow was weak, half-hearted. The friend turned, astonished, and raised his arm to defend himself, crying out in his pain and fear, but there was no pity in the young man's heart,

235

and he struck again. The second blow silenced his friend's cries, and the third crushed his skull. Then the young man skinned the bear, and with its claws he raked his own shoulder..."

"No! You can't have!...there was no one else!..." Gronu was crawling now, trying to escape him, and for the first time Finn felt pity. Yet remembering his father and his murdered friend he went on, reminding Gronu of the thing he had done; the thing he had thought unwitnessed, but which was seen from her hiding place by a young girl whose curiosity had drawn her to the mountain, and who fled in terror to fall at Finn's feet in the fearful storm that followed.

That which Shani had told Finn after saving him from the snows could never have been told to the tribe—to declare Gronu's guilt would have been to condemn her in the same breath. Yet that same knowledge, revealed thus to Gronu, struck terror into his soul. In truth, the horror of it had haunted him, preying on his mind even in his years of triumph. He was as superstitious—for all his bravado—as any in the tribe; the thought that the God he had rejected had chosen Finn as the instrument of His vengeance robbed him of his wits.

Not daring to approach, the people on the ledge had heard nothing of Finn's words, and could only wonder what madness had seized Gronu. They, who had seen many wonders, now witnessed one more. The man whose word had been law, longer than the youngest among them could remember, now raved and cursed on the ground, ripping up handfuls of grass. Suddenly he seemed to notice the cloak on his back, and tore at its binding, struggling to be free of it. It seemed for a time as if the bear had come to life once more and he grappled with it—as he claimed to have done all those years ago—until, victorious, he kicked himself clear and ran, shrieking, into the night.

CHAPTER
THIRTEEN

▲ ▲ ▲
▲ ▲

IT WAS SEVERAL DAYS before the tribe was ready to move. They were accustomed to packing up and moving, they had done it twice a year for as long as there had been a tribe, but this time it was different. From this migration there would be no return; nothing could be stored away against their coming back. Even the sacred objects had to be removed in great secrecy from Sanu's cave and prepared for carriage to their new home. The whole camp was in turmoil as tents were collapsed, belongings were strapped to sleds, and parties of men came and went from the ledge to trap and fish for food for the journey. None were busier than Finn and Shani; she moving among the women telling tales of the new land and reassuring backsliders; he giving advice, describing the route and main landmarks to the hearth leaders and, where needed, backing up their authority. That authority had been much undermined in recent years. Gronu had assumed all the responsibilities of leadership, and his passing had left a people enervated and unsure of themselves. Finn was constantly being called upon to make

237

decisions and pass judgment, and increasingly was driven to wonder whether the former independence of the hearths would ever be restored. Remembering the loose ties that had bound the old tribe and the way authority, never strong at the best of times, had come and gone with the seasons, it pained Finn to see how they all now looked to him for every decision.

Nevertheless, there was a new spirit abroad in the camp, discernible wherever Finn went. People sang as they worked, and greeted each other in the old, formal ways that had fallen into disuse. Old enmities were buried, old rivalries forgotten. Even those who had sided most closely with Gronu were accepted once more into the bosom of their hearths and fell again under the sway of their rightful leaders. Here and there people who had not talked to each other for a long while smiled shyly and exchanged greetings, as though both had survived some dreadful ordeal or been awakened from some horrid dream. Nor were the old neglected, as they had been; those too frail to walk were to be carried, with the very young, and those who could took their share of the work alongside their families.

At last, when Finn and Shani had begun to feel that it would never happen, the tribe was ready, lined up on the ledge in their hearths, calling for Finn to go to their head and lead them into the forests. It was Shani, though, who went first. Along with encouraging and advising the women, she had been much occupied as the days passed in calming Fleetfoot who, feeling the onset of Autumn, was growing impatient and awkward. It was to her that the buck responded best and her he would most readily follow. Therefore it was agreed that they would take the lead, starting off long before the tribe and waiting for them at the halting places she and Finn had marked on their downward journey.

Finn waited until Shani and Fleetfoot were well out of sight. Taking his place at the head of the column, looking down the lines of people burdened with their belongings, he received from each hearth leader the signal that all was ready. He turned

238

to Sanu. From his seat on a litter held shoulder-high by four strong men, Sanu called forth Annu's blessing on their journey, imploring Him to assist His people's passage through the forests that they might live in their new land, in accordance with His will. Then, the prayer over, Finn signaled with his spear and led the Burnt Shins in procession down the scree and into the trees. The parting was not without sorrow; they sang a sad song sung by hunters far from home as they descended, and cast many a backward glance for as long as the ledge could be seen. They were leaving the place where the Burnt Shins had been born, lived, and died since the beginning of the world, and knew that they would never see it again.

As they passed up the valley they looked to their right up the mountainside to the burial cave where the bones of their ancestors lay; every member of the tribe had been up there over the past days to weep and talk to the dead, promising to return whenever possible to honor them. Even though he had severed his links with this place years before, Finn suffered too at the memory that Hann and Mata lay there; over and over he had to remind himself that men's spirits did not rest with their bones but hunted forever with Annu. He drew comfort, too, from the thought that in saving their people from destruction he did Hann and Mata all the honor they would have wished.

They passed the Sacred Mountain on their left. It had played a great part in the life of every man in the tribe and would continue to do so, it being agreed that the initiates would still be brought there when the time was ripe. Finn thought, as he passed it, of the dreadful deeds that had been done there, deeds of which the tribe could never know, and of the burden of guilt he had borne for so many years until freed of it by Shani. He for one was glad to leave it behind him and, as if in sympathy with this secret thought, the tribe soon broke into a joyful song. Before them was unknown territory and a new life, a better life than that which they had left, if Finn was to be believed.

Just before dark they came upon Shani waiting where they had agreed—Fleetfoot grazed contentedly close by—and set up temporary camp for the night. Rations were meager though spirits were high. Before dawn they packed and continued their journey. Burdened as they were by their possessions and the old and the children, the tribe made slower progress than Finn and Shani had managed alone. Finn had allowed for this, breaking the journey into easy stages. But he was not prepared for its effect on those few still inclined to question his wisdom. Nor had he allowed for another factor that made its appearance at the end of the third day. It was almost dark when, amid the confusion of setting up camp for the night, Laela came up to him and drew him to one side, glancing suspiciously over her shoulder as she did so.

"Some of the men are meeting tonight," she said. "The whisper went up and down the column. After everyone has eaten and settled down to sleep they are to slip away down to the stream."

"What for?" asked Finn. "If they have something to say they will be heard."

Laela shrugged. "I don't know what it is about—they met last night too—but judging by those involved I would say that little good will come of it." That said, she slipped away as quickly as she could to rejoin her family in their struggles with the tent.

At their meal that night Shani was full of her exploits and her problems with Fleetfoot who, feeling the onset of the rut and perhaps, sensing that every step took him closer to home, was growing daily more unruly. After a while she sensed that Finn did not want to talk and fell silent, retiring to their tent, and leaving him alone in the dark. The camp was quiet; nothing could be heard but the rushing of the stream and as time passed Finn began to wonder whether Laela's tale had not been simply another camp rumor. He was tired, as they all were; finding himself nodding he was about to creep away to the tent,

240

ashamed of his suspicions, when he became aware of crouched figures moving about him in the darkness. Knowing that immobility was the best cover, he remained rooted to the spot as the shapes moved from tent to tent, assembled into one group of—he guessed—a dozen and then passed silently down toward the stream.

It was difficult ground to follow them across, full of dry bracken, but the sound of the stream and their own noise helped him. He lost sight of them for a while, but found them again by the stream where they were seated in a circle talking, with much waving of hands. Whatever was being said, it was clear that they were not all in agreement, and the talk went on for some time before they all rose, stretched, and turned once more toward the camp. Seeing that they must come near him, Finn backed into thicker cover, taking his eyes off the group for a few moments. He looked up just in time to see a group of three detach itself and start down the bank. He glanced back at the main group—it seemed no smaller than before. He was puzzling over what it meant when the rearmost of the three figures turned to wave to them.

Even silhouetted against the moonlit water behind, there was no mistaking the figure of Gronu, broad shouldered and taller by a head than any but Finn himself. This, then, was the purpose of this gathering in the dead of night—Gronu was following. Some that followed himself and Shani were still uncertain in their loyalties. The main group passed by Finn so closely that, had he chosen, he could have grabbed one of them by the ankle. The throat would have suited him better, he thought, but he fought down his anger, trying in the darkness to recognize them as they passed. It was futile, and the thought that they would no doubt reveal themselves in time brought him little comfort. As silence settled on the camp once more, Finn crept back to his tent and lay down beside Shani. Long into the night he wondered what form their disaffection would take.

In the morning he told Shani of what he had seen. Much as

it pained him to dampen her spirits with bad tidings, it was a relief to him that he no longer had to bear such burdens alone. She took the news well. Almost immediately she left him to wander among the women and the families as they made their preparations. By the time it was light enough to move she was still among them, with Fleetfoot still grazing in the trees a little way from the camp. The hearths were packed and lined up facing the direction they must march, and Finn was keen to be off. He strode impatiently over to where Shani stood with Laela, looking down the line.

"You had better be off," he said, "or it'll be dark before we reach the next camping ground."

"Tell that to them!" Shani nodded to the tail of the column where were gathered a sizable body of the younger men. They were addressing the people nearest them, pointing back down the valley in the direction of the river, drawing a larger crowd with every passing moment. Finn, striding down to confront them, was overtaken by groups of men and women from all the hearths, curious at the delay and eager to learn what had caused it. Joining the crowd that had gathered, Finn was not surprised at their faces. There could be little doubt that these were the same men he had watched the night before. His only hope lay in the fact that their meeting by the stream had obviously been far from unanimous; some among them seemed more unsure than openly hostile.

"That is our way!" the foremost among them was saying, pointing the way they had come. "We have come far enough. We are for home!"

From the mutterings among the crowd Finn could see that there was some sympathy for this view. But to his relief others were shouting, "Our minds are made up!" and "We follow Finn!"

"You follow him to your deaths!" the man replied. Finn stepped forward.

"I seem to hear another speaking through your mouth!" he

said. The men looked abashed, uneasy that their secret had been discovered. Finn was about to say more. But before he could speak another among them shouted, "Finn, you had your say in the great cave. Stay silent now. It is for us to follow you or not as we choose. And we choose home."

The crowd began to stir. Someone else urged, "Even as we speak the herds are massing on the grasslands. We should be going out to meet them, preparing for the kill, not fleeing off into the forests in pursuit of dreams."

With a great shout many of the crowd crossed over to join them. Emboldened, they began to cry out, "Join with us! Come home while there is still time!" The hearth leaders were silent; the authority that Finn had so painstakingly rebuilt vanished at the first crisis. The whole tribe were assembled now, most of them gathered around Finn, but a sizable and growing party, including many of the men, around the dissenters. They had touched a chord in many of the hunters' hearts with their talk of the massing herds; they had invoked that blood lust that seized them at the killing grounds, and with it were drawing away many among the best of them. Even now their minds were not made up. Some of them looked apologetically at Finn across the divide, or avoided his eyes altogether. Finn was at a loss; as one had rightly said, it was for them to decide—he had said so himself. He had said all that he could say at the cave. If they would not go with him he could not force them. Gronu might prevail after all.

"If you go back you go alone!" This was Laela, who had stepped from the crowd with a large gathering of women at her back. "We have buried too many of our children to have faith in your judgments. We follow Finn!"

Angrily, the hunters called on Laela to be silent. But the women rallied to her support. "What are you afraid of?" called a mocking voice from among their ranks. "Are you afraid that in the new land you will have to take up your spears again and become men?"

"Or do you fear not having Gronu to do your thinking for you . . . ?" called another.

The forest rang to their arguments as the two parties traded insults and all tried to make themselves heard at once. Finn stood aside, uncertain whether or how to intervene. Suddenly silence fell. Unseen in all the confusion, Shani had led Fleet-foot round to the rear of the column. There they both now stood, a little apart but visible to all. Pretending surprise at what she saw, she walked forward among them, leaving the buck in the trees behind her.

"We came back," she said calmly, "wondering where you were, why you did not follow?"

"We are not following you anymore!" growled a voice from among the defectors. "We are going home!"

"Then you go without your wives . . ." cried Laela. "We have come too far to turn back now."

Shani listened calmly to this exchange, then turned to confront those who had gathered about Gronu's men. "What is it you fear, that does not frighten the women?" she asked.

"We fear nothing!" said their leader. "*They* don't understand. We feel it is foolish to forsake the deer we know, for those we have only heard of!"

Shani turned away and shook her head in a show of disbelief. "And what of him?" she demanded, pointing to where Fleetfoot paced back and forth in the trees. "Did we conjure him from the earth, did he fall from the skies? Or do you think I sewed him together out of skins on long Winter nights?"

There was laughter on both sides of the clearing at this, but the man remained obdurate. "He is but one!" he said. "We have only your word that there are enough for us all in this new land you speak of."

"What reason have we to deceive you?" Shani appealed to the crowd at his back. "Still more, what reason has *he?*" She pointed again to the buck.

"Look at him! He grows restless as we wait about here. He

244

knows what lies ahead. He knows that in the valley we seek there are many more like him. He grows fat, and eager for the rut. You men all know what stirs him at this time of year . . . unless Gronu did *that* for you too. . . ." Even those hunters who had been most vociferous against Finn, only moments before, laughed in spite of themselves at this—Shani had always been popular.

"He has the wit to follow his womenfolk. . . ." she concluded. "If only you did too!"

Without waiting to see what effect her words had, she strode from the clearing and, coaxing Fleetfoot along with her, set off in the direction they must travel that day. Following her example, not daring to look back, Finn walked to his place at the head of the column. An age seemed to pass as he waited for Shani and Fleetfoot to pass out of sight while he listened at the same time to the confusion behind him. He knew that to look back would betray a lack of confidence that could prove fatal. He waited until there was complete silence behind him, then gave the signal to move. It was much later, passing up and down the column as was his practice, that he discovered the whole tribe, even the defectors, still with him. Now he knew what Shani had been doing that morning as the hearths had been preparing. As they ate that evening, she confirmed it. After basking in his praise for a while she tossed her head, as though it had all been nothing, saying, "We knew it was coming. It's not only the men who have their meetings!"

Although he felt sure that they had won over most of the waverers, and that even the rebels were more frightened than hostile, Finn kept a watchful eye out that night after the camp had settled. Nor was he surprised to see a party, though a much smaller one, slip away into the trees as on the previous night. He made no attempt to follow, knowing that he would be lucky indeed to get close enough to hear what was said. Instead, he might be unlucky in the extreme if he were to fall into Gronu's hands. As to what drove Gronu now, other than destructive revenge, he could only speculate but there was no doubting the influence he still commanded. The problem of Gronu would not be outrun, or ignored. In his innocence, he had hoped Gronu would stay away, living out his life as an outcast or, robbed of his wits, die in the forest. That would have absolved him of responsibility. But it was patently not to be—sooner or later the problem would have to be faced. The only answer that he could think of was an answer that terrified him.

He was occupied with these gloomy thoughts when a heavily muffled voice behind him whispered his name.

"Don't turn!" said the voice as Finn started. Frightened as much by his own violent thoughts as the eerie whispering at his back, he trembled, feeling in the dark for the shaft of his best spear.

"I have been with the others, with Gronu, at the stream..." said the voice, while Finn struggled in vain to recognize it. "He is saying that the buck is your talisman, the source of your magic. He means to kill it after dark tomorrow. Once the camp has settled he will come in with his companion."

"They were three last night," whispered Finn.

"They are only two now, Gronu and one other. Pretending to be for him, I offered to help. I am to stay at the door of your tent and stop you if you try to leave. Only I shall not be there."

"And the others?"

"They will do nothing. Gronu frightens them, he acts strangely, talks wildly, but he may yet win and then they will have to face him. So they will wait and see—it is between you and him now."

"How many of you were there down at the stream?" asked Finn. There was no reply. He waited for a while, then whispered, "Are you there?" But the man had vanished into the night. Finn considered what he had been told. He had noticed that morning, when they had thrown off Gronu's first challenge, that some of his old adherents were a good deal less

246

wholeheartedly committed than they had been in the cave. Presumably this man was one of them; yet there was always the possibility that this was an elaborate trap to lure him to his death. Overall, though, it seemed unlikely. He did not doubt for a moment that Gronu intended his death eventually. But Finn doubted whether even his staunchest confederates would join him in murder. Besides, if they meant to kill him, there were easier ways and it would little profit them to forewarn him. No, Gronu would kill the buck, destroy the symbol that had so captivated the people, and then try to win them back. If he succeeded, no doubt Finn would mysteriously disappear one night, as Rann's brother had done. However Finn looked at the problem it came down to Gronu—without him there would be no opposition, nothing to prevent their leading the people to safety and prosperity. With him, they could never be at peace.

Later, in the tent, having told Shani what had passed, Finn first gave voice to the thought that had troubled him since the moment he had first seen Gronu by the stream.

"I have to kill Gronu," he said.

"You can't!" Shani's shocked reaction had been his own at first. But he had weighed the problem, examined it in every light, from every angle; and there was no other way.

"He means to kill Fleetfoot. You know what that would do. How else do I stop him? While he lives everything we are trying to do is at risk."

"And if you kill him, what difference is there between you and him?"

Finn shook his head. "This is different. I must do it not for my sake or even yours, but for the sake of the tribe."

"How different?" she insisted. "Do you think he didn't say that when he killed Rann's brother, or the others who disappeared?"

"He killed Venn, as good as killed my father—he led the tribe astray. . . ."

"Gronu was right." Shani's last words, delivered quietly and

247

calmly, stunned Finn into silence. She went on, "He was right. The time *had* come for great changes. The old men would have sat and prayed till we were all dead. Where were the hearth leaders today when you needed them? Gronu had the wit to see it, and the courage to act. He was wrong, badly wrong, but whatever else he may have done, he was trying to save his people, just as we are now."

Finn was appalled. "How can you compare *us*...?"

She cut him short, impatiently. "Ask yourself this—if the tribe had not first followed *him*, would they now be following *you*?"

Finn slumped against the tent wall; suddenly he could see that she was right. Seeing the effect of her words she drew closer to him, pleading in his ear, "We go to a new life, a new world. Don't stain it with murder at its very beginning. Go against Gronu, as you must. Catch him, stop him somehow, but for the love I once bore him, and the love you had for him too, spare his life."

There was quiet in the tent for a long time before Finn spoke again. "As always you have spoken true. But this time, for the first time, I must stop my ears to it. He must die; one life for the good of all." He prepared himself for her next onslaught. But he did not expect the form of it.

"You have been leader of the tribe for three days..." she said softly, lying down and turning her face to the wall, "and you are starting to think like him already!"

They did not speak in the morning but dressed in silence and went their separate ways. Nor did he see her at the midday break, and they ate their evening meal in continued silence. Night fell, and the camp settled to sleep. After the exhausting day, few had any wish to sit talking around fires. No word had passed between Finn and Shani since the previous night. Before he went to the glade where Fleetfoot lay, however, he knew there were things he must say to her. Shani was not asleep. He found her seated, wrapped in her deerskin, facing the tent door.

248

He took his place beside her, and they sat in stillness for a while, communicating wordlessly the love they felt.

At last he spoke. "If I should die . . ." He got no further. Her answering sob stopped him; he fumbled for an easier way to say what he must. There was no easy way, so he said again, "If I should die, you must lead the people. Find a man, a good man, out of Hann's hearth . . . my hearth, if you can. If you guide him as you have guided me, the people will be safe in both your hands."

By the light of the lamp he could see the tears stream down her face, but there was more that he had to say.

"When I used to go out to hunt, I always asked your blessing, for luck. I do not ask it now for I know I shall not have it . . ." He paused, hoping that she might bless him, after all. But she dropped her head to her knees and sobbed out loud, as though each breath caused her pain.

"Mine has been a hard life and full of sorrow," he whispered, "but for the years we had alone together in the valley, I would gladly have lived a hundred such lives."

He left her there, weeping, and had lifted the tent flap and was halfway out when he heard her voice behind him.

"If one of you *must* die," she said, "let it be Gronu."

Outside, he remained crouched for a while where he was, letting his eyes adjust to the darkness, listening for sounds of movement. He knew that this was his most vulnerable time; if last night's warning had been a trap they would spring it closed now. He tensed himself, ready to dive for cover at any moment. Gradually the blackness around him became gray and the menacing shapes that had threatened on all sides became trees and bushes. The whisperer in the night had been as good as his word—he was not on guard. Even so, Finn took a circuitous route, stopping and listening often in case he was followed, until he came to the glade where Fleetfoot remained. He chose a spot downwind from where the attack would come, and settled down to watch and wait. The forest was rarely silent even at night, and this night was no exception. Fleetfoot himself browsing, the wind in the trees, odd sounds from the camp, as well as any number of night creatures—Finn heard them all, tensing at each noise, then relaxing as he identified it. Only the wind worried him, rustling the trees and the undergrowth, providing perfect cover for Gronu's silent approach.

Time passed. Fleetfoot grew restless, Finn grew tired. Gronu and his companions would have been able to travel faster than the tribe, could have arrived well ahead, lain up, eaten, and rested. Finn began to wonder now whether this was Gronu's plan—to wear him down with constant alarms until he grew careless, and then to strike. He was wondering how many nights like this he could last, with long days' treks in between; wondering also whom among the hunters he could trust to relieve him at his task. Then he heard a sound that came from no animal. It was a sound that Finn, now used to hunting alone, had not heard in many years, but it was a sound he recognized at once—a tongue-click, a signal between hunters. It came from downwind and over to Finn's left, telling him that he was between them and Fleetfoot. Quickly he weighed the situation —they were two against his one. But he had the advantage that they were not expecting him to be there. His aim was to kill Gronu; he anticipated little trouble from the other once that was done. But if he waited until they came to him the two of them would overwhelm him. He must work his way round behind them, and hope that it was Gronu he came upon first. It left their way to the buck open, of course, but he decided to risk it, hoping to kill Gronu before they killed the deer.

A race began, conducted by moonlight, a race of which two of the contestants were unaware. Still as figures on a cave wall, all three crouched, spears poised to strike, waiting for a gust of wind before moving cautiously, their legs lifted high, feeling the ground with bare toes as they went. Round they went, slowly circling—two figures intent on the deer that lurked in the shadows, the third hunting the hunters. The other two were noisy, Finn thought—stalking was a lost art and they had not been taught by Hann. He was grateful now for the hours he had spent, creeping, aching spear arm raised, in pursuit of his father, wary of the stinging shower of stones that would come his way if detected. The thought crept into his mind that Hann would be horrorstruck to see his skills used against human prey; but he drove the thought out, nerving himself for the kill that must come.

Fleetfoot moved. He emerged from the shadows, out into the moonlight toward the spears of the men who hunted him, stopping just out of spear-cast, blissfully unaware of danger. Knowing the beast as he did, Finn knew that its next move would bring it within spear range. If he shouted now, scaring Fleetfoot away, he would at once become the hunted himself instead of the hunter. The wind died, and the figures all froze, but Finn, pausing only for a moment, continued to work his way slowly up behind the nearer of the two figures. If only it could be Gronu! That way he could kill him swiftly, then shout and warn the deer, confident that Gronu's companion would take off into the night. The other man might try to kill the deer; but only Gronu had murder in his heart. By the time the wind blew once more Finn was close enough to one of the two to reach out and touch him, but still he could not tell which he was. Then the wind drove away a cloud, the moon suddenly brightened the scene below, and Finn saw that the man to his front was not Gronu. Gronu was farther away out of reach, tangled in a thicket, silently trying to struggle free to get a clear cast. Watching him struggle, Finn cursed his luck, and did not see Fleetfoot move toward them. Slowly the figure in front of him rose on his haunches, spear raised—the buck was in range, and the man's arm came back to throw.

Not knowing what he would do next—knowing only that he must save the deer—Finn reached out, closed his hand softly round the end of the man's spear shaft, and pulled it sharply toward him. The man cried out in surprise and anger as he fell

251

over backward to sprawl at Finn's feet. From the corner of his eye Finn saw Fleetfoot dart for cover; then Gronu burst from the bushes toward them, his spear arm drawn back. The man at his feet sprang up with a curse, seizing Finn's waist in a wrestler's hold, and both crashed into the trees. The moon had vanished; feeling for the man's face, trying to force his head back to break his hold, Finn suddenly felt the man go limp. He slid to his knees, his hands still at Finn's waist but now clutching it for support. Finn stooped to hold him. "Dead!" the man breathed into his face before his head fell back. As Finn released him he rolled away, Gronu's spear sticking from his side.

Dropping to the ground while he groped in the dark for his spears, Finn looked and listened. Gronu had vanished—he had cast recklessly at the shadows before him, indifferent to his friend. Now he would be wondering which of them he had killed. Finn waited. Gronu must approach again. He clicked his tongue, mimicking their signal; and something stirred in the trees over to his left. Noiselessly Finn drew himself to his feet, selected his best spear—he knew it by touch—and poised himself to throw. This was the moment he had dreaded the most, the moment when his spear must bite human flesh. But he knew that it must be done, and he meant to do it quickly and well.

When Gronu broke cover he was stepping forward cautiously, holding aloft a second spear. Finn could see him ducking and rising, turning his head, trying to pierce the gloom, still uncertain whether it was friend or foe that slumped at the foot of the tree. His right arm poised forward, measuring the distance, Gronu raised himself on the balls of his feet as he moved in on the inert figure before him. His back was to Finn—a clear target. Finn knew that he must strike now, before Gronu saw who lay there and dived for cover. Yet he could not. He could not kill him like this, from cover, as though he were a beast.

"Gronu!" he bellowed. Gronu turned and saw him. Both

cast at the same time. Panicked, Gronu had thrown wide. Finn felt the spear pass by him as he saw his own strike home. At Gronu's scream Finn sank to his knees, thinking it was all over. But in his anguish he too had thrown wildly; with a cry Gronu pulled the spear from his shoulder, and blundered off through the trees. Taking up the fallen spear Finn sprinted in pursuit, cursing Gronu for not dying, cursing himself for not killing him, cursing the whole world.

Behind him in the camp he could hear the confusion caused by Gronu's screams; ahead he could see Gronu disappearing into the trees, heading for the stream. Wounded and afraid, he was making no attempt to move silently. When he stopped Finn could hear him thrashing about in the undergrowth. He knew he was gaining on him; ignoring the cries from the camp, he plunged on after him, fighting his way through the tangle of branches that tore at his face and arms. He saw the stream, and Gronu struggling down toward it. Finn's cloak had caught in a thornbush. As he struggled to free himself, he looked up just in time to see Gronu stumble. As he fell something cracked beneath Gronu; whether it was bone or branch Finn knew not. He knew only that this was his chance. Slipping out of his entangled cloak, he raced over to the fallen figure and raised his spear, ready to strike.

This was worse than he had ever imagined it. Standing over Gronu, he could see the blood that oozed from the wound in his shoulder, the same blood that now had dripped from Finn's spear point. Gronu was already past words; his face was mad, fearful, like that of a wounded animal in a trap.

That seemed to make it easier. Finn was about to finish him when a look passed across Gronu's face that chilled his blood. He smiled, only for an instant, a bitter, sly smile that seemed to mock Finn with what he was about to do, and he remembered Shani's words, "You're thinking like him..." He stayed his hand.

"Finn!" A cry from behind, from the direction of the camp,

distracted him for an instant. In that instant Gronu kicked his legs out from under him, scrambled to his feet, and leaped into the stream. When Finn rose again he could hear him splashing across and climbing the far bank.

"Finn!" Men from the camp, alerted by the noise, had come in search of him. Pausing at the bank of the stream he turned in their direction. "If I am not back by dawn, go on. Shani will guide you!" he shouted, then snatching up his cloak, dropped into the stream in pursuit.

Wounded, lamed by his fall, and crazed with fear and pain, Gronu made slow and noisy progress. But he knew where he was going. Finn was forced to stop and listen every few paces; besides that, he was tiring fast. They stumbled on through the night, Gronu stuffing his mouth with leaves to keep from crying out, Finn moving warily, fearing a trap yet anxious to have done with the whole dreadful business. At times when he stopped, Finn could hear Gronu ahead sobbing and gibbering —and he recalled the face that had looked up at him by the stream, the face that had frightened even his former friends. The sky lightened imperceptibly. Finn could follow now by the splashes of blood on the leaves. They began to climb; as he had guessed, Gronu's bolt-hole was in the rocks, where his own had always been. He stopped to listen, heard feet scrabbling on stones, and then, for the first time since the chase had begun, silence. Peering through the sparse tree-line in the direction of the last sounds, he could see outlined against the graying sky a rocky ledge. He sank to his knees to catch his breath, listening all the time for the sound of further movement. There was none, and Finn felt sure that Gronu had reached his lair and gone to ground.

He was equally sure of two other things; he himself could go no further, and he did not relish the thought of following a wounded but still dangerous enemy into those rocks in the dark. Soon it would be dawn; time enough then for the reckoning, if Gronu lived that long. Slipping back down into the trees, he placed his back against a stout pine facing up the slope toward the rocks, drew his cloak about him, and slept.

He awoke shivering and covered with dew to a grim, wet morning. Climbing painfully to his feet and stretching, he crept cautiously to the edge of the tree-line. To his astonishment he saw a thin column of smoke coming from among the rocks where Gronu had disappeared the previous night. Either Gronu had thrown caution to the winds, assuming he had lost Finn in the forests, or this was a trap.

Finn took no chances on his approach, working his way round the side of the mountain, dragging himself up wet rocks that grazed his knees and elbows. The day was well advanced before he had crawled to a position from where he could observe the small ledge, less than a stone's throw ahead and below him. Gronu was damp and bedraggled, seated at the ashes of an extinct fire, chewing distractedly at a hunk of meat. Behind him was an overhanging rock that would have afforded shelter, yet he looked as if he had sat out in the open all night. He was unarmed, and had no spears at hand. His wound was undressed; dried blood caked the shoulder of his smock and matted his long dark hair. He seemed lost in a world of his own. When he reached for a handful of twigs the pain in his shoulder seemed to surprise him, and he probed the wound as though seeing it for the first time.

In his pain and bewilderment, he did not at first see Finn standing on the rock above him. But, far from leaping and fleeing at his approach, Gronu leaned forward, narrowing his eyes as if uncertain who this stranger might be. He looked old, his face drawn by pain and fatigue. Sensing no threat, Finn lowered his spear; as he did so Gronu's face at last lit up with recognition, and he smiled. It was not the twisted leer of the night before; the face that smiled at him now was the face of his old friend, the brave, good-natured boy at whose fireside he had sat, and who had shared with him the triumph of his first kill. Smiling at him from behind that mad, tortured face

255

was the Gronu he had known and loved. Gronu reached down and took a hunk of meat—as he had that night lifetimes ago by the river—and held it out to Finn. For the first time Finn glanced down, noticing the remains of a carcass scattered around the fire. Human remains. Retching, Finn fled the ghastly place. Not heeding the feeble protests from behind, he stumbled down the hill and into the forest, plunging, frantic, through the trees and bushes until he fell to the earth broken and weeping.

▲　　▲　　▲

It was almost dark before he had recovered sufficiently to sit up, head in his hands, still shaking, and force himself to think of the future. Gronu was no longer a threat, that much was clear. Even if he survived the wound and the hardships that faced him alone and mad up there, he would never again lead the tribe, if he could even remember that there was such a thing. Shani would have led them to the next camping ground by now; he would make haste to rejoin them. He would tell any who asked that Gronu could threaten them no more. The thought gave him strength; he rose shakily, took up his spear, and started to hobble painfully toward the valley bottom. Just before he descended he glanced back one more time, and caught sight of Gronu seated, unmoving, where he had left him.

Finn knew at once that he would have to go back. This solution was too easy, too much in accord with what he had hoped for. To salve Shani's and his own consciences he had prayed for a resolution that did not involve killing Gronu. He had prayed that Gronu would die or disappear—just not be there one day and so absolve him of responsibility. But Gronu had not gone. He was on that ridge where he might live and suffer for weeks, months, even years. If Gronu, the boy who had been his friend, could have foreseen that human remnant seated on the ledge he would have begged Finn to spear him there and then. Up there—for all his faults and all his crimes —was a fellow man, sorely wounded in body and soul. Could he deny Gronu, through his own cowardice, the kindness he would show to any wounded beast?

He killed Gronu cleanly from behind. Stirring the ashes of the fire with a piece of bone Gronu had not heard him approach, and he fell forward without a sound as the single spearthrust broke his neck. Finn buried Gronu and the grisly remains of his companion side by side in shallow graves on the mountainside. Wrapping Gronu in his own cloak, he laid upon his chest the spearhead that had slain him, then breaking the shaft, flung the pieces to the wind. Their graves sealed, he prayed to Annu to speed their journeys to the dreamworld. Like Hann's first-born, Gronu would be whole there where there was no sorrow, and would hunt forever with his ancestors. For a long while Finn sat on the bare hillside in the rain remembering, as was fitting, past kindnesses and happier times. Then, at last, he wept for Gronu's companion and for Gronu, who had been his boyhood friend, of whom great things were promised, who had tried to rise above his God, and had fallen lower than a beast.

CHAPTER
FOURTEEN

STILL BRUISED, still shaken by his ordeal with Gronu, Finn stood by Shani on the ridge that overlooked their valley, and felt again the power this place had to heal him. They still talked of it as "their" valley, and for the moment, as the long winding column of men, women, and children toiled up behind them, it still was. Yet that was about to end; soon the people they had led here would spill down into it and make it their own. Finn found himself hating them. They would poison the air with their jealousies and bickering; poison the earth with the bodies of their dead. They would fish in the stream where he had taught Shani to fish and bathe in the lake where he and she had swum in that first golden Summer. A part of both their lives would die the moment the others set foot on the valley floor. He felt in that moment that the best part of his life had passed, and he wished that he and she could go on somewhere new, somewhere where no one could follow.

Yet all was as it should be, and Shani's bright smile reminded him that this was the moment they had planned, striven and suffered for. Hers was the only happy face, though, as the people climbed onto the ridge and lined up on either side of them. Despite all his warnings, despite all that Shani had said passing among the camp fires the previous night, he could see the disappointment on the faces that filed past him. They had struggled for so long, uprooted themselves from all that they held dear, had prayed, dreamed of this moment for so long that it was bound to fall short of their hopes. For all Finn's counsel to the contrary, they had hoped to find a land filled with Reindeer with herds stretching as far as the eye could see, not, as now lay before them, an apparently deserted valley, no different from many others they had passed through since leaving home.

Shani was among them immediately, pointing out the stream, the mountain pastures, and the valley where they had spent their Winters. She seemed to be everywhere at once, and her infectious good humor was yet again helping the awkward moment to pass. Then halfway down the slope, almost overlooked, Fleetfoot bellowed. The long journey and the people who had fed and tended him were forgotten as though they had never been. Scenting his own kind and his own land, he raised his muzzle till his antlers lay across his back and trumpeted his joy to the treetops. Silence fell on the ridge as, his song finished, the great buck galloped down the slope, to be swallowed up in the forests below. It was as though this beast had been sent by their God to lead them to their new world; his task completed, he had left them now, to rejoin his kin. Suddenly all along the ridge prayers of thanksgiving were being offered up to Annu. Their devotions done, the people turned to Finn and Shani who led them singing down the hill.

They camped that morning by the stream; in the days ahead they would move to the site that Finn had chosen for the tribe, subject to the approval of the Elders and hearth leaders. By now they were well practiced at setting up camp. Each man, woman, and child knew the tasks they had to do. Even so, it seemed to take forever. Every other halt had been a mere stage in the journey, and the land around of only passing interest; here every hill and gully, every stick and stone was a part of their new world. Distracted as the people were, tents rose and then fell, fires flared and died and flared again, and it began to look as if they would still be floundering there when darkness came. A tent of Finn's hearth sagged and listed, and the people nearby jeered. Then seeing the cluster of men and women around it staring up the hill they turned in that direction. All down the line of the camp others did the same, as more tents fell, and bundles of kindling dropped to the ground, and the whole people stared in awe at the silent spectacle above.

Deer—more than a man could count—were running across a hillside high above them; within the forest, a forest of antlers. A great shout filled the air as the men rushed for their spears. The women had raced to the fires, and Finn hastily gathered the hearth leaders around him. Now was the test of their authority, the time that would decide the future of the tribe. One bout of heedless slaughter now would set them on the path to a destruction as certain as that which they had just escaped. Strict orders were given—rules prepared by Finn against this very moment. They would go out under their hearth leaders, would take only one doe chosen from among the weakest, for each family group. Leaving the rest to live, to breed, to propagate the herd. After the men had gone out an anxious silence settled on the camp, broken only by the distant cries from above. Fires were banked as a gesture of faith and tents finally erected, but scarcely a word was spoken until the first hunters came home dragging their prey behind them. The whole tribe clustered round then, inspecting their kill with cries of surprise and joy. Even these, the weakest of the does, were sleeker, fatter, than any they could remember from the grassland herd. In ones and twos they came down from the forest now, and the crowd thinned and scattered to the fires. The blood-stained ground and the butchered carcasses hanging from the boughs, the bright faces, eager round the fires, and the fresh meat hissing on the spits—all proclaimed that the Burnt Shins had come home.

They feasted long into the night, the great fires throwing sparks up to the stars, lighting the greasy, laughing faces, the

261

bloated supine figures and the children running without fear from hearth to hearth. Boasts and stories passed across the fires, and songs—the old ones known by all, of hunting and of love, and new ones, many made up there and then, about Shani, Finn, and Fleetfoot. Sitting together at their own hearth they heard them all, Finn embarrassed, ill at ease, Shani reveling in the praise, accepting adulation as her due. At last to Finn's relief there arose from somewhere a song he had not heard in many years, and had once feared never to hear again. It was the oldest and the simplest of their songs, telling of the love of their God, the beauty of their world, their sheer joy at living, proclaiming to the heavens who they were—they were the children of Annu, they were the Burnt-Shinned people, they were the Reindeer people.

▲   ▲   ▲

Warmed by the afternoon sun, Finn lay in the shade of a tree and dreamed of Venn. Venn waited for him in the dreamworld, smiling, holding out the spear that Hann had made. Finn grasped the spear in both his hands, and swore brotherhood as before. Together, laughing, they ran down to the lake where dead men wash away their earthly sorrows. There was another waiting for them by the water's edge. It was Gronu; he reached out to embrace them both and hand in hand the three walked out into the water. Then, when they had bathed, they lay upon the grass and laughed at a bad dream they had all had, in which they had fought, known guilt and suffering, and shed each other's blood. Just as Finn saw Hann, a small boy at his side, come running along the shore toward him he awoke. His disappointment did not last long—he often saw and talked with Hann in his dreams, dreams that he knew were too vivid not to be true.

At last he sat up, stretched lazily and looked out over the meadow. In the distance, far below, he could see the shimmer of the mountain lake where the tents of the Burnt Shins had blossomed every Spring since he and Shani had led them into the valley. The women and children were out gathering, and the woods around the camp rang to their laughter. The world seemed filled with children these days, noisy, sprawling, fat little children everywhere he went; he relished the few quiet moments he could snatch up here. He listened to the women's voices calling the young ones to order, thought he heard Shani's among them, and smiled to himself. His first thought on leading the people here had been wrong; the best days had not been past, they had lain ahead of him, he was living them now. There was no telling when or why they would end. This was his thirtieth Summer, and though a little stouter than he had been, he could still beat the youngest of the men to the mountaintops. Only last month, Laela's father-in-law, in his fifty-second Summer, had carried his own grandson's eldest child up to the fawning grounds. The people had thrived and the herd had grown; only the wolves had had cause to regret the Burnt Shins' migration. Six Summers ago men of his own hearth had discovered a place where the ground had fallen away some time in the distant past; it formed a natural bowl in which deer could graze enclosed by walls of rock, guarded from wolves with fire and spears by the youth of the tribe.

A noise over to his right distracted him. A young buck, the velvet hanging in strips from his antlers, was rubbing them against a tree to be free of it. The buck saw him, stopped, and then went back to work, unconcerned. Fleetfoot, though still an object of veneration among the Burnt Shins, was now by no means the only Reindeer who visited the camp. Shani had done more by naming that fawn than she had realized—she had marked a new relationship between them and Man. Finn shaded his eyes to see the deer more clearly, then clicked his tongue irritably. The beast was ear-marked. He had fought ever since they had entered the valley against the practice of ear-marking live beasts, but despite all his best efforts it was spreading. Whenever he gathered the other hearth leaders to harangue them on this point they would nod sagely and agree wholeheartedly, all the time planning where they would hide their own beasts until his anger blew over. Lately Finn had stopped trying. He spent much of his time judging disputes over Reindeer, with hearths, families, even individuals laying claim to beasts that had once belonged to no one but Annu. Men prided themselves now not on their prowess at hunting, fishing, or running, but on how many deer they could lay claim to—as if a man could be judged by what he had! He and his father had never owned more than they could carry—their two spears and the contents of a skin bag. Were they not worthy men?

It was understandable, of course. There was very little real hunting these days. The chosen deer were killed easily enough, and the task of guarding the herd fell mainly to the boys. How then was a man to show his prowess? He could show off to the women at the fishing, or swimming in the lake, but what else was there to judge him by? Yet it was the youth that worried Finn the most. They grew more restless and discontented with each passing year. Last Summer a few of them had taken off into the forests, farther than even Finn had journeyed. They had returned with tales of a tribe of forest primitives and exaggerated accounts of an obviously bloodless battle between them. Already they were talking of "protecting their territory," and even some of the older men whispered at night—when they thought they were not heard—of raiding them for wives. Wives!—there was choice enough here for any man. What they missed was the thrill of going out after prey with their spears, the comradeship of the hunting band, its secret language, signs, and rituals. Not that the rituals were neglected. Stories of the old times, including Finn and Shani's now, were still told around the fire; Sanu had passed his knowledge to a young man of the tribe; and the boys still went to the Sacred Mountain in their fourteenth Spring. The men danced the Reindeer dance Spring and Autumn, to invoke Annu and plead with him to protect the herds. But the old urgency was gone, and the great feasts were more a symbol than a necessity.

He had been wrong, Finn knew, to suppose that everything could stay the same. Though he had fought to preserve the tribe and the old ways from the forces that had threatened to destroy them, in so doing he had changed things more completely than even Gronu had wanted. Was all this pleasing to God, he wondered? What would Hann have made of it all? Even as he thought of his father, his son who bore the same name emerged from the trees at the far side of the meadow. This was already the little one's sixth Summer, and he had broken away from Shani's gathering party to chase a butterfly. Now, seeing his father, he abandoned the chase and ran across to him; disturbed, the buck slumped off into the forest.

Shortly after their return to the hearths, Shani had happily found herself pregnant and in the years that followed Finn became a father more than once.

Finn grunted as the child clambered onto his chest, crying, "Why do you come all the way up here when you don't have to, father?"

Finn rolled, ditching the boy onto the soft moss. "To get away from little boys who ask too many questions!" he said.

Hann sat up, frowning comically. "I'd never come up here. It's too far! . . . We came up for the buckwheat," he added as an afterthought.

"There's some back there. Go and pick it." Finn nodded toward the trees where the deer had stood, where a patch of it grew at the edge of the meadow.

The boy shrugged. "We have enough now." Although, with his reddish-brown hair, he resembled Finn he had his mother's impatient streak.

"Why can't it all grow in one place . . . ?" he demanded suddenly, "instead of scattered all over the forest. I've been walking all day!"

Finn laughed, remembering the boy's mother as she struggled with mats and bowls, complaining all the way to the valley. "The grass grows where it pleases," he replied.

"Well, I wish it pleased to grow down by the lake, then I could swim and play all day."

There was time enough, Finn thought, for the boy to learn that the world could not be ordered for his convenience. He lay back, closed his eyes, and let Hann grumble on.

"*Make* it happen, father!..." The boy tugged at his arm, forcing him to sit up once more. "Make the buckwheat grow down by the lake, all in one place. Everyone listens to you!"

Finn shook his head, laughing. "There are some things even I can't do. I can't move mountains, or trees... or even buckwheat."

"Hann!" Shani's voice sounded from across the meadow, and the boy burrowed into the undergrowth behind his father.

"Hann!" Still calling, she wandered into the open space before the trees. Bathed in sunlight, she made a sight that still stirred Finn as it had by the fishing pool when they were both children. The years had been kind to her; she remained as lithe and slender as ever despite her three children, the eldest of whom now snuggled into the moss and leaves in his father's shade.

Seeing Finn she laughed. "Another bolt-hole!" She called to him, and her voice echoed round the glade. Finn smiled guiltily and shrugged. "I've lost Hann somewhere..." she said as he stood up and brushed himself. "Did he come this way?"

Finn stooped to pick up his cloak. "Not while I've been here!"

Shani seemed unconcerned. "No doubt he will make his own way back." She turned and headed back to the trees, calling over her shoulder, "We're going to bathe, are you coming?"

Finn rose and started across the glade toward her. At the edge of the trees Shani stopped and looked round Finn back to the mossy bank where he had lain. "Tell him to come too, the work's done now!" she said loudly.

The two disappeared, laughing, into the forest, and the small boy crawled from his hiding place, brushed the twigs from his hair, and set off after them. Halfway across the glade he stopped, stared angrily for a while at the buckwheat blowing in the breeze, and then ran unsteadily down the hill.